One In A Million

By
Barbara Keaton

Parker Publishing LLC

Noire Passion is an imprint of Parker Publishing LLC.

Published by Parker Publishing LLC
12523 Limonite Ave., Ste. #440-438
Mira Loma, California 91752
www.parker-publishing.com

ISBN: 978-1-60043-053-4
First Edition

Manufactured in the United States of America

Cover Design by Jaxadora Design

Other Titles by Barbara Keaton

Love For All Seasons
Nights Over Egypt
Cupid
Blaze
By Design
To Love And Honor (Anthology)
An Unfinished Love Affair
All I Ask

One In A Million

By
Barbara Keaton

Chapter 1

Deena Wall stepped out of the cab and looked up at the old station house. She guessed circa 1950s, from the looks of the large once beige, now dingy grey bricks. Opening the dull Plexiglas doors, the walls were painted white, with a navy and white checkerboard boarder near the ceiling. She followed the blue sign with white lettering and a single arrow informing her to stop at the sign-in desk. She glanced to her right and noticed a long wooden bench stretching from wall to wall. Her eyes scanned the wall to her left; pictures of the city and FBI's most wanted were plastered neatly, top to bottom, along the wall. Coming to a stop in front of a large imposing desk, she stood there until the desk sergeant noticed her.

"Good afternoon, Sergeant, I'm Deena Walls." She looked into the grey eyes staring back at her. "I'm here for my client, Kasha Bentley."

Detective Charles Henry Harris turned at the sound of the authoritative voice, curious as to who would posses such a strong, yet mellifluous voice. He faced the owner of the voice and saw her standing near the desk, a pair of black rimmed glasses perched on her small, pert nose. He watched her as she stood erect, one hand resting on the desk, the nails painted a warm bronze. He let his eyes travel to the top of her hair and began a slow descent, stopping where the desk stopped—at her voluptuous bust.

He looked at her eyes. She was watching him watch her.

"Detective Harris here can help you." The desk sergeant stated while pointing behind him. Charles stepped forward, past the sergeant in time to hear him whisper, "she's out of your league," ending the crass statement with a chuckle. He ignored the laced words and put his hand out to her. "Good afternoon, I'm Detective Harris. How can I help you today?"

He pulled his hand back when she glanced down at it and then looked up into his eyes as her fingers drummed on the desk.

"I'm Deena Walls. I understand you are holding my client, Kasha Bentley. I need to speak with the arresting officer and/or the detective handling this case as well as see my client. Can you make that happen?"

He was summarily cut off when he didn't immediately respond, her light eyes captivated him. "Well, if you can't assist me, then please go and get the commander." He wanted to laugh as she tilted her head to one side and pushed her glasses further up on the bridge of her nose.

This sister is fine, but she's trying to punk me.

Charles cleared his throat and dismissed the amused look plastered on the desk sergeant's face. "Ms. Walls, I *am* the detective handling the case. Now, if you'd have a seat for a moment, I'll be with you and will take you to your client."

What he was about to do he knew was wrong, but there was just no way he was going to let her get the best of him. Not, Charles Henry Harris, the third.

"Detective Harry why are you playing these stall tactics?"

He nodded his head slightly to one side, wondering had he heard her correctly. Had she just butchered his name?

"It's Detective Harris. And there's no stall tactic," he lied. "I'm gathering some information here and then we will go up when I'm finished." He watched her poker face and knew she was good at what she did for a living. He'd sure hate to have to meet her on a witness stand. The only evidence of any emotion was the slight tick in her right eye. "Please have a seat over there." He pointed to a row of benches behind her. "And I'll be with you momentarily. I assure you, your client is well."

"Umph, as you say Detective Harry."

"Harris," he replied, the last letter of his name came out as a hiss. Upon hearing snickers from the group of officers and other personnel he turned and narrowed his eyes. The disturbance quieted.

For twenty minutes Charles gathered papers and moved around several logs, every few minutes looking up at the attorney who he'd only seen on television a couple of times, once when she'd defended a wealthy local family in a wrongful death suit and had been interviewed by every news outlet in Chicago. He had watched her answer questions with ease. The second time, she had been interviewed on a local program about her decision to become a lawyer. That time he sat and watched as she smiled and answered questions, but for some reason her smile never quite reached her eyes and back then he found himself wondering why.

Thinking of the times he'd seen her on television, he'd decided she was much prettier in person. He looked at her again. *Nah, scratch that she's gorgeous*. The tug in the pit of his stomach grabbed his attention. He looked at his watch. He'd had lunch a few hours ago, so he wasn't hungry.

"*Mrs*. Walls, please follow me," Charles said as he came from behind the desk and walked over to where she sat.

He watched in rapt awe as she rose, damn near floated, from the row of wooden benches, her feet encased in what he guessed were three-inch heels supported by what appeared to be average sized feet and supple calves. Her suit was the color of fire red, which fitted an ample bosom, cinched at her small waist and adorned by a multi-colored scarf draped around one shoulder and secured with a gem encrusted, circular pin. Her hair, which was curly and wild about her head, seemed to be the only thing out of place, or then again, he found the curly mane fitting to the lioness who had just trampled on his territory.

Time for the lion to tame the lioness.

"It's not Mrs., Detective. It's Ms," she said as she stopped to stand in front of him. He looked down into her eyes, the color a surprising, attractive contrast to her smooth mocha chocolate coloring. Her eyes reminded him of honey—honey brown.

"Ms. Walls," he repeated. "Come this way please." He gently took her by the elbow and resisted smiling down at her as she looked up into his face. He was really pushing it, he thought, but for some inexplicable reason he couldn't help himself. If he could have put his hand around her waist without either her smacking the taste from his mouth or being charged for inappropriate behavior he would have done it. He shook his head. He was really tripping and he knew it was time to get it together. He had an attempted murder case to solve.

Charles kept his hand at her elbow as he escorted her through the security doors to the bank of elevators situated behind the desk. He pressed the up button and waited, praying for the first time in months for the elevator to have one of its slow moments—he was enjoying the look and smell of one Ms. Deena Walls.

At the whoosh of the elevator doors, he frowned then stepped to one side as people departed. "After you," he said as he waited for her to step into the elevator.

The ride to the fifth floor was silent as he watched her from the corner of his eye. He didn't want to talk, he didn't want to stare. Heck! He didn't want to do anything to bring this short time to a quicker end. He was enthralled and perplexed. He tried to chalk it up to her being a star attorney and nothing more. But when she looked up at him he saw an unnamed emotion flash between them.

Moments later, the pair walked off the elevator and Charles had her follow him down a maze of hallways and cubicles to the interview rooms. Once they had come to the door with the number six on it he stopped.

"Your client is waiting for you in there." He opened the door and watched as she walked in. He was still standing in the doorway when she met his eyes.

"Thank you Detective Harry. That'll be all," she dismissed him.

Deena inhaled deeply. She knew it had been a long time, but dang she didn't think three years was that long to go without when you were really hoping to find that one; yet, she'd had to use that extra reserve just to hold herself in place and not show the fine detective that he was getting to her.

When he approached her, she thought him a tall, chocolate candy bar, his voice low, deep and slightly gravelly had grabbed her attention. She watched him walk toward her, his back ramrod straight, his shoulders squared. The sleeves of his shirt were rolled up over his forearms. His handsome face was accentuated by a neatly trimmed mustache. She was hypnotized. He reminded her of one of those fine brothers from the Rundu calendar, and was build like one too. *And his eyes.* Deena was drawn instantly to them the closer he got. She thought he had the most sensuous deep, dark brown, almost black, eyes she had ever seen which had a hungry look, almost predatory look to them. She swore his eyes could start a fire. Mix that with the wicked, hefty scent of his cologne and she was hypnotized.

Damn he smells good.

She leaned her shoulder against the door to the interview room briefly and inhaled quickly. Time to put on the game face she mused. Besides, she knew if she continued to stand in such close proximity to Detective Look N Smell Good, she'd loose the good sense she'd inherited from her momma and daddy.

What in the heck is wrong with me?

When she stood up after he'd called her name, she watched as he had looked down at her, a slight smile on his fine face. And when she challenged him he had rightly put her in her place. Brownie point number one—she didn't like a man who could be easily intimidated—no matter what.

At the elevator, after she'd stepped in and stood over to the corner of the small contraption, she watched him from the corner of her eye as he stood there, slightly in front her, trying not to turn his head to watch her, opting instead to watch the numbers light up on the overhead panel. They had ridden in silence, with Deena looking at the back of Detective Harris's head, his hair cut neat and close. She resisted the urge to reach out and stroke what looked like smooth flat curls about his head.

Deena had curled her top lip and nodded her head curtly right before she trailed behind him toward the interview rooms. She watched his rear as he walked.

Umph, he's got a football player's butt.

In the room she finally looked at her client, Kasha Bentley.

"I didn't do it, Deena. I didn't shoot that guy." Her client insisted as she jumped from the chair and hugged Deena tightly. Deena glanced around the small, bland interview room with the one-way mirror. She knew they were being watched. "You've got to get me out of here."

"Okay, sweetie," Deena soothed as she led Kasha back to her chair then pulled one of three chairs lined against the wall up to the side of the table close to Kasha and then sat down. She looked at the young woman and noticed the strain in her cinnamon face and the fear in her deep blue eyes, made so by contact lenses. Kasha's make up was smeared, the mascara from her eyes made her look garish.

"First, I have to arrange your bail, but right now we're being watched and I'm going to ask you to refrain from speaking any further about the incident."

"But Deena, I didn't do it. I told them that."

"Kasha," Deena leaned forward and looked directly into the young woman's eyes. "Please do not say another word. Let me work on the bail then we'll talk once you're released." Deena placed her index finger to her mouth and watched as Kasha nodded her head in the affirmative.

Deena pulled out her blackberry from her purse and began dialing a number. "Kimmie, I've made it to Area 3. Have David come on down, I think it's going to be a long evening. And go ahead and close up for the night. Thanks, Kimmie. Goodnight." She put the instrument back in her briefcase.

She stood and walked over to the two-way mirror and knocked. "Detective, I know you're there. Can you please step in here?" She walked back over to the table and faced the door. Several moments later the door opened.

"Yes, Ms. Walls."

Deena couldn't help herself as she looked him up and down. In all of her years she had never laid eyes on a finer specimen of a man and she had been around some good looking men—some of the finest in the entertainment industry. She guessed him to be at least six feet four, with broad shoulders, a wide chest and long legs. His face, covered in a neatly trimmed beard, was the color of warm cocoa, his dark eyes piercing. His white dress shirt sleeves were rolled up to showoff well-formed forearms. And when he looked at her as if he could see straight through her to her libido, she wanted to scream—the glare so penetrating she felt as if he were trying to put her under a spell. She had to get a grip, she well couldn't afford any Vulcan mind tricks.

"Detective Harry," she purposely pronounced his name incorrectly. He may be fine, but she didn't have to lose her mind and let him know it.

"Harris, Ms. Walls…"

She waved her hand. "Can you please tell me exactly all the charges Ms. Bentley is being accused of and when will bail be set? As you know, my client is a very popular recording artist and her safety is paramount to me."

"And the health of the man she shot is paramount to me." He stared at her, his smooth eyebrows met in the middle. She'd angered him and wasn't sure if that was a good thing or a bad one, but right now she couldn't quite grasp the sudden attraction to the detective. She also knew she didn't have time for any dalliances or distractions in her life.

"Detective Harris," she said, deciding against butchering his name again. "Unless you charge my client, you cannot continue to hold her." She looked at her watch. "And according to your own booking papers, she's been here for almost 8 hours already."

"Ms. Walls," he began and then stepped further into the room closing the door behind him. She watched him as he slowly waiting squad car for the trip to the city's main jail for suspects who were charged with committing serious criminals.

"This is going to be a long night." Deena blew out as the elevator doors in front of her opened. She looked down the hallway once more as David, Kasha, Detective Lee and that tall drink of water, Harris, disappeared around a corner.

Chapter 2

"Deena Walls speaking. How can I help you?" Deena spoke through the receiver as she pushed stacks of files from one end of her desk to another. She was partner and co-owner in the family's legal business, which was a hodgepodge of stuff, from her bail bondsman, slash private investigator, baby sister, Dionne, to her oldest brother, Darius, who taught law and ran the legal assistance side of the conglomerate, ending with her brother David, who was a partner with her. The four of them, with Deena being the oldest girl, the second child, made up Walls & Associates.

Their parents, both retired lawyers, were graduates of Howard University's school of law where they had met. Together, they built the business, which in the beginning had been run from the basement of their first home, to become the current multi-million dollar law firm it was today. Jedidiah and Deena Walls had instilled in their four children that they could be and achieve whatever they'd set their minds on.

"How about you come into the office, Mr. Swift, next week? I'll have my assistant, Kimmie, put you on my calendar. Hold on." Deena instructed Kimmie to give the caller, who was a wealthy, international meat wholesaler looking to add an addendum to his will, a date over the next two days for him to come in and discuss his latest changes. Deena had to chuckle. Mr. Swift deleted and reinserted his children in and out of his will each time they did something to displease him. She wondered what and which one of his three grown children had transgressed this time.

Deena pinched the bridge of her nose, in an attempt to head off a tension headache. She bent her head down then placed her forehead into the palm of her hands. She'd been going at it non-stop for nearly two days, for that was how long it had taken Deena and her brother to bail their client out of jail. Something in Deena's gut told her this was one case that would be the test of her mettle. For the past year, Deena had been thinking of changing directions all together. Since she'd become a mentor at the Juvenile Detention Center over two years ago, she'd begun to have a serious change of heart in just who she should defend in the legal arena. Sure, the high-profile, high-paying clients had taken her to points and places she may not have otherwise traveled; but defending them had also left a strange unseen film across her entire being. It wasn't anything unsavory—Walls and Associates didn't believe in unethical behavior—but the clients seemed more and more ungrateful.

"Deena, your dad is here for lunch."

"Thanks Kimmie," she responded into the intercom and then gathered her belongings. It was Friday and she was not going to return to the office. Her plan was to have lunch with her father, which would last at least three hours, then hit the gym and end her evening with a bag of microwave popcorn and a good movie.

Deena walked to the outer lobby and watched as her father held court with the recent law students hired as interns for the summer. He was animated as usual—his body language and use of his hands to make his points was one of many things he had used when he was a practicing attorney and then a circuit court judge. She enjoyed watching him just as she had when she was a youngster and had observed him litigate several cases; his most famous was when he defended a group of home owners who'd been discriminated against. It was this case that had made her want to be a lawyer.

"And if you look up the constitution of any state in the Union, you'll notice a resounding theme of immutable rights," she'd heard her father say as she approached him. Deena smiled. This, she mused to herself, was her almost twenty years ago when she'd worked for her parents and had listened with rapt amazement as they'd told of being on the edge of voters' rights, civil rights and all rights in between. Both had admitted to being idealistic, but would not change a thing.

"Hey, Daddy-O!" Deena laughed as she called out to her father. "Wrap it up, Your Honor and let's get going. I'm starving."

"If you would eat right in the morning and then partake in a light snack, you wouldn't be so hungry." He said as he kissed his second born on the cheek. "How's my favorite girl?"

"I'm well. What's mom up to today?"

"She's working on some project with the sorority. What do they have you doing?"

"Fundraising," Deena responded as she wrapped her hand around her father's bicep. At 70, Deena thought her father in great shape. Since his retirement from the bench five years ago, he hadn't slowed one bit. He lectured several times a year, swam daily and boasted that he and his wife had a very healthy sex life. Deena cringed at that last thought. Sure she was no Pollyanna and knew fully about intimate matters, but she didn't want to hear, much less imagine the intimate nature of her parent's relationship.

"Where to today, Daddy-O?"

"How about we go to that nice café on Cottage, Ain't She Sweet?"

"Sure," Deena said as they stepped out onto King Drive and headed to her car, her latest toy, a two-seater, convertible, CLK63 AMG Mercedes Benz.

"Girl, you too old to be buying these death traps."

"Get in and buckle up," Deena ordered, ignoring her father's lament. Each time he saw the sleek sports car he had the same reaction. This was one of the few extravagant items she allowed herself. The car reached 80 miles per hour in five seconds and Deena, being a lover of speed, had opened it up several times on long stretches of road late at night. Her top speed had been one-hundred and twenty miles an hour. She giggled to herself. *Jedidiah Walls would have a mini stroke if he knew that tidbit of information.*

Deena cruised through the changing neighborhood with ease. She marveled as she watched the new mixed with the old, evidence of gentrification everywhere. When she came to a halt at the traffic light she watched as several youths crossed in front. They pointed and nodded their heads as they admired the midnight black sports car. She waved at them and noticed one of the kids whose face showed no emotion as he lagged slightly behind the group. She watched his eyes, the blank stare, and could only imagine what he was thinking. Her eyes took in the rest of him, the too saggy dark jeans slung below his behind, the navy and grey hooded sweat-shirt, which hung just right about his head, his grey and navy designer gym shoes.

The group was still meandering across the intersection as the light turned green. No one bothered to honk their horns.

Moments later, Deena and her father pulled up outs de of the café. Once inside, they both placed their orders and th n sat at a small table near the window. Deena sat and listened a her father started their lunch-time conversation by telling h how she needed to get re-married—give love another try. Sh knew that for the next three hours she'd get a loving lecture fro her father, but he also knew, like everyone else in her immedia family and a few close friends, Deena was afraid to take t t trip down lover's lane having divorced five years ago followi a very short nuptial.

Just as she predicted, three hours later, Deen nd her father emerged from the café. As they reached her car, ark, four-door sedan pulled up behind them. Deena paused the occupants stepped out of the car. She was grateful for dark glasses as she retrieved them from her purse and slipped t onto her face. This was the second time in three days that 'd laid eyes on Detective Charles Henry Harris and her react was no different than the first—explosive.

"Well, Ms. Walls, nice to see you again." e walked over to where Deena and her father stood on sidewalk while Detective Lee nodded in their direction an en headed into the café.

"Umm, not so sure I can say the same," eena replied, a smile on her face as she waved at Lee. She gl ced over at her father standing near the passenger door. She oted the amusement in his eyes. He'd always said that out of l of his children, Deena had inherited his quick wit and biting ngue.

"Judge Walls," he stepped over Deena's father. "It's a pleasure seeing you again." He said s he took Mr. Walls's hand in his and shook it. "It's been a whil ."

Deena watched her father eyes narrow and then a look of recognition as he pumped the detectives hand up and down, patting his back loudly.

"Yes, I remember. You were one of my last cases. If I remember right you were a rookie detective back then. So, how's the department treating you?"

"Very well, sir. I'm still in violent crimes, but it's not bad." He glanced over at Deena before returning his attention to her father. "And though the hours can be grueling, the work is still what I want it to be."

"Good to hear, son," he responded. "You know, I don't remember if you're married or not."

"I'm not married, sir. Divorced," he looked over at Deena again and then wanted to laugh at the horrified expression on her face at her father's question of his marital status. "And I have a son, age 15 going on 40."

"That's how kids are. And that was how Deena was when she was growing up, always in a hurry." Jedidiah laughed. "So, how do you know my Deena?" He leaned his hip on the side of the vehicle, crossed his arms about his chest and waited for his response.

Deena rolled her eyes upward. She knew that gesture meant they'd be at that same spot for at least another ten minutes or so, give or take how Detective Harris answered his probing questions.

She walked around to the passenger side and leaned next to her father to watch the male bonding session in play. And she used the time and their conversation as an uninterrupted opportunity to enjoy an unobstructed view of the handsome man whose face had slipped in and out of her mind no less than once an hour since meeting him. She watched his mouth move as he spoke, his white teeth with a slight overbite, which oddly she found to be quite cute on him.

The afternoon sun cast a warm and sexy light across his handsome face as she took in more of him, observing the laugh lines around his full lips, his jet black eye brows rose with his eye movements. She studied his body language—confident, sure of himself. Admittedly, she liked what she saw even though she didn't want to. Add to it all, he smelled *delicious*; she thought as she closed her eyes and inhaled deeply.

Her eyes rested on the fullness of his smooth lips, shaped perfectly, sort of like L.L. Cool J's. She wondered if they'd feel as smooth against her own—against her bare skin. As she continued to watch him, he was like an accelerant to her flame, which rolled across her face, down her chest to settled in the core of being, threatening to engulf her.

Deena forced her eyes from his lips to the way his broad nose moved when he spoke and then to the twinkle in his eyes when he laughed, the sound rich, vibrant and genuine. She had to smile as the laugh lines around his sensuous mouth were more pronounced. When he moved his head, she noticed the diamond stud in his right ear. She'd never dated a man who wore an earring. But on him it gave him sort of a rugged edge in a daringly sexy way. She guessed the gem to be at least one carat.

"Well, we'd better let you go." Jedidiah Walls said reaching out to shake Detective Harris' hand again then reached into his pants pocket and retrieved one of his business cards. "Here's my number. I golf on Saturday mornings. You do play golf, don't you?" He asked and then continued when Detective Harris nodded his head in the affirmative. "Great. Join Deena and me tomorrow. We tee off at 7." He pushed the card into the detectives hand and then waved as he got into the two-seater.

Deena eased from her place and walked around to the driver's side of her car. She watched him as he watched her, a hint of mirth shone in his eyes.

"What, detective?"

He walked over to where she stood and looked down into her face. He was tempted once again to pull her into his arms, but this time he wondered how she would taste, how they would taste mingled together. He forced his eyes to settle on where he knew her eyes rested hidden behind those dark shades that had allowed her to check him out. He wanted to tell her that he knew she had been checking him out.

"How well do you drive this death trap?" He asked her.

She placed her hands on her hips and leaned toward him. She inhaled deeply and came away with a hefty scent of him, his cologne wrecked havoc with her senses causing her brain to freeze momentarily before she was able to utter a word. She batted her eyes rapidly, perplexed, for this was truly a first.

"Umm, I don't think you and I know each other well enough for you to be questioning my driving abilities." She opened the car door and slid behind the wheel.

"Yeah, but we could." He said as he leaned over to peer at her though the open door.

She stared up at him, his smile a dazzling Colgate kind of smile, and she fought to tap down the shiver that had begun a steady descent up her body. He shut her door, tapped the top then walked around the front of the vehicle, waving at her father as he did.

"He's a nice guy, Deena," her father said.

She shot him a pensive look. "Don't start Jedidiah Louis Walls. I don't want to hear it."

Later, following a grueling session of boxing, Deena headed home, where she showered, ate a small dinner then sat down to check her emails before popping some popcorn and settling down in her home theatre to watch a video. The sound of the ringing phone captured her attention. She looked at the caller ID and smiled. It was her sister, Dionne.

"Hey, girl, when did you get back?"

Dionne, the baby of the family, was eight years younger than Deena. Though all the Walls children favored their mom, Dionne looked more like their mother than anyone, with her caramel complexion, shoulder length hair and honey-colored eyes.

"Yes, I'm home; finally. This one was tough. The guy tried to taze me."

Deena sat back and listened as her sister told her about of the fugitive she had chased half way across the country. His bounty had been half a million dollars, of which a quarter of that belonged to Dionne and Walls Bail Bonds Inc. When it came to family and money, Deena wasn't always so sure which one came first to Dionne. Still she was proud of the sister who upon first glance many thought was a pushover, but when provoked, Dionne, who possessed a black belt in Karate and stood an inch over five feet, could bring a man three times her size and weight to his knees. Her fiancé, Steve, a bounty hunter himself, said that was what attracted him to her.

"Dionne, I wouldn't tell dad about this one. He'll have a fit."

"Don't I know it; even Steve raised the roof over it. But, I'm okay," she responded then changed the subject. "Hey, I heard that Kasha was arrested for attempted murder?"

Deena leaned back in her chair and began to outline as much of the case that she could adding she and David would be working the case together.

"And what gets me is that she isn't being very forthcoming with information. The guy she's accused of shooting is in a coma and you know if he doesn't make it the charges will be upgraded to murder one. You know I'm going to need you to do a little snooping for me. I'll send you what I have so far."

The sisters spoke for another twenty minutes, catching up on family business and the personal happenings in their respective lives. They ended by assuring the other they'd be at the Sunday family dinner with maybe some shopping the upcoming week.

Deena sighed loudly when her phone rang again. She paused as the light, indicating it was the business line ringing, flashed. She looked at the caller ID and saw the call was from the Chicago Police Department.

"Walls and Associates, how may I help you?"

It was Deena's turn to man the hotline. Each family member took turns personally fielding the incoming calls after hours, which could range from serious inquiries to folks who had seen the recent business advertising on cable television—not that they needed another client.

"I'm looking for Deena Walls?" the deep voice spoke into the receiver.

Deena grabbed onto the receiver and held on as the voice seeped into her. She

shook her head. *Umph, umph, umph – what a crime to have a voice like that.*

"Speaking, how may I help you?" She hoped her voice was steady.

"Good evening, Ms. Walls. I hope I'm not interrupting anything important. This is Detective Harris from Area 3."

"It depends, Detective Harris," she replied hoping to sound more authoritative and then realizing maybe she hadn't sound so due to the slight chuckle she'd heard. "What can I do to you? I meant, what do you need?" came her flustered response. She blew out an exasperated breath. "Detective Harris why are you calling me?"

"I thought I'd call and tell you the victim has taken a turn for the worse. They don't expect him to make it the rest of the night."

Deena closed her eyes, shook her head and said a silent prayer. Not good, she thought as a million and one items rolled around in her head at the possibility of having to prepare for a capital case, something she'd never done before. Yet, even with that thought, there was still something in her gut about the whole thing that didn't quite resonate with her.

"Thank you, Detective Harris. I really appreciate your call."

"Do you, now?" he asked, his voice lower. Deena opened her eyes and watched as the screen saver, a 3D graphic of her sorority's crest, floated and then rolled two and fro on her monitor.

"Yes, I really do. But I need to go now. I need to make a few calls."

"Running—I see. I'll call you back if there are any further changes. Good night, Ms. Walls. And I look forward to seeing you in the morning."

"No, you won't see me tomorrow, Detective. I've another engagement and won't be joining my father for golf. But you have a great time with my dad. Good night." She hung up the phone and thought about the man on the other end.

Jeeze. And his voice is even sexier on the phone.

Deena called David and told him of the recent change of

events. They made arrangements to meet at the office on Sunday before the family dinner to discuss their next move if things turned tragic.

After checking for emails and fielding a few more phone calls, Deena shut down her computer and headed to her home theatre. Popcorn in hand, she settled down on the overstuffed couch in front of the large-screen television, hit the play button on the remote and absently watched as the opening credits to the movie rolled on the screen. Her thoughts rolled to those of Detective Harris, how he'd stood over her while they were in the elevator, his dark, deep brown eyes as he sat across from her in the interrogation room and the way he'd smiled at her outside of the café. Deena knew she didn't any distractions right now and all he'd be was a distraction—albeit a super sexy fine one.

Later as she attempted to sleep, Deena tossed and turned, sleep coming in spurts and filled with odd dreams. When she'd dreamed of Detective Charles Harris, she awoke fully. She tried to shake the sensuous feelings the dream had left behind for she couldn't understand how she could be so instantly attracted to him when no man, not even her ex husband, had ever gotten to her in that manner so quickly. Besides, Deena reasoned, a man that damn fine has got to be attached—he's too good looking not to be. Her eyes widened with the thought that maybe he was on the down low. *Nawww,* she stated a loud. She wasn't the least bit homophobic, but she shook her head just the same at the thought and sincerely hoped not.

Chapter 3

Charles sat at his desk while his mind played a video, for the umpteenth time since laying eyes on her, of Deena sitting in the bland looking chair in the interrogation room, her shapely legs crossed, her light eyes blinking as she had spoke to her client.

He'd watched her expressions change, like seasons, as she spoke. He liked the way she looked up close, her near-nutmeg complexion clear and even—no make-up—he liked make-up free women, and her small nose, which twitched when she became excited.

The one time she stood and walked to the water fountain, he just about lost all senses. He had never seen a woman walk like she did. Her hips did a rhythmic dance, a sway to some imaginable beat—some tune. He loved it. Wanted to watch her walk everyday if he could. He couldn't believe his eyes when he saw her, in his station house, on his turf and knew it was a one in a million opportunity. How often do you get to arrest the clients of Deena Walls—partner of one of the most successful law firms in all of Chicago?

And when she stood near him, the top of her head barely reached past his collarbone. Charles liked short women and he couldn't believe his luck when he spied her earlier outside of the café. He had to steel himself against grabbing her and pulling her close as she had looked up at him, her eyes shielded behind those dark sunglasses. He'd watched her closely, as she crossed her arms in front of her. The motion was supposed to ward off danger, but Charles courted danger—even danger that came in a small package of dynamite named Deena.

Charles shrugged his shoulders, attempting to dismiss her and all thoughts of her. Besides, he reasoned, he wasn't trying to get all tangled up with her or any other woman for that matter. He was tired of the games most women played and their inability to just let go of past hurts. He wanted a woman who could not only hold her own, but was mature enough to let the past be the past while embracing the future. Yet he couldn't get his attraction to the dynamite attorney out of his mind and he found it somewhat disconcerting.

"Man, I got it bad," he said loudly. Lee appeared in the doorway and smiled. "Not one word from you. Here me?" he barked then turned his attention to the stack of papers on his desk.

"Hey, I've got nothing to say, Chuck." He held up his hands. "Look, I'm ready to call it a night. What about you?"

Charles closed the file and returned it to his active pile. He'd been working on several cases for the past ten hours and he was tired. He was glad for the upcoming Saturday, a day he saved for doing errands and hanging out with his son, Corbin.

Besides, he thought to himself, he was golfing with Judge Walls, Deena's father and he knew Corbin, who was on the golf team at his high school, would enjoy hanging with the retired judge, whom Charles found to be quite animated. Charles couldn't help but laugh at the memory of the judge who had run his court room by the book and didn't suffer fools, be it attorneys, cops or defendants. But he was also equally as comfortable using funny quotes and antidotes to get his point across.

He thought of Deena again. His gut instinct told him she was not what he saw, that beneath the veneer her emotions ran deep. His curiosity piqued and he wondered just how deep she was, how much of what he saw was really her and how much she kept hidden—protected. Charles had a feeling Deena kept a lot hidden. He rolled that last thought around and wondered why he even cared. Still it was something about Deena that woke him up and caused his blood to stir, right below the surface.

Charles looked up at his partner. "Yeah, I'm about finished here." He stood, stretched and then grabbed his blazer, slipping his arms through the sleeves. Lee turned off the lights as he and Charles stepped out into the hallway. They both joked and waved, stopping at cubicles to speak with fellow officers and detectives as they made their way to the door that led to the stairway. Both preferred to take the stairs for not only health reasons, but because a perp had tried to assault a female officer in the stairwell a year back. And even with the installation of cameras and stringent security measures, personnel continued to take the stairway as an extra precaution.

"What you got going on tonight?"

"Lee, I've got a date," he looked at his partner and then tried to hide his laughter when his partner raised his eyebrows. "...with a washing machine." He laughed as he headed for his private vehicle, a Ford Explorer.

"Man, you need to get a real life."

"Look who's talking."

Lee pointed to himself and then shook his head. "I've got a date, tonight, and her name is not Tide and she doesn't smell like a dryer sheet."

Charles couldn't help but laugh at his partner and closest friend. Lee, as he called him, had first been his partner when they were rookies, where they'd hit it off immediately, and then years later when they'd both became detectives in Violent Crimes. Lee had made it a point to teach Charles all about his Chinese culture while Charles had introduced him to the three cultures that made up his heritage: African, Cherokee, and Gullah.

"One day, Lee."

"Umm, but I did catch those looks between you and that attorney. She's good looking, Chuck, but she's no dummy."

"And she's got a razor sharp tongue," he replied and then thought about her shape. He shook his head as the thought of her up close and personal gathered in his mind. He did find her great to look at, and the little sparing match they'd had seemed to fuel his curiosity to find out as much as he could about Ms. Deena Walls.

"Be careful, dude," Lee pounded Charles's fist with his, embraced him and then headed for his own vehicle. "I'll call you on Sunday to see if you're up for some gladiator."

"Sure, just give me a call. I'd be more than glad to kick your butt some more," Charles responded and then laughed even harder when he thought of the last time they'd played PlayStation II. Lee had been beat not only twice by Charles, but nearly a half dozen times by Corbin.

Charles waved as he put his vehicle in drive and pulled from the rear lot of Area 3. He slid in a CD of some reggae and bopped his head to Shabba Ranks as he listened to him brag about being the king.

Finally arriving home on Chicago's south side, Charles rolled into his garage, shut off the engine and sat quiet for a moment. He looked at the vehicle next to him and smiled. He was just about finished restoring the 1965, black on black, drop-top, Pontiac GTO.

Rebuilding cars had been one of his hobbies since high school, when he had taken auto mechanics and body shop. He was so good at it, he'd been offered jobs even before he'd graduated from high school, but he knew his mother, Winnie Harris, would have had a stroke had he not gone to college. And it was his mechanical acumen that helped pay his way through college—he fixed everyone's car, from the president of the university to the dean of students. Charles had made enough money to not only pay his tuition, room and books, but to keep some money in his pockets.

Charles allowed his hand to slide down the side of the vintage vehicle; its smooth contours and curves reminded him of Deena. He opened the driver's door and slid onto the seat, wrapping his hands around the steering wheel. He was just about complete—only a few modifications left. He'd be finished well before the beginning of the upcoming season of the vintage auto shows held at various locations around Chicago.

He rested his head back on the headrest and closed his eyes. He could image himself rolling down the street with Deena sitting next to him, the breeze flowing through her curly hair, his hand resting on the back of her seat.

Charles sat up.

"I'm tripping," he said aloud as he climbed out of the car, shutting the door behind him. He closed the garage door with the automatic opener. He thought of his ex-wife. The car was just one of the many things he and his ex-wife didn't have in common. But Charles held no animosity toward her for he had been and still was a man who lived by truth and the truth was that they had been mismatched from the start; it was something that neither had wanted to admit it back then. The marriage didn't last five years. But he was grateful for the one great thing he did get out of the marriage—Corbin.

He glanced over at his elderly neighbor's yard, the weeds and grass reminded him of a mini jungle and he was tempted to make noises one would hear in a dense jungle. He reminded himself to cut their grass and conduct a little weeding when he his mowed his own lawn.

"Hey girl," he greeted the large Rottweiler who met him at the rear door. "Where's Corbin?" The dog perked up as she ran toward the stairs leading to Corbin's room. Charles followed behind, taking the stairs two at a time. He looked at the large poster of Beyoncé on the closed door—sounds of the Hip Hop princess could be heard loudly through the closed door.

"Corbin," he called as he knocked on the door and then opened it. He looked at his son, the boy who had come to live with him the moment he'd turned twelve, dressed in baggy jeans and a white t-shirt. Charles had agreed with his ex-wife when she insisted he raise their son into manhood. She moved to Florida not long after.

"Hey there, son," Charles said as he held out his arms. He watched as his son rose from his prone position on the full-sized bed and stepped into him for a hug. "You okay today? How was school?"

Corbin returned the hug before stepping back. "I'm good, Dad, and school was okay. I only got a C on my biology test though."

Charles sat at the desk where his son's computer rested. He smiled when he noticed the screen saver was as a collage of pictures of their trip last summer to Africa. Charles and Corbin had started taking two-week vacations every summer when Corbin had come to live with him.

"So, what do we need to do to get a better grade?" Charles asked as he glanced around the room, taking in the contents. He never wanted to spy on his son, but he did make sure he knew what was going on. He'd even started helping Corbin clean his room weekly.

"I was freaked out, Dad, when they brought that pig out to be dissected."

Charles laughed, for his son was definitely a chip off the old block. As a detective he'd seen death—from decomposition to a body riddled with bullets—but he'd never been able to handle the coroner's office and the autopsies homicide detectives sometimes had to witness. This was why he'd never entertained homicide.

"Was there another option?"

"No. It was the pig or bust."

Charles rose from chair. "Well, you may need to try for some extra credit work to make up for the grade." He headed toward the door. "Do you have any homework?"

Corbin shook his head 'no' and followed his father out of the room. They walked down the stairs and headed to Charles' bedroom, near the rear of the oversized brick bungalow. This was their daily routine and since Corbin's arrival Charles had altered much of his bachelor life, learning to cook, clean and keep female company to a bare minimum—actually more like non-existent. He'd had two real dates and a few dalliances since his son had come to live with him three years ago, but nothing really serious. It seemed as if each time he thought he met someone he could bring home, something would happen and they'd split up.

"We're going to have to work on that biology. What else is going on?"

He began preparing for their evening run, easily slipping into one conversation after another. Charles looked at his son and noticed the hair on his face seemed thicker than it had been a week ago and the hair on his head needed trimming. He made a mental note to trim his hair on Saturday after the golf outing.

He watched his son as he leaned against the dresser and told him about some upcoming party at a friend's house and how all the kids from school would be there. Charles paused and looked at him. They'd been having the conversation about sex and birth control, but he knew from the constant phone calls and messages from girls he needed to make sure his son's head was screwed on tightly. Not only did he not want to be a grandpa anytime soon, he also didn't want his son to catch any type of sexually transmitted diseases.

"Are you ready to go for a run, girl?" Charles spoke to the dog as he scratched behind her ears. At eight-months-old, the Rottweiler was considered a puppy and he had affectionately named her Sweetie because of her easy and sweet demeanor.

Sweetie barked. "Okay, girl, go get your leash and meet me back here in ten minutes." He laughed as Sweetie raced off to retrieve her leash while Corbin headed back to his bedroom. Charles removed his revolver, a 9mm, nickel plated Glock, unloaded it and placed it into a locked safe under his bed. He removed his clothes, replacing them with his workout gear.

Moments later, they emerged from their rooms, father and son, dressed in long shorts and sleeveless T's.

Sweetie sat near the rear door, her leash in her large mouth, waiting for Charles. He took the leash from the dog, placed it around her neck and then led her outside.

Corbin's long legs broke into an easy stride and Charles knew he had to run a little harder to keep up. He didn't mind though, this was one their favorite times together which allowed them to spend uninterrupted quality time while catching up on the events in Corbin's life. After they'd jogged for several blocks, they switched directions and headed to the neighborhood park.

Charles knew few if any people would be in the park at nine at night and he could let Sweetie loose as he and Corbin jogged around the track.

An hour later, Charles, Corbin and Sweetie headed back to the house. After instructing Corbin to give Sweetie some water and let her out in the yard, he headed to the shower.

Later that night, as Charles and Corbin sat in the basement to watch television, Sweetie situated firmly between them with her large head resting on Corbin's thigh, Charles glanced up from the newspaper he'd started reading to the screen. He watched as the words rolled across the screen announcing upcoming community events. He leaned toward the television when he saw the announcement about an upcoming dinner where Deena Walls would be receiving an award. He knew the organization and the husband of the executive director.

He picked up the cordless phone nearby and began dialing. He drummed his fingers on the arm of the couch. When the party answered he dismissed with the pleasantries. "How much are the tickets to that upcoming fundraiser honoring Ms. Walls?" Charles nodded his head as his frat brother gave him the information. "And I'll be at the same table as she is?" He smiled, his right eye brow raised. "I'll be there and I owe you one, frat. I really do. And do me another favor. Don't tell her I'll be at her table."

He hung up the phone and then looked at Corbin, who was looking squarely at him a broad smirk plastered across his face. Charles wanted to tell him to mind his own business that he knew what he was doing, but didn't because in large part he wasn't quite sure what he was doing himself or why.

"What?" he asked as he raised his hands.

Corbin laughed at the gesture. "Like you tell me, 'somethin's 'a cookin'".

Chapter 4

"The only reason you're going to see me tonight is that I'm the guest of honor, otherwise you wouldn't be seeing me." Deena spoke to her sorority sister, Karen LaFontant, who was the executive director of the Juvenile Mentoring Unit. Karen, a former juvenile probation officer, started the unit several years ago to address issues faced by juveniles being adjudicated for crimes. Her unit, one of its kinds across the United States, sought to provide wrap-around services for juveniles, many who were also the center of nasty, custody battles between the state and their parents. Deena had started supporting the unit first by donating money, but when Karen had talked her into becoming a mentor and she had met the first of three mentees, Deena was hooked.

"Whatever, shippee." Karen laughed. "Just have on your 'come get me' shoes. Gary has sold seven tables to his frat brothers and a few of them are quite single."

"So?" Deena groaned thinking of how Karen and her husband, Gary, would probably try and fix her up with some funny looking dude with too much cologne, too much ego and not enough common sense. She forced the thought of the possible blind date out of her head.

"So, it has been several years, Deena. And in that time I can count on one hand, minus a finger or two, how many real dates you've had. And girl, I'm afraid to ask you again how long it's been since you've got your groovy cool on."

Deena twirled around in her seat. She stared out onto Dr. Martin Luther King Drive and watched as CTA buses and people rushed up and down the street. She snickered and thought about what her soror had just said and she knew Karen was right. But every time a man tried to get too close, Deena began to have serious reservations and would abruptly end things, no matter how promising. And she didn't even want to think about intimacy. She didn't even want to go there. No way.

Besides, once bitten, twice shy.

She thought about Detective Harris. She hadn't heard from him since last week. The victim had stabilized even though he was still in a coma. On Sunday during their family dinner, which was also the day following the golf outing the detective had with her father, her father had talked non-stop about the smart, good-looking detective who was destined for higher places within CPD. Her father had ended by informing her he seemed to be a great father and was a divorcee, just like her.

"Now tell me. What are you going to wear tonight?" Karen's question brought her out of her momentary reprieve.

"I'm thinking of a white number or maybe that short black dress I bought when we were in Puerto Rico last year."

"Deena, wear the black one. You've got great legs and the dress will show them off just right. Girl, I'm going to have to put a fire extinguisher and some ice water at your table to put out the heat you're going to be attracting." Karen laughed.

"You're crazy, Karen. You know that. But, I've got to run, I'll see you later."

"Thanks, sister. I really appreciate the support. Love you."

"Love you, too," Deena responded. She hung up the phone and returned to her work. She met with two new clients and took an urgent call from one of her mentee's, a 15-year-old female name Serena whose mother had left her with an elderly relative. Serena, a pretty bright teen with a high IQ, was being held in juvenile detention for shoplifting and battery. After assuring the youngster she would indeed be in court with her when her date arrived, she made a mental note to stop at the nearby convenience store and pick up some toiletries for Serena and several of the other female youths she mentored, all who were being detained for one reason or another.

By the end of the day, Deena was tired and ready to head home. Visions of soaking in her Jacuzzi tub danced in her head; but she had to get ready for the fundraiser/award ceremony for the Mentoring Unit.

As Deena readied herself for the evening's activities, her right hand kept itching. It signaled one of two things: money or a golden opportunity.

Deena stepped out of the building where she lived in the two-story penthouse unit and into a waiting, white Lincoln Towne car she hired for the evening to take her to the posh Swiss Hotel for the evening's affair.

"Wow, brother, you're looking quite prosperous," Gary greeted his fraternity brother and friend with the secret handshake hidden behind their chest-to-chest embrace.

"Same to you. Where's the woman you stole from me?" Charles looked over Gary's head and the pair laughed. "You know you took my woman."

Charles and Gary had gone to college together and had pledged Omega Psi Phi during their sophomore year. Gary had met his wife nearly ten years ago when the alumni chapter they belonged to held a fundraiser with the fraternity's sister sorority. They'd met Karen at the same time, but clearly she was interested in Gary. When they married five years later, Charles hadn't been able to make their wedding in Jamaica because he had been working on a high profile case surrounding a rash of violent assaults.

"You know what they say: finders keepers loosers weepers." Gary patted Charles on the back. "But I do think I've redeemed myself by placing you at the table with the one and only Deena Walls. And do know she is not only my daughter's godmother, my wife's best friend and soror, but I must think awful highly of you, for I got calls from a few other Frat wanting to sit at her table." Gary chuckled and turned toward the entrance to the ballroom. He whistled low and Charles turned to face the door.

"Dayum," Charles muttered under his breath as he watched Deena walk into the ballroom, her normally wild, curly hair, which he actually liked, flowed in a layered look framing her face. She had on a sparkling black, spaghetti-strapped dress, the hem resting several inches above her knees and giving him and every other man in the room a healthy view of a pair of gorgeous, well-formed legs.

He swallowed the large lump forming in his throat. He removed the white handkerchief from the breast pocket of his tux and dabbed at the moisture forming along his brow.

"My God, what did I ask for?" he'd asked aloud before he

could catch himself. He looked at Gary who only shrugged in response.

Charles decided to make a beeline for the men's room. He needed to regroup, to try and get his self together before sitting next to Deena. He couldn't remember the last time a woman had gotten under his skin to the point of making him feel like a schoolboy on a playground asking to play along. The emotion was both foreign and admittedly a little scary.

After using the facilities and washing his hands, he left the washroom and headed back into the ballroom. He inhaled deeply and pep talked to himself as he made his way to the table he'd be sharing with one of the most beautiful women he'd ever had the pleasure of being insulted by.

Deena stepped inside the elegantly decorated ballroom and looked around at the scores of people who had gathered to support the Juvenile Mentoring Unit. For nearly 10 years, the mentor program had been the last life line for juveniles who had brushes with the law.

Deena spotted Karen across the room standing next to her husband, Gary, a public defender at the juvenile center. The two had met and married five years ago and Deena thought they complimented each other, both supporting the other, while strengthening the other's weaknesses. She smiled as she watched them move effortlessly through the ballroom, heading to their table. They were truly the couple of the century, which is how Deena playfully referred to them. She hadn't been jealous of her best friend and sorority sister, but she often secretly wished she could find a mate like Karen had.

By the time Deena arrived at the table, those present were laughing as Gary told one story after another of his job as a public defender. The table, which sat ten, was situated near the front of the ballroom, close to the band and the platform where Deena would deliver her acceptance speech.

She noticed an empty seat on her left and she wondered who would sit there, for she'd been entertained by a slender, cream in your coffee colored man who sat next to the empty chair and was leaning over it, his hand possessively draped across it.

Deena was being polite as the man, who identified himself as Larry, chattered endlessly and she hoped he wouldn't move over. She was being even more polite when he asked her who was sitting next to her and she shrugged her shoulders. She wanted to tell him: *not you*. She didn't want to come off as mean, but this

Larry guy was not her type and she could tell he was attempting to come on to her.

As the band kicked off the start of the festivities and Larry began to ease his way over onto the empty seat, she got a whiff of a familiar scent just as she heard the deep, luscious voice.

"Good evening, Ms. Walls," he said as he looked down into her upturned face. He noted the astonished look and was pleased that she seemed pleasantly surprised. "Brother Larry, I do believe you are trying to slither into my seat." Charles yanked at the seat which caused Larry to nearly topple over. "Thanks for thinking it needed warming," he shot at Larry as he sat down.

Deena raised her eyebrows taking in the way his tuxedo fit him perfectly, the cut of the single-breasted jacket accentuated his wide shoulders before tapering down to hang just above his thighs. The deep purple cummerbund matched his bow tie.

Charles claimed the seat next to her.

"Good evening Detective."

"My name is Charles. Some folks call me Charles or Chuck."

"Which would you prefer?"

"I'll take Charles over Harry, which, as you know, is not my name."

Deena smiled and nodded her head. She was owned that one.

"Okay, how about I call you Charles," she said and looked into his face, his beard and mustache neatly trimmed as was his closely cut, curly hair. Her eyes roved over his right hand and she noted the clean, short nails as well as the bandage attached at the fleshy part of his hand. She pointed to it. "What happened to your hand?"

"I cut it trying to remove a crankshaft."

"I bet you were trying to remove it with one of those short wrenches."

He blinked several times.

"Yeah, how'd you know?"

Deena chuckled at the surprised look on his face. Very few men outside her ex-husband and the men in her immediate family knew she liked to tinker with cars. "Let's just say I know a little sumptin-sumptin about cars."

"Can you cook? Clean? Dance?"

Deena laughed and nodded in the affirmative to his litany of questions.

"Then, will you make me an insanely happy man and marry me?" Charles took her left hand in his. She could see the sparkle in his eyes and the mirth that shone on his handsome face. She laughed as she slowly removed her hand from his, the jolt of electricity from his touch that shot up her arm caused her to flinch and she didn't want him to see the effect he was having on her.

With his humor and that wicked scent he wore, a piece of the wall she had erected fell away as he held her attention, never letting Larry get another word in edge wise.

"Would you like to dance?" Charles stood and held his hand out to her. She glanced across the table at her friend and soror and knew that they were on display. Deena then looked up at the face staring down at her and much to her surprise she placed her hand in his and rose, allowing him to lead her to the dance floor. Charles wrapped his strong arm around Deena's waist as the slow strings from the live quartet began to play.

Deena tried to resist placing her head on his chest, but lost the will to do so when he pulled her closer, her breasts flush against his upper torso, heat radiating between them. She felt it, the electricity; the heated flame of desire as it fanned itself around her. She didn't dare look up, not sure she wanted him to see the look in her eyes, instead she closed her eyes and swayed to the music, her mind whirled as he hummed against her hair, his fingers lightly massaging her waist.

"And if I didn't say so, please accept my apologies now, for you look stunning in that dress."

Deena blushed. She had hurriedly dressed, sweeping her hair up into a chignon with ringlet curls hanging around the nape of her neck and cascaded down the sides and front of her face. The short, fitting black spaghetti strapped dress, adorned with small iridescent beads, gave an appropriate peek of her bosom and shapely legs. And her black *poi de sio's* pumps were just the added touch she wanted to achieve. She was glad she listened to Karen.

When the music ended, reluctantly Deena stepped away from Charles, but his hand never left her waist as he guided her back to their seats. Holding her seat until she sat down, Charles allowed his hand to brush lightly across her shoulders. Deena shivered lightly.

What in the world is the matter with me? She wondered.

Once dinner had been served and most folks were working on the desert, Deena rose to give her speech. She stepped up on the stage and headed to the microphone. Looking out she glanced around the crowded room. When she looked at the table where she'd been sitting, her eyes fell on Charles as he sat forward in what seemed to Deena as one of expectation. What did he expect of her?

By the time she'd delivered her speech, which spoke of the need to continue to protect juveniles while balancing their needs and the needs of the public, and then accepted her award, the crowd were on their feet, giving her a standing ovation. And when she headed toward the edge of the stage, she was met by the strong hand of Charles as he escorted her back to the table.

Deena had to admit she hadn't enjoyed herself this much since she and her family had gone to Disneyland last year on a family vacation where she'd spent a lot of time with her brothers' wives and their children. But the burning question in the back of her mind was; would he run once he knew the issues she dealt with on a regular basis.

❦

"You were the belle of the ball," Charles stated as he held his hand out to Deena, assisting her from the high step of the SUV. "And that was some speech you gave. I didn't know that both of your parents were attorneys."

Deena nodded her head in the affirmative. For the entire evening, she'd allowed Charles to make a fuss over her, helping her with her chair when she'd rose to deliver her speech, to going back and forth to the bar retrieving drinks for the two of them. Deena listened to Charles as he told her stories that made her laugh and he had listened intently to her as she talked about her family. But it was when he'd look at her, an odd gaze to his dark eyes that had her wondering, caused her pressure to rise and her pulse to run erratic. And when he'd held her in his arms, her head resting on his chest, his arms wrapped securely, protectively and seductively around her, she'd become lost, not sure if she ever wanted to be released from the warm shield he provided.

She had inhaled his scent, the cologne mixed with his natural body essence—her mind swirled and even as she looked at him now, she found herself wondering who this man was. The one who on this night made her feel as if she was the only one who mattered, plied her with a generous amount of attention and looked at her as if she was the only woman in the entire room. And when he'd asked her how she arrived and she told him, he insisted that she cancel her hired car and allow him to escort her home. Right before they departed the hotel's ballroom, Karen had come up to her.

"You two look great together," Karen whispered into Deena's ear. "He's single, straight, and is really a great guy. I'd approve if you took him home and had your way with him."

Karen laughed out loud at the incredulous look her words left on Deena's face. She would not be having sex tonight, or any other night. And it wasn't that the sexy-ass man standing near her didn't bring some ferocious heat that seemed to pool at her core every time he so much as tapped her hand—she just didn't want the heartache—she'd had enough to last her two lifetimes.

After they left the hotel, Charles had offered to have her wait while he went to get his vehicle. She refused and began walking with him. She hadn't known how far away he'd parked from the hotel and her feet began to protest the three-inch heels as one block turned into two.

Charles looked down at Deena. "You should have stayed put. I didn't expect anyone to ride with me, so I parked at a meter. Here," he stopped and knelt in front of her. He removed her shoe and began massaging her foot. She rested her hands on his broad shoulders, closed her eyes and moaned loudly.

"Oh, my gosh!" she exclaimed. "Man, you should go into business."

He laughed loudly. "You think?" He looked up at her and watched as her eyes fluttered open. He winked at her then placed the shoe back on her foot, repeating the action with the other foot. "There, that should last you. I'm just another a block away."

"Thank you," she replied as they walked side by side, their hands bumping.

Finally arriving at the SUV, Charles opened the door and held out his hand as Deena climbed into the front seat. She watched him as he crossed the front of the vehicle then slid in beside her. She could see him steal a look at her and then smiled at him when she gave him her address.

The normal ten-minute ride took thirty as they laughed and talked, with Charles getting stopped by every traffic light on Michigan Avenue.

Deena had to admit she had really enjoyed his company and wondered why he didn't have a girlfriend. Karen had said he was single and her father talked about his son, who'd accompanied them on their golf outing. Her thoughts were interrupted when he pulled up in front of her building.

"Wow, you live here?" He asked and watched as she nodded her head up and down. "Must be nice," he murmured as he stepped from the vehicle and walked around to the passenger door. Opening it, he looked up at the high-rise. "What floor do you live on?" He held his hand out to her.

"Top." she mumbled. This was always the way it started with her and men. They would see where she lived, come inside and then their minds would play tricks and they'd make the crazy assumption that if she could afford a 8,000 square foot, two-level penthouse, then what could they give her. None stuck around to find out.

"Well," he said and then looked down into her face. He noticed her eyes were cast downward. "Ms. Walls, I must say I had a great evening. Did you enjoy yourself?"

She looked up at him and smiled. He was leaning over her looking into her face expectantly. His smile and that wicked cologne that had made its way onto her dress began to do a tap dance on her senses that would make the Nicholas Brothers look like rank amateurs.

"I did. And thank you. Most times those things are so boring it's like watching a can of paint dry. But you made the evening fun, so I owe you."

"I'd like to collect. How about dinner on Friday? Say, seven o'clock. I'll be right here." He said and pointed to the ground.

Deena wondered had she heard him correctly? Was he inviting her out to dinner? Weren't they on opposite sides of the fence? Especially since Kasha's arraignment was in one week and Deena planned on using some of Charles's own tactics against him, like his interrogation of Kasha before she'd arrived.

She looked up at him as he watched her expectantly. Their night had been great, almost magical and if they had met under different circumstances she would consider going out with him. But seeing as how she had a case to win while possibly decimating Charles in the process she didn't think their dating would be too great an idea.

"Charles," she opened her mouth and saw the look in his eyes change from mirth to caution as if he knew what she was going to say before she said it. "I'd love to, but you and I both know that when this whole case goes to trial, I won't be your favorite person."

"And you're sure of that?"

Deena chuckled. This brother didn't quite know who she was. Out of hundreds of cases in all her years of litigation, she'd only lost one and that was due to her lack of experience. Deena didn't plan on loosing—she knew that a deal would be what she'd end up with after ensuring a few of the charges were dropped or lessened.

"I'm quite sure."

Charles tilted his head to the side and began laughing. "Woman, I like your style. But for me none of this business is personal. You'll have to toss the kitchen sink at my momma's head for me to take it personal. But I think there's another reason."

"What?" She asked and watched as Charles leaned his large, masculine frame on the side of his SUV.

"You're afraid that if you go out with me one time you won't be able to get enough of my charm and animal magnetism."

He twisted his mouth and then crossed his arms over his chest. Deena chuckled as she watched his cool stance. She liked him, liked how he looked, how he smelled, how he'd held her and knew a part of what he was saying was true—she was afraid. Deena didn't want another man who started out sweet and good and nice only to end up trying to rule and control her. She would not be caged ever again like Seth had tried to do.

"You're funny, detective…"

"Aww, shoot, we're back to formalities?" He interrupted her.

Deena rolled her eyes at him.

"Go ahead, Ms. Walls."

"I just don't think it's a good idea for us to go out right now."

Charles grinned at her. "But after the trial is over, maybe you can find time to hang out a little and let your hair down like you did tonight." He reached out and tucked a strand of her hair behind her ear, his fingers lightly grazing the side of her face.

Deena shivered. She wanted to lean into him, to feel his fingers caress her face, to pull her into an embrace. No, she chided herself, not going to be charmed this time.

"Thank you, Detective for a great evening and for seeing me home." Deena began backing up toward the entrance.

Charles stepped away from his SUV and extended his arm toward her. Deena shrugged her shoulders as she decided to slip her hand around the bend at his elbow. She marveled at the solid feel of him as he walked her to the entrance of her building.

"I would escort you to your door, but from the looks of this place, security isn't an issue," Charles said as he looked up at the camera trained on them. He glanced into the dimly lit foyer then down into Deena's upturned face. He wanted to kiss her so bad he could have sworn his lips were aching. Instead, he tapped her hand then took it in his and kissed the back of it. "So, I'll bid you a good night. And I'll see you in court."

"Good night. And again thank you."

"It's been all my pleasure, for sure. Good night." He waved over his head as he walked back to his SUV. Deena stood in the lobby and watched him walk, his gait strong, assured and super sexy. He waved again as he entered the vehicle then disappeared down the street. Deena stood there for several moments until another couple entered the lobby.

Turning, she headed to the elevator, placed her key into the indicator and waited as the elevator ascended to the 35th floor. At her floor, she stepped off the elevator and walked down the short hall. Opening the door, she stepped inside, shut the door then placed her keys in the glass bowl that sat atop a maple table before heading further into the condo.

Deena walked over to the floor-to-ceiling window and leaned against it, her eyes absorbing the striking beauty of the August night, the bright full moon and sparkling stars. She wrapped her arms around herself and thought of the many nights she'd stood in the widow and dreamed, sometimes with tears in her eyes as she thought of the pain of loving someone so much that one was blinded to all there was to really see. She didn't want to love like that ever again, and though Charles was gorgeous, sexy and attentive, she had no intentions of getting involved with him or any other man. Besides, she reasoned, she found it so much easier to just be alone. She knew how she felt and knew she'd done the right thing by not encouraging Charles.

Deena sat on the chaise lounge nearby. She looked up in time to see a falling star. Quickly, she closed her eyes and made a wish before she could catch herself. She was amazed at the wish—to be fearless in relationships.

After twenty minutes, Deena headed to her bedroom. As she readied for bed, the scent and thought of Charles firmly in her mind, she slid in between the cool sheets. She gave up trying to remove him from her thoughts and gave in to the fantasy that seemed hell bent on taking residence in her conscious while making her remember that she was not only a woman, but a woman who at one time had loved deeply and passionately.

"Why did I let him rob me of that?" Deena whispered as she rolled over on her side and closed her eyes. She forced the thought of Seth from her mind, opting to refocus and allow Charles's image to invade her.

Chapter 5

"Why are you finding it so difficult to tell me the whole truth, Kasha?" Deena said as she paced around the conference room. Several times she had come close to losing her cool with the young woman, for she knew, based on some preliminary investigation of her own, that there were several people in the apartment of the housing complex where the incident had taken place.

Deena sat down and looked around the table. Across from her sat Kasha, David and Kasha's agent, a young guy from Los Angeles named Juan-Carlos Valdez. Deena knew Juan-Carlos from some business she'd handled for several of his clients and a pair of mutual associates, but outside of that she really didn't know the smooth-talking man with the warm olive complexion sitting across from her, his grey silk tailored suit hanging on him just right.

Since agreeing to represent his latest client six months ago, Deena had found herself nearly babysitting the young woman, bailing her out of one problem after another. It had gotten so bad each time she received a call concerning Kasha she'd come to expect the worse and was relieved when it was good news.

"Let me begin, Juan-Carlos, by telling you that the charges against Kasha, coupled with the fact that she won't even tell us what happened..." She pointed to herself then David. "...the night Mr. Williams was shot remain a mystery, which really doesn't bode well with the CPD, us or her case. And although Mr. Williams is expected to survive, he's still in a coma and may be that way for years to come."

David blew out a breath hard. "Once we've finished this case, Mr. Valdez, Walls and Associates will no longer represent Ms. Bentley."

Juan-Carlos jumped from his seat and found himself staring David squarely in the face. Deena hadn't flinched. She was an excellent boxer and David was a black belt in Tai Kwon Do. She made a tent of her fingers and watched the stare-down between the two men, even though David was a few inches shorter. David won.

"Sir, I suggest you have a seat," David ordered, his voice dangerously low. Out of the four siblings, David was the one a person least wanted to ever cross. While Darius and Deena could be a little mouthy, and Dionne more kick-butt, David was the quiet one of the brood and when provoked could strike, physically or mentally, with an accurate blow. Deena looked at Juan-Carlos and recognized the view of reckoning.

"As I was saying," David repeated as he sat back down. "Walls and Associates will represent Ms. Bentley in this upcoming criminal case, but all other business will be summarily discontinued. You will receive your retainer back and we've drawn up another agreement for the criminal work only. Is this understood?"

When David and Deena had met that Sunday, both had the sneaking suspicion that something with Kasha wasn't quite right and given that she hadn't even told them what had gone on in that apartment, only added to their suspicion, which was further piqued with the arrival of Juan-Carlos in Chicago.

Deena looked over at Kasha, her head hung low as she sat quietly listening. A former homeless teen, Kasha had a voice that could make angels cry and the Devil of a deal to give away the souls collected. And her exotic beauty—a beautiful bronze complexion—made many people openly stare in awe. But Kasha also had personal demo ns chasing her and Deena had tried several times, in vain, to get the girl to agree to go to counseling. She thought about Kasha's words on the phone the day of her arrest.

Even the matter of where she lived had been a problem. It took them a month to get the truth. Juan-Carlos had asked Deena, as a favor, to help Kasha find a place to live. Then there was the issue of her true identity and birth date that arose following a late-night into early morning party where it was reported that underage drinking had taken place. That's when Deena found out she was 18 and not 21 as she had claimed.

Other issues cropped up, like missing clothes at promotional shoots to shoplifting at department stores and her refusal to leave behind the street element that seemed so intent on making sure Kasha never realized her dreams because they were angry she dared to have any dreams at all.

Kasha had been non-stop drama and Deena found herself doing more bailing out and smoothing over than she liked.

Deena's Blackberry vibrating at her hip brought her back to the meeting at hand. She glanced at the number then hit the send button.

"Hey Karen," Deena began. "I'm in a meeting. Let me call you back later."

She disconnected the call and turned her attention back to the group assembled. She looked over at David, whose face was tight with anger. "Juan-Carlos," Deena began as she stood again. She knew her movements was making Kasha nervous, which is exactly what Deena wanted. She needed her to understand that years of her life were at stake, for the best they could hope for was attempted murder, which in the state of Illinois was a felony that carried no less than 10 years in a state prison. And the penal facility for women was no joke.

"Walls and Associates, as you may know, is a family owned firm created by our parents. Over the past forty years, this firm has worked hard to establish a solid reputation." Deena paused and looked Kasha squarely in the eye before continuing. "The legal profession is often viewed as a seedy business teeming with attorneys of questionable mores. This is not something we have ever participated in, nor will we. Your client's refusal to help us defend her is difficult at best and we're tempted to drop her now, but we also finish what we start. It is against our better judgment, but we will represent her. But do know this." Deena stopped in front of Kasha. She watched the young woman wring her hands one over the other. "If we find out she's withheld key components to this case as a means of covering for someone," she paused, her eyes glanced around the room. "We will drop her ass so fast she'll spin and you'll feel it all the way in La-La Land." Deena slowly turned to rest her stare on Valdez. "Are we clear?"

The question was simple and Deena looked from Juan-Carlos to Kasha, who had raised her head and met Deena's stare. Deena thought she detected fear in the young woman's eyes.

"Good," Deena said when Juan-Carlos nodded his head. "Well, let's get started. We've a lot of ground to cover."

For four hours Deena asked many questions about the day leading up to the incident. The arraignment was tomorrow and she had to have more than she did when she stepped into court.

When she asked for the names of the occupants of the apartment, Kasha shook her head and then looked at Juan-Carlos. Deena had noticed several times while she questioned Kasha that the young woman had glanced over at Juan-Carlos as if he had the answer. As far as Deena knew, Carlos hadn't been in Chicago. Or had he?

"Juan-Carlos, where were you on the evening of the incident?"

"Hey," he threw up his hands. "I'm not the culprit here. Why do you need to know where I was at?"

Deena looked at him and felt it. She glanced over at David and they both nodded slightly. Juan-Carlos was a part of this whole fray somehow and they needed to find out as much as possible as soon as they could. Kasha's first court date was in a month.

"Why don't we take a break for today?" Deena rose from her seat, picking up her note pad. "Kasha, be here at 9 in the morning. Juan-Carlos, we won't need you; you and I can talk later. Are you staying at the Hilton?"

Juan-Carlos looked from David to Deena. From the look on his face he wasn't too keen on not being present when the pair planned to talk to Kasha again. "I'd like to be here when you question Kasha."

David rose from his seat. "That won't be necessary," he responded as he dismissed him with a simple wave of his hand. "We won't be asking her anything about the incident; we'll be preparing her for a different life." David walked to the door, paused and then turned. "A life behind bars." He turned the knob, stepped out the open door and was gone.

Deena watched Kasha's expression as she looked first at Deena then to Juan-Carlos and finally at the spot near the door where David had just left following his parting statement. Yet, this was Deena and David's exact plan. They intended on making Kasha understand all that was at stake.

"I didn't do anything!" Kasha looked at Deena. "How can I go to jail?"

Deena shrugged her shoulders. "Well, at the least you can be an accessory. And don't forget the other charges. Those are pretty serious." Deena headed to the door. "You need to think on what it is you want. Truth and freedom or lies and being locked up with a burly sister trying to make you her wife." Deena raised her eyebrows as she nodded her head then exited the conference room. She made a mental note to contact Dionne for she needed some additional detective work done and so far her sister had uncovered some tidbits she didn't think Charles knew.

Charles. She thought about him for the umpteenth time since they'd been at the awards dinner. A week had passed and it seemed as if every minute of each day she'd thought about him. His scent was branded in her senses and his sensuously wicked smile was etched in her mind. She needed to get Charles off her mind, which was easier said than done she thought, especially since they'd be seeing each other first thing tomorrow morning at Kasha's pre-trial hearing.

❧

Charles looked up at one of the last vestiges of public housing. This was one of the few remaining ever since the city decided housing people one on top of the other wasn't such a grand idea.

He and Lee had gotten a tip earlier about a cache of money and some drug deal that had gone wrong which led to the shooting of Eric Williams. The same informant stated that Kasha Bentley had been there as well as some of Brother Barnett's boys.

Charles wondered if Deena knew that tidbit of information—information Charles was surely going to use during the pre-trial hearing in the morning. He'd thought a lot about Deena since the awards dinner and his phone call to her when it seemed as if Eric Williams would meet his demise. Since then, he couldn't seem to shake the searing impression she'd left on him that there was a lot more to the beautiful Deena Walls. In spite of the circumstances, he was truly looking forward to seeing her in the morning. Shoot, he mused, she didn't know this wasn't personal—it's all business. His mind wondered back to the victim, Eric Williams, who had a rap sheet forty Chicago blocks long; yet, it still didn't mean he deserved to be shot and left for dead. But in looking over his rap sheet and notes made by prior arresting officers and prosecutors, Eric had been associated with Brother Barnett on several illegal occasions.

He shook his head at the name Brother Barnett. What a crock, for the man he knew as Winston Barnett was far from acting like anyone's brother. He knew the man well, having not only arrested several of his mob members, but he had gone to high school with him. Yet, for as long as he'd know him, they'd always been on completely different sides of the law. Numerous times Charles had arrested Barnett's cronies but he'd never come close to arresting Barnett himself and that was something he'd promised himself he'd do before he left the force and he had at least ten good years left. Still, with this case, he'd hope to put Barnett and his illegal band of cronies out of business.

Charles and Lee stepped out of the tell-tale, department issued sedan. He knew the car screamed "cops" but he didn't readily care as he and Lee headed up the front walk of the building. He nodded his head at several of the men who loitered around the entrance. He knew several of them: one was an informant; another was a former dealer turned addict; and then another he'd arrested so many times they were on first name basis. But most of the folks knew him and Lee and gave them both their due props. They didn't act like super cops or *Robo Cop*, they were men who treated everyone with respect and demanded it in return.

"Little Mike, what's up?" Charles clasped hands with one of his former perp's.

"Sup, Chuck. Lee. Wha ch'all doin' here?

"Taking a look around at 1216," Charles replied and glanced around at several

people ear hustling on their conversation. Good, he thought, time to let Brother Barnett know he was on to him. This was his case and this time, Barnett is going to see the inside of a jail cell for a really long time because he knew Kasha hadn't been alone and also knew the young woman didn't have the temerity to commit murder.

He continued his conversation with Little Mike. "Some serious shit went down up there and I came back to look over a few things I may have missed." Charles said, though they all knew it was a ruse, but he still had to play it all up.

"Heard that," Mike nodded. "Later ya'll," he said to all present and then began walking away.

Charles watched him walk away. He knew that was his way of saying that though he may know something, he wasn't quite ready to get involved. He made a mental note to contact him in a few days.

"Let's go," he said to Lee as he looked at watch.

Charles wanted to curse—loudly—as he and Lee began walking up the twelve flights of stairs that would lead them to the floor where the incident had taken place and where they knew their informant would either be hiding or would leave behind a way to contact him. Either way, Charles was truly irritated. He couldn't even begin to fathom how folks lived in a building where the halls were too dim, moldy and smelly; and, the folks who were responsible for cleaning up the place he didn't even want to go there.

"Dang. How many more?" Lee asked as he huffed loudly, drawing in large gulps of air. "I'm going to need hazard pay."

Charles laughed at his partner as he looked behind him. Lee stomped up the stairway. "You need to run more," Charles said as they stepped up on the beginning of the sixth flight. "This would be a walk in the park if you did."

"Hell, I need to. Why is it the doggone elevators never work when you got to go up more than two flights?"

They continued up the stairs, their conversation somewhat muted, their ears trained. As they finally made it to the 12th floor, Charles thought he heard the sounds of someone crying. He slowed as he reached the landing. The sounds of crying followed by what sounded like muffled screams became more pronounced.

"You hear that?" he asked Lee just as he stepped up behind him. The sounds came again and both men drew their weapons as they crouched down in the stairway. Charles felt something crawl across his shoe, but didn't make a sound as he tilted his head toward the sound and then motioned with his weapon forward.

The scream came again, but this time it sounded different. At the fire door, Lee came around Charles and slowly opened it, squatting low as he peered down the hallway. He pointed toward the end of the hallway and Charles nodded his head.

Lee stood slowly as they both crept down the hallway where the noise had seemed to come from. Charles said his prayer, the one he always recited when danger lurked, and continued. When the muffled scream sounded again, both men ran quickly stopping at a door near the end of the hallway. Lee pressed his ear to the door. He nodded, stepped back; his weapon trained over his head, then kicked the door hard, the lock giving way as the flimsy material splintered. Charles rushed in first, his eyes scanning the scene in front of him. He wanted to shoot the man standing over a woman, his pants hanging around his ankles, her's torn from her, blood flowing from her nose and mouth.

"Step back from her, man, or I'm going to kill you." Lee's voice was deathly calm as he came around Charles's right side. "Do it now," Lee ordered, his voice even.

Charles watched as the offender's hands rose up above his head. "Man, she's a crack head. She don't mean nothin'."

"Whatever! Step away from her." Lee sneered as he stepped boldly up on the offender. "Put your hands together behind your head."

"What about my pants?"

Lee snatched the offender's hands, pulling them roughly behind his back. "Now you're concerned. What about her?" Lee asked the rhetorical question. "And don't you dare answer that. Get on your knees." Lee pushed the offender down by the shoulders until his knees met the bare floor.

Charles held his weapon in one hand and held out his other to the woman. "Come here, ma'am. Come over here to me." His voice was strong, but low as he watched her eyes dart from one man to the other—he could see the fear and distrust plainly shining in them. "We're cops. We're not going to hurt you." Charles took a tentative step forward. He watched as she scrambled to her feet, her pants fell from her. Charles wiggled out of his blazer as she got closer. Once she reached him, he placed it around her. "I need to call for help," he said to her. "I need you to go into my pocket and hand me my cell phone."

The woman nodded and did as he asked. She refused to look at him as she handed him his cell.

"Thank you. Let's go out into the hallway." He led her out of the empty apartment. After speaking to dispatch, he asked her name, but she refused to respond opting to stand next to him as they both leaned against the wall. When she slowly slid down to sit on the dirty floor, Charles looked down at her. Under her bruised face, the ruddy color he took to have once been a warm cinnamon, he guessed her to be no more than twenty, if a day. He took in her tattered appearance and wondered who she belonged to, her once pink, sleeveless blouse, torn and dirty, with stains of various sorts patch-worked about it. Her hair, tinted blonde on the ends, was matted to her head. He watched as she wrung her hands, the movements erratic and agitated—he knew she was feigning. Charles made it a habit of never asking addicts why or what, he just gave them what he could legally provide them at the time—a temporary reprieve from their seemingly ongoing situation.

As if she knew he was observing her, the woman looked up and met Charles's eyes. He was taken aback, for her eyes were sad and vacant and he thought of Corbin, thankful the boy was in his life and prayed that the Lord would allow him to remain so until his son no longer needed to depend on him.

Without thought, he put his hand out to help her up as the sounds of footsteps and the sounds of police two-way radios greeted them down the hallway.

"It's going to be alright. Trust me."

The young woman nodded and clutched her hand tightly into Charles's. He smiled slightly at her as a female officer approached them.

They spoke for several moments, with several other officers dragging the offender from the vacant apartment, as the female officer came to stand in front of the young woman. Charles, whose hand was still clasped by the woman, heard the officer ask the woman her name. He was relieved to hear the woman speak her name: Christina. The officer disappeared then returned several moments later with a bag.

"You're in good hands now," Charles said as she released his hand and followed the officer into the vacant apartment. Moments later they emerged with Christina wearing a velour-looking, black sweat suit and a baseball cap.

He watched as she walked slowly behind the officer, her head bent as she eyed the floor beneath her. He prayed for the best knowing that whatever happened to Christina from this point on was totally up to her.

The apartment Charles and Lee had come to investigate further was two doors down and they headed for it. As they stopped at the apartment, Charles looked up in time to see her stop, then turn. He heard the woman say "thank you." Charles smiled slightly and nodded his head at her.

Lee watched the exchange and then looked at Charles. "Dude, lets hurry up and get what we've come for. I've had way too much excitement for the day."

Chapter 6

Deena crossed the busy street and headed to the criminal courts. Next to her walked her brother David and their client Kasha. Over the past twenty-four hours, Kasha hadn't been out of Deena's sight—they had spent the day at the law office and the night at her parent's house. During that time, Deena's mother and father had taken turns telling Kasha what would happen and why if she refused to state the entire truth surrounding the incident. Their advice was to no avail—Kasha was still mum about who else was in the apartment and why; but, most importantly, she still hadn't said who shot Eric Williams.

Deena looked at Kasha as they stood waiting their turn to go through the metal detectors. Though Kasha was dressed in a simple black suit and white blouse, her youthful face free of her normal make-up, her eyes darted around in fear. Deena wanted to shake the girl until either her head snapped off or until some good ole fashioned common sense crawled up into her head. She just couldn't understand why she would take the fall for folks who would let her. Deena's attention was snatched to the present when she got a whiff of the cologne that told her Charles stood less than five feet behind her.

"Good morning, Ms. Walls," he said.

She heard the deep rasp of his sensuously decadent voice. Goose bumps rose hard and fast as she turned to face the man of her dreams—literally. She had dreamed of him twice in the past four days.

"Good morning, Detective Harris," she responded looking up into his dark eyes. "Where's your partner?"

"He's here already, probably in the court room talking to the DA."

She watched as he stepped past her to speak to David, their hands shaking as he told David about how their father had spoken highly of him. "And you too, Deena. He really talked a lot about you."

Deena cringed. She knew her father had probably told him every story about her life, from her birth to what she'd done the day before their golf outing. But Jedidiah Walls never apologized for bragging on his children—he'd tell anyone who'd listen all about them and his five grandchildren. And with David's wife expecting again, he'd have yet another grandchild to add to the litany of stories he told on a regular basis.

Deena thought of her three nieces and two nephews whose ages ranged from sixteen to two. She loved children, and along with Dionne, tried to spend as much time a she could with her brother's kids. When she'd married, the first thing she wanted to do was to get pregnant—thank God that never happened. She couldn't see sharing custody with Seth, much less having to see him for any reason.

She looked up at Charles. Even though he was talking to David, he hadn't taken his eyes off of her. She took in what he was wearing, a pair of tan slacks, black cap toe shoes, a black blazer and a white button down shirt with a tan and black tie, the slip noose loose at his neck. She noted that tufts of chest hair peeked out from the tops of his shirt. Deena shook her head—she found chest hair highly sexy.

"Sounds like a plan. My son will love it. I'll call you in a few days," she heard him say to David. He then moved closer to her, leaned down and began to whisper in her ear. "Have you reconsidered? I guarantee you'll never regret it." He stood and smiled down at her, then walked over to where members of the various law enforcement agencies entered, their weapons placed in a tray. He smiled at her as he watched her watch him as he walked through the metal detectors next to the ones she'd just stepped through. When she cleared the detectors, he was standing nearby watching her. Once their eyes met, he winked, placed his weapon back in the shoulder holster hidden under his blazer, and then disappeared through a set of doors marked for law enforcement only.

Deena was just about to ask David what he and Charles were talking about when her attention was drawn to the vibration of her Blackberry. She looked down at the caller-id.

"Hey Dionne, what you got?" Deena spoke lowly into the phone. She'd had Dionne and her fiancé, Steve, doing major undercover work on this case. She knew Kasha was afraid of someone and she needed to know who in order to cop a plea and get her into a protection program if necessary.

"Girl, find someplace quiet. I've found out a real bombshell."

"I'll call you right back." Deena hung up and put the Blackberry in her purse then walked over to David. She told him Dionne called. He nodded and informed Deena they would be in the office of the state defense attorneys, several were friends of theirs.

Deena looked around and wished for the old enclosed phone booths as she spied the women's restroom. She rushed to the bathroom and selected the last stall. She placed paper on the seat, sat down and removed a legal pad from her legal briefcase before she pulled the Blackberry from her purse and called her sister back. "Okay, spill it."

For over twenty minutes Deena listened as her sister went on to tell her what she had uncovered about Eric Williams and his dealings with a low-level street gang who was possibly fronting for a much more sophisticated criminal organization. Word had it, according to Dionne, the whole situation got out of hand when a drug deal went bad due to Williams' insatiable greed.

"And Deena, hold on to your Coach purse."

Deena heard her sister's sharp intake of breath.

"Eric is Kasha's brother."

Deena inhaled deeply and then rolled her eyes. "You have got to be kidding me! Damn." She stood. "Now it makes too much sense. She's covering for her brother."

"Yeah, but I think there's more here," Dionne said. "The deeper I began to dig, the more doors close."

Deena stood, placing her pad back into her briefcase. "Oh, sis, you've done great. Keep trying to dig up more, but be careful." She looked at her Rolex watch. "I've got to get upstairs. Court is in twenty minutes. Thank you, baby sis—I love you."

"Love you, too."

Deena stepped out of the stall and rushed to join David and Kasha.

"Is there an office we can step into real quick?" Deena asked

David and then walked over to the office he pointed to. She motioned for him to join them. Once Deena closed the door, she cornered Kasha.

"Why didn't you tell us Eric Williams is your older brother?"

"I understand that your future wife has entered the building," Lee teased as Charles approached him standing outside of the courtroom.

"Oh, we've got jokes this morning." Charles replied as he headed into the courtroom, followed by Lee. "Ready?"

"Man, this case is gonna blow. You sure you ready? I mean, your future wife may be mad at you."

Charles smirked at Lee and then thought about what he'd said. The last thing he wanted was for Deena to be mad at him. Shoot, he hadn't even talked her into going out with him yet. He thought about what she was wearing. His eyes had just about dropped from his head when he spied her strutting across the street, the way her hips swayed as she walked toward the court building, the perfect fit of her skirt, the way the short jacket rested right on top of her perfectly round behind. And the high-heeled pumps accentuated the toned muscles of her calves. And once he'd stepped up close to her, the smell of that wicked perfume—a vexing concoction of citrus and red freesia—worked his pulse rate up several notches to the point tiny beads of preparation rolled down the middle of his back and caused his groin to tighten.

But he knew he'd have that reaction for it was nearly the same one he'd had the night of the awards dinner. He tried to prepare himself and so far he wasn't doing too badly—he hadn't had the urge to run to the bathroom. *Damn, I've got to get a grip.*

And so what, he thought, today we're on the opposite sides of this case. But that wasn't going to be a deterrent to his plan to continue to ask her out or be in her presence—he planned on wearing her down. Slow walk her, as his father called it. Yeah, he was going to slow walk her right into...

"Is everyone here?" asked the bailiff as he entered the courtroom from the ante-chamber at the front of the room near the judge's bench. Charles had been told that the judge hearing this preliminary part of the case was one who took no prisoners of any kind. The judge had already made her position known when she'd sent the bailiff out—the proceedings would begin on time.

Members of the prosecution team waved their hands just as

the door opened and in entered Deena followed by David and Kasha. Charles watched as Deena's persona filled the room—her head back and held high, her shoulders rounded. He could see from the set of her smooth jaw that she was there to do battle in a war that no one would really win. A youngster's life was on the line and another one's life was hanging in the balance. Charles continued to watch Deena, noting the nuances of her movements, like when she paused at the wooden railing that would separate the spectators from those directly involved in the court proceedings. She looked at the two prosecuting attorney's for the state assigned to find her client guilty—her mouth a slight smile, almost smirk, as she put her hand out to both attorney's—two men. Following the gesture, she waved to the bailiff, hugged the court secretary and introduced herself to the stenographer, placing a business card in her hand. Yeah, baby was working this room and Charles was impressed.

But when it came to him, Charles knew deep down what Lee had said about her was true—this woman was no average sister and he knew that he had to bring his "A" game to the table. He was going to start today by showing her just how tough a witness he could be.

The sound of the bailiff's voice brought all to attention and the prosecution and the defense team rose at the entrance of Judge Willamena M. Hall.

"Have a seat, ladies and gentlemen," came the judge's light voice.

Charles knew that the voice was only there to fool those who had never set foot in her court before. He'd been there before and knew Judge Hall was no pushover and he had personally watched her when she cited three attorney's for contempt due to continued bickering with each other.

"Detective Harris," Judge Hall called out. "Good to see you on this case. I take it you are prepared as is the defense?" She looked at Deena and David. "Ms. Walls and Mr. Walls—please give my best to your parents." She ended with the prosecution. "Attorney Lacowitcz, please ask your counterpart Mr. Johnson how we do things here in my courtroom."

All parties nodded and waited as Judge Hall looked over the various papers in front of her. Several times she looked up at Kasha who had glanced over her shoulder numerous times to the door behind her. Charles thought the gesture odd, as if she had been expecting something or someone.

"Let's proceed. Kasha Antoinette Bentley, please step

forward," Judge Hall began. "The charges brought against you are quite serious. Today we will decide, based on your attorneys and the state prosecutors, the best way to proceed, either with a bench trial, that's just me, several witnesses, and the attorney's present here today. Or a trial by jury, which will include twelve people, your peers, who will hear all evidence in support and against your plea to the charges set her before you. Do you understand?"

Kasha nodded her head up and down.

"Dear, I'm afraid I do not understand head nods. You will have to speak in this courtroom. Again, do you understand what I've said to you?"

"Yes, your honor," her voice came out shakily.

"And are the attorneys standing to your left your chosen counsel?"

"Yes, your honor, they are."

"Then Kasha Antoinette Bentley, how you do you plead to the count of…"

Deena interrupted the judge. "Your honor, my client pleads not guilty to all charges and we wish to waive the right for a trial by jury and move for a bench hearing once all pre-trial motions are heard."

"So noted. Does the prosecution have any objections?"

"None, your honor."

Judge Hall looked through several pages, made markings on some and then shuffled the papers neatly in front of her. She looked directly at Kasha.

"Court will adjourn until one month from today, same time. At that time we will proceed with the bench trial. Any motions will be submitted prior to that date, so I expect no last minute machinations and theatrics. But I do expect for all parties to be prepared and ready to proceed. And Ms. Bentley, do not leave the state of Illinois or the United States. Understood?" Judge Hall banged the gavel and then rose, leaving the court room.

Charles remained seated. He did not want to give up the unobstructed view he had of the woman who seemed to vex him—the temptress who had no idea the effect she was having on him. And if he ever got her alone again…

❧

Seth Scott sat in his office listening on his phone.

"Boss, Kasha's been with those attorneys's all night and now they're in court."

He rubbed his aching forehead. He had too many secrets.

"Don't let her out of your sight. We've got to get her before she talks. Do you have a man at the hospital?"

"Yeah."

"Then it's time to up the ante on this whole thing. Brother Barnett is tired and now so am I. You take care of her and then find that damned Juan-Carlos and bring him to me."

Seth slammed down the phone. In all the years of being Brother Barnett's *consigliore,* he had never been ordered by him to become directly involved in the day-to-day business. And he had no intention of sullying his hands or his expensive suits dealing with the low underlings. He understood that Brother Barnett was angry at having that young punk, Eric, attempt to continue to skim off his profits and that last little game was the breaking point. But still, the money wasn't something that would have broken the bank—one hundred thousand dollars—it wasn't paltry, but it sure wasn't something Barnett was about to forgive even though the man spent damn near that in one day as if he was spending a twenty dollar bill.

The sound of the phone broke his thoughts. "What?" he responded angrily into the telephone receiver. He listened intently to the report from one of his own personal foot soldiers who were also tracking this Juan-Carlos guy. Something about him bothered Seth. He didn't care for Juan-Carlos and had advised Brother Barnett during their evening meal last night to cut the guy loose as soon as was possible. Brother Bennett hadn't replied just nodded his head as he finished his meal.

"Very good," Seth said. "You and your boys keep an eye on them all. There's something in the wind that just doesn't sit well me and I'm going to find out just what it is. Call me back in an hour."

Seth hung up the phone and went back to work. He found the whole thing—working for Brother Barnett, supporting his mother and siblings and trying to find a way out quite hilarious—in a tragic comedy sort of way. He'd never intended on getting in this deep, but with each step, he found himself further entrenched in the maddening underworld of organized crime.

Chapter 7

Deena headed back to her office. The first part of her day had been long and draining, and she knew that the next few weeks were only going to get longer. To make matters worse, she was disappointed in her performance this morning in front of Judge Hall. She'd been too distracted, first by Kasha's continued silence. Silly girl! Her whole life was about to play out for one long stint in a jail cell and she was covering for folks who probably deserved to be locked up. And then Dionne's news about Eric Williams being Kasha's brother—that little tidbit only left Deena angrier when she mentioned it to Kasha. She honestly wanted to strangle the child. Even though she'd admitted that he was her brother, still, that simple child didn't bother to utter anything else that would aide in her defense.

Then added to it all, was that irascible, arrogant, fine assed Charles Harris. Deena rolled her eyes heavenward. She thought about how good he had looked wearing just a simple pair of pants, shirt and blazer. Admittedly, she wanted to faint when he'd walked up to her, his cologne swirling around her head and doing things to her body. And when he whispered in her ear—she almost lost it. The heat had rolled up and down her body like a rollercoaster on twirling tracks—up down, sideways, and to and fro. So of course by the time she entered the courtroom and felt his eyes on her, she was beside herself and almost blew it when

Judge Hall asked Kasha about her plea and whether she wanted a bench or jury trial. Kasha wasn't supposed to say as much as she had.

Her thoughts went back to Charles. A part of Deena wanted to say yes when he'd asked her out again, but she felt he didn't know what he was asking for and knew once she ate his ass up on the witness stand, he was going to change his mind about her. Most did. She hadn't found a man yet, including her ex, who could handle a sister with a little pizzazz and some self-confidence.

Deena stepped inside the building housing the law offices with her thoughts on what her sorority sister Karen had said about Charles. She also thought of the opportunity she'd had to really see him up close when they were at the awards ceremony, how he'd been such a gentleman, how funny he'd been and his undivided attention to her. But to Deena the true question was would he still be interested in her when he found out some of her deepest fears, the ones she wrestled with continually.

She shook off the thoughts and willed the day to get better, knowing it would

once Mr. Swift arrived. She was actually looking forward to his visit, for knew his story about why he wanted to change his will for the thousandth time would be one to hear.

"Good afternoon, Deena. Here are your messages." Kimmie followed Deena into her office and sat in the chair across from her. "Karen called. Your mom called. And a Detective Harris called."

Deena looked up. She had just been thinking of him.

"Did he leave a message?"

"No, but he left his number."

"Did anyone from the media call?"

Kimmie shook her head. Deena was surprised and grateful for the way the police department was handling the case for not one word of Kasha's arrest had made the news outlets. She knew a story of this magnitude could cause some irreparable harm to Kasha's career, which was just getting started. But Deena didn't want to think about that right now, she had a client on her hands who refused to cooperate, a defense she had to prepare and a too fine man singeing her brain.

"Kimmie, have the paralegals meet David and I in the conference room."

For over an hour, Deena and David related details of the case against Kasha and the young woman's stand on the case. When they finished, satisfied the team understood what they were facing and the best way to precede, Deena headed back to her office to prepare for Mr. Swift's arrival.

"Wow," Deena said as she rounded the corner to her office. "Those are really beautiful flowers. Kimmie, you got a date we don't know about?"

"No, ma'am, those are for you," Kimmie said, her brown eyes lit up like beacons. "They arrived a few minutes ago and I didn't even get a chance to peek at the card."

Deena sat down at the chair near Kimmie's desk. She looked at the large bouquet of yellow and purple tulips and removed the card attached to the cut crystal vase.

"If today was any hint, then I'm looking forward to your grilling. Detective HARRY."

Deena laughed loudly, remembering her intentional butchering of his name when she'd first met him. He hadn't been rattled in the least bit and she had to give it to him—he hadn't been intimidated and had actually put her in her place a few times.

"They are beautiful," Deena said as she rose. She picked up the vase and headed into her office. She refused to look at Kimmie, who followed her into the office.

"Okay, come on. Spill it."

"Spill what?" Deena set the flowers on the corner of her desk. "There's nothing to spill. I got flowers. That's all." She smiled broadly, her face flushed. No one outside of her family had ever given her flowers. Well, she didn't count her prom date or the little nerdy kid down the street who'd brought her a bunch of dandelions when she was ten.

Deena smiled as she thought of the man who'd taken the time to send her what she would consider a "forget-me-not" gesture that would him at the forefront of her mind. She picked up the phone and dialed the office number listed on the business card he'd given her.

"Violent Crimes, Detective Harris speaking."

She listened to the voice. Even with its authoritative tone, she still found it wickedly sensuous and sinfully sexy. "Hello, Detective, it's Deena Walls. I just called to thank you for the beautiful flowers."

"You are most welcome, Ms. Walls. And if you'd agree to go out with me, I'll send you as many as your office can handle."

Deena laughed. "I told you, once this trial starts you're not going to be so interested."

"Says who, Ms. Walls?" he chuckled. "Look, we've both got a

job to do and I have no doubt, based on what I saw of you today, that you are great at what you do, but if you haven't noticed, I'm a big boy—I can take care of myself."

Deena closed her eyes and remembered the strong feel of his large hands as they massaged her tired feet the night of the award ceremony. *Big boy indeed.* She opened her eyes.

"So, let me show you. What about this Friday night?"

"Charles," she said his name on a sigh.

"Yes, sweetheart, what do you want?" he replied, his deep voice deeper. Deena imagined feeling the breath of his words caress her ear lobe. Heat of the most searing kind rushed down her chest to settle at her core. She crossed her legs.

"I tell you what, Ms. Deena, how about I send you a little teaser? Besides I've got to go—I have another case I need to work on. Call me at home after you get my teaser. Talk to you later, sweetheart. Bye."

Deena held the phone to her ear, the sound of the dial tone reverberated in her ear. She was giddy, felt like a school girl and she hadn't felt like that in a long time. She wondered what he was planning on sending her next.

Charles glanced at Lee as he placed the receiver on the desk phone. He knew his partner was going to have something to say the minute he hung up. He'd begun his slow walk of Deena and so far he was pleased with the results he was achieving. If he didn't know any better, he'd heard her giggle. And to him that was a good sign and he hoped what he had planned for her would get him closer to his goal: getting to know her up close and in person.

He envisioned her lounging back with the phone to her ear, a rare smile to her face. He'd never really seen her laugh heartily, though he heard it over the phone. When he'd seen her smile, for some reason it didn't seem to reach her beautiful eyes and he wondered who or what had put such pain in her eyes. He knew that if given half a chance, he'd be the one to erase it and replace it with something better.

He smiled when he'd heard her use his first name versus his surname or professional title. He liked that, the way his name sounded as it rolled so easily from her lips. Charles shook himself out of his day dream of her and began to busy himself refusing to look up at Lee who was now leaning on his desk. Charles finally looked up at the sound of him clearing his throat rather loudly.

"What?"

"Slow walking, ugh?" Lee chuckled. "I know that was Ms. Walls you were talking to, so what's going on?"

"Just upping the ante a bit." He reached out to the next file on his desk as his mind tried to conjure up her expression when she'd receive her next gift.

"Come on, what'd you do, man?" Lee sat down in the chair and crossed his legs. Charles looked up into his best friend and partner's eyes which were wide as he waited for Charles to fill him in.

"Nothing to tell, Lee—nothing at all. But I promise you that when she goes out with me on Friday night, you'll be the first to know. Deal?"

"Deal!" Lee pounded Charles's fist. "Just remember what I said. This one is no pushover."

Charles nodded. This he knew well and had every intention of showing her that he not only respected her as a woman, but as a professional who was serious about her job. He actually admired her for sticking by a client who was less than cooperative.

He wondered if she knew Eric Williams and Kasha Bentley were siblings. Charles chuckled. She probably did. He then wondered how much more about Ms. Bentley and her sibling had she discovered. He had been surprised to find out the two were related, but wasn't surprised to find out the reason Eric took that bullet to the head—stealing money from drug dealing gangsters wasn't a smart move, especially if a person wanted to live. But some things didn't add up, like why was Kasha at the housing project at that time of night, and why was her brother skimming money from Brother Barnett when he was a mid-level dealer himself? And even though he'd gotten those bits of information from one of his informants, he still felt as if something was missing.

He knew based on how he thought Deena worked, that Kasha would need to cop a plea and be placed into protective custody—the plea would only work if she cooperated. She had to know this, but still Kasha refused to tell what she knew, even with a possible offer of immunity and protective custody. If she had agreed, today would have been a wash and he and Deena could have very well been on their way to dinner.

Charles called up Eric's probation officer. He needed to know all about Kasha Bentley's big brother and the best way to do it was to dig up his entire life story.

As he listened to the probation officer outline Eric Williams as a really smart man, he also painted him as someone who was impatient, often taking the easy way only because he couldn't wait for outcomes.

At 25, Eric had spent the last ten years of his life in and out of the penal system, first as a juvenile where he was remanded to Warrenville until he turned 18, then two years later at Statesville for manslaughter, possession with intent and several weapons charges. His last charge, two years ago, was for attempted murder and he'd had a private attorney who'd gotten him off on a technicality.

Charles thanked the PO as he shook his head. *Yeah, there's more here, he said to himself, and I'm going to find out just what it is.*

Deena leaned back in her chair; her eyes glanced over to the cut crystal vase filled with the tulips. Her heart was racing—fast—as her mind flittered over his words, the humor in his tone, the deepness of his voice, and resulting goose bumps that rose hard and fast at the mere sound of it. She thought of her last date, which she had met at a conference, and shook her head. Anton Green had been at the annual Chicago Bar Associations conference and when she'd been introduced to him by fellow colleagues, he'd seemed harmless; but, as she got to know him, she found him self-centered and more than a little neurotic. But what rattled her most was his abrasive behavior and that was something she swore that she'd never be bother with again. Her ex-husband had been brutish and abrasive and the emotional pain he inflicted was just as bad as the physical.

Deena shook her head. She wasn't about to go down that road again, either thinking about it or feeling sorry for herself. It was what it was she mused and then looked up in time to see Mr. Swift enter to stand next to Kimmie's desk. He removed his grey felt fedora, then handed Kimmie a box of Frango Mints and a single red rose. Deena watched as he bowed at the waist, taking Kimmie's hand in his to kiss the back of it. Kimmie giggled like a school girl. He'd been smitten with Kimmie ever since he'd been a client—some fifteen years.

"Mr. Swift," Deena headed to the outer office. "I'm ready if you are." She watched him as he winked at Kimmie and then headed toward her. With a small kiss to her cheek, Mr. Swift stepped past Deena to stop at the coat tree near the door. He hung up his hat, removed his blazer and then walked over and sat down at the table situated near the corner of her large office. For a man nearing seventy, Mr. Swift looked more like a very young fifty.

"How's my favorite Barrister?"

"I'm well, Mr. Swift. How are the pigs?"

He chuckled at her question, which had been long standing between them, for it was pork and its by-products that made him a very rich man.

"They are fat and making me richer, as usual," was his patent response. "And now I'm ready to make that young filly out there a very wealthy woman if only she'd agree to marry an old, idealistic man such as myself. She'll want for nothing," he said out loud as he leaned back in his chair to look out into the outer office. He smiled broadly at Kimmie. "Yes sir. Never have to work again and I've got the little blue pills."

"Umm, Mr. Swift," Deena exclaimed as she tried to hide her smile. "Aren't you married?"

"Not for long."

Deena shook her head as she closed her office door. Mr. Swift was on wife number four and she wondered what this one had done. Since he'd been a client she'd handled two of his divorces, both with substantial payouts to the women even though he had a pre-nuptial agreement. "Does this mean I'm filing again, Mr. Swift?"

He looked at her and nodded his head. She could see the pain shining clearly in his warm, sea-green eyes. Deena had long established that he was in love with being in love, but once the honeymoon wore off, he found himself wanting. She understood the feeling of being less than satisfied emotionally and physically, but she was nowhere near as impetuous as he was—she'd figured once was enough.

"Okay, well I have a copy of your pre-nuptial agreement with Cindy. Do you have her lawyer's info?"

He nodded his head. "Sure do. And give her nothing outside of that agreement. I've got proof that she's been sleeping with that lazy, revolting son of mine."

Deena looked up and into his eyes. She wasn't sure if he was fishing for a real reason or that what he'd just said was the truth. "What type of proof do you have, Mr. Swift?

"These," he replied as he reached into his briefcase and pulled out a stack of photos. "They meet up every Wednesday at the Marriott for a little love in the afternoon." His tone was even, devoid of emotion, but it was his eyes that told a different story.

Deena felt sorry for him. Sure she thought he was eccentric and a little paranoid, but she knew he didn't do infidelity so the pain in his kind eyes was real. She reached out and patted his hand.

"Don't worry about a thing. I'll take care of it," she said as she pulled the pictures to her, glanced at the first one which showed his wife, Cindy, and his son, Alexi, in a naked embrace. She placed them in a manila file folder on the table. "As for the will, are you removing Alexi?"

"You bet I am. I've already fired him." Mr. Swift looked out of the window. "How long will all of this take? I'm going to head to the Mediterranean for a month or so."

"About two weeks to get all the paper work completed and filed. By the time you return Alexi will be out of your will and you'll be on your way to being single again."

He tapped his index finger on the table. "Very good." He nodded several times as he rose from the seat across from Deena and then smiled. "You know you are a very beautiful woman. Seth was a fool."

Deena gave a slight smile at the compliment, but reserved her right to refuse to comment on just what type of fool Seth had been.

"Then I guess that's it." She rose to her feet then walked over to the coat tree and retrieved Mr. Swift's hat and blazer. Returning to his side, she held the blazer for him and then handed him his hat. The pain she witnessed had never been there before and she shuddered. "You okay, Ari?" She'd never called him by his first name before.

He smiled sadly at her. "I will be." Then he turned and faced her. "You know, Deena, I loved them all, in my own way, but I never cheated on them—never laid a hand on any of them with anything but love. The only thing I'm guilty of is being too busy making money. I've got some rotten kids that I don't even like and a wife, damn near forty years my junior, who's a whore." He inhaled deeply. "Make sure you have Dionne watch my home when that tramp moves out. I'll give you a list of what she brought with her. That's all she's to leave with." He tipped his head then headed out to the outer office. Deena listened as he bantered playfully with Kimmie. No one would ever suspect he was mending a broken heart.

Once he'd left the office, Deena had Kimmie hold all her calls. She looked at the calendar–it would have been her sixth wedding anniversary had Seth not committed the ultimate act of betrayal.

"Nope, won't give in," Deena said aloud as she focused her attention on the file folders resting on top of her desk with Kasha Bentley's name on them. She was busy trying to find a way to get the foolish young woman to tell what she knew so that Deena could keep her jail time to a minimum. She knew that the very least, Kasha would have to do jail time for her role—whatever that role had been.

By the time the day ended, Deena was tired. She left late and decided to skip her boxing class. As she waited for the city bus, she looked around at the faces of the various people waiting at the service stop. She wondered, just as she had as a child, what their stories were.

She played the game she had as a child, guessing, based on the person's face and eyes, what their story was. She thought of Charles and for the first time since meeting him had wondered what his real story was. She knew he was interested in her, but he, like her, at one time had been married and was now divorced.

Her thoughts filtered in and out as she boarded the city bus that would take her home. She placed the ear buds of her iPod into her ears. Deena loved music and hummed along as the first song, an old Elton John cut, began. She watched as people strolled along Michigan Avenue, enjoying the warm spring day and thought it'd be a nice day to head to the park, take a book and enjoy the first real break from Chicago's cold, windy winter.

At her stop, Deena alighted the bus and walked the short half block to her building. She checked her mail box and saw a note from the doorman informing her of a package. She wasn't expecting anything, so she was wondering who had sent her a package.

"I have a notice in my mailbox that there's a package for Walls?" she said to Sergio, the doorman on duty.

"Yes, ma'am. It's a little large. I'll have one of the guys bring it up to your place."

"Thank you, Sergio. I'd appreciate that."

Deena took the elevator to her apartment and once inside she happily kicked her shoes off and padded barefoot across the gleaming wood floors. Walking into her den, she anchored the iPod to a set of speakers so she could continue her mini Elton John concert. Deena headed to the kitchen at the sound of a knock on the service door.

One of the maintenance guys stood there and at her request deposited the large box on her kitchen table. She searched for a return address and finding none, she grabbed a pair of kitchen shears and began cutting the tape from the box. Once she had the tape removed, she opened the box and smiled broadly at the contents.

Deena removed a large wicker picnic basket, sat it on the Pergo floor and then sat down beside it. She opened it and began pulling out the contents. Two Waterford crystal wine glasses, an expensive bottle of white wine, wrapped containers of various cheese and several packages of assorted crackers. Deena looked for a note and when she couldn't find one remembered what Charles had said to her earlier.

"Oh, no he did not," she smiled as she stood up, taking the basket in hand as she headed to her briefcase where his card was. She picked up the cordless phone from the marble coffee table and dialed the number he'd indicated was his home number.

"Hello, may I speak to Charles?"

"Speaking. How are you, Deena?"

"I'm well, Charles. I got the basket, it's really nice. Thank you so much." Deena laughed and then stretched out on the chaise near the floor to ceiling window. "You don't give up easy, do you?"

"I'm a detective, so I'm not one to walk away so easily. Besides, it's not in my nature to give up. Now, Ms. Walls, want to add a few more goodies to that basket and hang out on Friday?"

Deena cast her eyes out over the view of Grant Park, Lake Michigan, and further northeast, the Ferris wheel at Navy Pier. A part of her wanted to say no, to push him to the safe place, to ignore the simple fact she was attracted to him. While another part of her was pushing her to get on with her life, that it was time for a change. And what better way to begin than with Detective Charles Henry Harris.

"Sure, Charles, let's add a few more items to the basket and hang out on Friday."

"Great," he responded, but didn't hang up. Instead they slipped into one conversation after another. And they spoke for nearly forty minutes allowing the conversation to flow between them and cover everything from the current warm weather to their respective jobs. Deena hadn't wanted to stop talking, hadn't wanted the voice seeping into her system to cease. She was surprised at his range of knowledge and found his deadpan humor so to the point where she had been laughing loudly.

"Charles, I've got to do a little work before bed, but I've really enjoyed talking to you."

"Same here, Deena. I'll be by on Friday at around six to get you. Shall I pick you up at your office or at your place?"

"Pick me up here."

"Will do. Good night, Deena. Sweet dreams."

"Same to you, Charles, I'll see you on Friday."

Deena depressed the end button and placed the phone on the

charger. She looked out over the darkening sky, the crest of the moon overhead as the city began to get darker. She thought of the gift Charles had sent and how touching as well as unusual it was. She hadn't met a man who liked to go on picnic's, which meant that Charles had a touch of the romantic about him. Deena wondered if he was into poetry and museums, full moons and sun rises, lounging and loving.

Well, she mused to herself, she was about to find out.

Chapter 8

The leather chair of Seth's office had become a torture device. "I do believe we're paying you too damned much money for Kasha's lawyer and her family to be digging up information that was supposed to be buried by now." At least the damn Walls hadn't found out everything yet.

"You didn't tell me that they were so determined," Juan Carlos said. "Besides, Kasha won't say a word. She doesn't want to spend more than a day behind bars. That little time she spent in the lockup scared her straight."

"Well, you need to make sure Kasha continues to keep her mouth closed. That sanctimonious Walls clan is unreal." He shook his head and then muttered lowly, with just enough force to make one believe that he'd blew out breath, "but had she only believed in me." Seth waved his hand in the air as he rose from the leather office chair. "Anyway." He walked over to the window and looked out at the street teaming with people who had one cent less than most folks. He noticed his reflection staring back at him. His caramel complexion was accentuated with what women called his "bedroom brown eyes," which were slightly rounded, an aquiline nose, his jet black hair trimmed to perfection and his slightly full lips, surrounded by a thin mustache made up the rest of the package: a male stripper's physique—he worked out every day except Sunday. Seth knew that he was good-looking, built like a brick, and he used it to his advantage both personally and professionally.

But the one thing he couldn't shake was his anger over his quick divorce, which had been granted in-absenteeism while he was in jail.

When he'd first met Deena, he knew she was his ticket to a different way of life. He had always wanted to be an attorney, but back then he had wanted to defend those who couldn't defend themselves; and that was what he tried to focus on in the beginning. That was until those who paid for his college and subsequent ticket to law school had politely informed him he would work for Brother Barnett exclusively, defending the ones who dealt in the underside of the world—provided vices of all kinds. Seth was their attorney, using his searing good looks and equally impressive mind to defend those who really should be inside jail cells. It was either that or stand idly by and watch as his family succumb, one by one, to the vices of the street. He had wanted to protect his family, especially his mother. And when Brother Barnett gave him his first retainer—more money his poor mother and siblings would never see in this lifetime or the next—he knew he had just sold his soul with redemption nowhere to be found.

"Look, Juan Carlos, I don't care what you have to do. Kasha must never reveal what went on in that apartment. Too much is at stake. All of our lives are at stake." When Seth had been first introduced to the record promoter, slash agent, Seth knew the old saying of keeping your enemies closer aptly applied. Seth found Juan Carlos, also an attorney, sneaky and ruthless with an ugly penchant for young meat. And because of his proclivities, Seth had purposely kept his dealings with the man limited. The last thing Seth wanted was to go to jail for something he didn't even indulge in—young trade.

"Well, I think the only solution to my problem, our problem, is to look for a permanent one."

Seth held up his hand. He didn't even want to hear it. The less he knew the better. But he also knew that Brother Barnett would be none too pleased to hear of the latest events surrounding this case. The missing money and drugs was still a thorn in Brother Barnett's side and each day he questioned Seth about it; which he thought was odd. He hadn't been this preoccupied with anything for the twenty plus years Seth had known him.

Seth wanted to scream. He was more than tired of defending Brother Winston Barnett's cartel of pimps, dealers, liars and thieves.

He thought about Deena. When he'd first met her they were both first year law students. Back then he had wanted to do what she was planning on doing—legal work that would help those who deserved it the most. He had been impressed with the Walls family, had wished his own had been like them—but life deals you the hand you are to work with. And he had loved Deena like no other—had never met a woman who loved with the passion she had. He had been her first and he took great pride in introducing her to love between a man and a woman. He knew then that once they graduated law school they would marry—he couldn't stand the thought of another man with his Deena.

Everything changed with graduation and with Brother Barnett's offer that really could not be refused. Seth went to work immediately, even before he'd passed the state bar exam. At first Seth tried to resist, but Barnett's insistence and his people providing him with too much of the good life he knew this was something he'd never get without struggling. Still, he'd kept it from Deena, even after marrying her. Yet, in the back of his mind he knew that once Deena found out the type of clients he really served she would leave him.

And she was so headstrong. Brother Barnett had said a headstrong woman would only bring a strong man down. So when he'd hit her the first time, a month after they married—he had thought he was putting her in her place. When he hit her the second time a few months later, after swearing he'd never touch her again, he found himself handcuffed to a hospital bed.

That was five years ago and he had yet to get over Deena. He knew the first time he'd hit her—it had scared her and to some extent it garnered the reaction he was looking for. She became somewhat docile, more quiet and not as quick to question him. But when he hit her that second time, he saw the hurt mixed with pure hate in her beautiful eyes and for the first time since he could remember, he felt genuine fear.

The first blow left his nose broken, the second left him unconscious. When he'd awakened at the hospital, her brother David had been standing near his bed. And for the second time in some 24-hours, he felt fear and knew the mistake was one he could never erase. He was a fool for listening to Brother Barnett in the first place—he had watched his step-father repeatedly go upside his mother's head on a regular basis and he hadn't liked it then. Even now, he could still see the cold anger in David's face when he leaned close and whispered in his ear to stay away from Deena or he'd pay with everything he had. Seth knew at that very moment he had lost the one woman who really made him believe in himself and had loved him with all she had.

Ironically, he was jealous of her. Her family did for her what he and his siblings should have done for their mother—provided her protection and solace. Instead, he and his family had stood around and watched The only time Seth had done anything, he'd done it after he'd hit Deena—he'd made sure his mother's tormentor would never again see light of day.

For his battering of Deena, Seth had been jailed, his paperwork lost for nearly two weeks. Her father used his powers to make sure he'd have a hard time navigating the system. During that time divorce proceedings had begun. Upon his release, Deena's whole family stood outside of Cook County Jail and watched him as he climbed into a cab. Nary a threat had been made, but the implication was just the same.

Seth brought his thoughts back to the present.

"Juan Carlos, I'm really busy today and I'm tired of you and this whole Kasha issue. Both have taken up more time than I'd like. When Brother Barnett asks me for an update, I'll have no choice but to tell him the truth." Seth wanted to laugh at his own statement. *Truth among thieves? What a crock.*

"Just tell him I'll have his money first thing tomorrow morning and that Kasha will be dealt with accordingly."

Seth stared nastily at his adversary waiting for him to get the hint and exit his office. He watched trepidation cross the man's face and knew the last thing this guy wanted was to tangle with one of Brother Barnett's enforcers. Seth had gotten one opportunity to see several of those brutes at work—that was all he needed.

Juan Carlos nodded his head and backed up to the door. He opened it without turning his back on Seth. Seth's expression never changed even when the man was gone. He turned back to the window overlooking Madison Street in the heart of the Westside. These were his people, the ones he really should be defending. He continued to watch as the beat cop, who was on the payroll, shook down a petty thief. Got to keep up appearances, Seth chuckled to himself.

Sitting down at his desk, he opened the desk drawer. Next to the nickel-plated.38 semi auto, with a pearl handle grip, was a picture of Deena. Since the divorce, he'd apologized to the picture but didn't have the nerve to apologize to her directly. Besides, he didn't want to meet up with her or her family, who wouldn't hesitate to put a bullet in his head for what he'd done to their

Deena. He didn't know who to be most afraid of—Brother Barnett and his brutes or Deena Walls and her family.

As he continued to study the picture, he became angry, feeling that if she had given him half a chance, tried to understand him, get to know the life he had led, the things he had seen, she wouldn't have been able to dismiss him so easily.

"Shit," he cursed aloud and then thought of how they had been married less than six months. He put the picture back into the drawer and slammed it shut.

"Mr. Monroe, a Miss Jones is here to see you," His secretary called over the intercom.

"Lissa, you can let her in. Thank you."

Seth watched as the door opened slowly. He smiled in spite of himself, for this was one of the better perks of the job.

"Seth," the leggy beauty called his name as she shut and then locked the door behind her. "I've been waiting to see you all day," her voice sang as she untied the belt that held her wrap dress together allowing the silky material to pool at her feet encased in four-inch stilettos.

Seth swallowed hard as his groin tightened with anticipation. His eyes narrowed as he watched her walk closer to him, dressed in those shoes, a pair of thigh-high stockings and nothing else, her full breasts moving in time with her swaying hips. He closed his eyes when she was mere inches from him and reached out to him, her long fingernails making a trail down the buttons of his French-cut shirt to rest on the visible sign of his hardness.

"You are ready for me." She said and then got to her knees, unzipping his trousers.

Seth threw his head back as the warmth of her mouth surrounded his girth and was nearly his undoing. He thought of Deena one last time and knew that no matter what, they would never be together again. But that didn't keep him from fantasizing.

Chapter 9

Images of Charles had stayed with her for the remaining three days prior to their date. During that time, he sent her emails, called and left her messages and spoke to her every evening. One night, he even sent her dinner.

Deena and Kimmie had been busy working on two cases. David and the firm's three paralegals had worked nearly non-stop trying to gather as much evidence and legal information as they could for Kasha's defense. The more information Dionne supplied, the more Deena understood that Kasha felt her life was in danger. Deena had called in a favor to a friend who worked at a half-way house one hundred miles outside of the city and arranged to have Kasha transported there.

As they worked on the defense the day before her date, Charles had called. Deena happily took a break to talk to him, settling down in her office, her shoes off and her feet tucked under her as she sat on the couch in her office. They spoke for nearly an hour, Deena surprised at the amount of time that had gone by. Once they ended the call, with Deena promising to call him once she arrived home, she resigned herself to return to her work. An hour later, a delivery man arrived with enough food to feed a platoon twice over from her favorite Italian restaurant, Maggiano's.

Deena smiled as she picked up the phone to call Charles. She got his voice mail, left him a message and then went back to work, taking a plate of chicken and fettuccini alfredo mixed with broccoli to her office. She propped up her feet on the desk and ate till she was satisfied. *That Charles is something else,* she'd thought then.

And when she arrived home, she called Charles, thanking him for the food, asking him how he knew Italian was one of her favorites. He admitted to contacting David, who had agreed to provide martial arts lessons to his son, Corbin.

Her thoughts returned to the present and how each day, she was becoming more and more accustomed to Charles—his laugh, his voice and his biting sense of humor. Deena was so used to hearing his voice daily she wondered if she'd ever tire of him. But each time she spoke to him, she became more and more anxious for Friday and their date to arrive. She then thought of Kasha.

Deena frowned as she thought of the latest news Dionne had unearthed. While Kasha had not been directly involved in the drug deal, she had been there when her brother was shot. According to some informant, Kasha had walked in on the deal that had just begun to turn bad.

Deena had called the half-way house where Kasha was hiding and had told her that she'd be over first thing Sunday morning to discuss the next steps in her defense. Kasha hadn't shot anyone, hadn't dealt any drugs, but she had seen who tried to kill her brother and that made her a witness to attempted murder in Deena's eyes and an accessory to murder in the eyes of the prosecution. But if Kasha talked, how long would it be before whoever was behind this whole menagerie would find her; or even worse, harm Deena for persuading Kasha to tell all she knew. Deena thought maybe the young woman knew too much. A cold chill settled across her, leaving her with a sense of foreboding.

Deena shook off the eerie feeling and picked up the phone. Dialing Karen's number, she felt the need to speak with her soror. After getting past what Deena called Karen's gatekeepers—her secretary followed by her executive assistant—she finally got her soror on the line.

"Okay, where have you been and why are you just now returning my phone call?"

Deena chuckled. "If you are able to, meet me at Honey Child's and I'll tell you all about it."

"Shoot, I need a day at the spa. Think she can squeeze us in? You know that place is always packed."

"Yup, made reservations in hopes that you could get away and Dionne is joining us."

"Girl, I will see you at Honey Childs in half an hour. And don't be late."

"Make it one hour. I've got to wrap up a few things and then I'm on my way. Besides our appointment is for 1:30."

"Sounds great. See ya, soror."

"Bye." Deena hung up then called her sister, making sure that she was still going to meet her at the spa. After her calls, she went on to finish the first part of the defense of Kasha Bently. She wrapped up her day with the filing of Mr. Swift's paperwork. Shutting down her computer and locking her office, Deena waved her hand over her head to Kimmie as she headed out to Honey Childs Spa.

"Hey, girl," Bambi, the owner of Honey Child's said with a smile as she embraced Deena. "How are my favorite girls?"

"Good," the trio chimed as they each took turns hugging the vivacious owner of one of Chicago's hottest spas.

Having been in business for nearly 10 years, Honey Child's boasted some of the most well known clients in Chicago, with rumors having it that Mary J. Blige and Kim Coles visited when they were in town. Located in the trendy Gold Coast, the three-story salon and spa boasted soothing brown and cream tones with gleaming rich silver tone accessories. It had become one of Deena's favorite tranquil get-away without having to leave the city.

Bambi held Deena's hand. "Sister, I love that suit. What's that? A Chanel? Or a Dolce and Gabanna?"

Deena stepped back and twirled, the pale peach skirt rested mid-thigh, and the matching scalloped blazer fit her perfectly. She looked down at her feet and they both laughed. Deena was wearing pink flip-flops.

"Now that's a fashion statement."

"You know I'm here to get me a manicure and a pedicure. I couldn't very well wear the Manolos.," Deena responded.

"Well ladies, I have a few new products I'd like to try on you. Are you game?" Bambi asked, looking at each one.

They eagerly nodded their heads in the affirmative.

"Great. One of the products is a new massage/rubbing oil. It's supposed to heighten the senses. The other is a new hair product that tames the frizzes." Bambi reached out to Deena's unruly mass of curls. "Like these." She laughed as Deena swatted at her hand. "Come on, let's get you ladies started. I'm so glad to see each of you."

"And we're glad to see you, too. Besides, I need it and I do need to get my hair trimmed."

"Anything you want, you know that. Jasmine will assist you guys from station to station," Bambi said as she raised her hand and motioned to a young woman dressed in black and white. "Jasmine, this is Deena Walls, her sister, Dionne, and their best friend Karen LaFontant. Please take great care of them. Start with some beverages to get them relaxed and then show them to the Relaxation Station." Bambi winked. "Deena's going to get her hair trimmed, so have Javier on standby once she's finished with her rub down."

Deena hugged her childhood friend and then followed Jasmine, with Dionne and Karen right behind her. After undressing and replacing their clothes with deep brown smocks, they headed to the private station, which was located on the top floor of the salon. As they entered the room, its walls painted a warm cream, Deena noticed that the décor had been changed since her and Dionne's last visit two months ago. The massage table was covered in a smooth looking brown cloth and the small pillow at the head of the table had the salon's emblem on it. The overhead recessed lighting added a calming ambiance. A small love seat, two matching chairs, in pale gold, and a round, blonde wood coffee table rounded out the furniture in the private room. The two masseuses worked quietly as Deena, Dionne and Karen began to talk.

"Okay, tell me all about you and Charles, and don't leave out a word."

"Yes, do tell." Dionne looked at Deena expectantly; her eye brows raised high, just like their father did when he was expecting a juicy story.

Deena inhaled deeply and thought of the man who had called her every day, several times a day, and who wouldn't allow her to lay her head on her pillow until she had called him to let him know she had arrived home safely. The past days had gotten so that she looked forward to awaking to his voice then going to sleep with his words on her mind. She wasn't sure what she would do when she saw him later—a big part of her just wanted to run into his arms and hug him, placing a wet kiss squarely on those full lips of his.

"Charles is the investigating detective for CPD on the Kasha case," Deena began as she looked at her sister. "He's also friends of Karen and Gary and is Gary's fraternity brother."

Deena looked from Dionne to Karen and back as she told them

what happened following the awards dinner, how he'd been sending her flowers, food and emails for the past week without fail and about the subsequent gift that led up to her agreeing to go out with him.

"Girl, how are you going to grill him on the witness stand after all of this?" Dionne asked as she stepped behind a screen returning moments later wrapped in a large white sheet. She lay on the masseuse table and looked up at Deena. "Does he think he's that damn strong?" Dionne snickered as she folded her arms under her head, allowing the masseuse to begin working on her shoulders.

"Shoot, I hear ya, Dionne. I hadn't thought about that," Karen chimed in as she readied herself for her massage.

Deena looked at them both, the soothing music in the background couldn't erase the niggling feeling in the pit of her stomach that said he wouldn't be able to handle it—that he would not only be angry at her once she finished with him, but that he'd refuse to see her. Yet, when she had raised that very issue with him, he insisted that she do her thing—that he wouldn't feel any differently; maybe more enraptured, he'd said.

"He said it won't change how he feels."

Dionne nodded her head, her eyes closed. "Hell, he ain't been grilled by a Walls yet."

Karen came to sit next to Deena. "Do you like him?"

She nodded her head as her face became warm with a blush. "And he is so sweet, Karen. Why didn't I meet this dude sooner?"

They both looked at Deena with wide eyes. She laughed loudly.

"Ya'll wrong, you know that? I don't mean sweet like that. He's solid. I mean he's caring in a way I need him to be. I don't sense any overbearing need to put me in my place, like I have a place I'm supposed to be. What's that all about?" came her rhetorical question, one they'd each asked each other a time or two during their dating woes.

"Girl, that was those un-evolved brothers you were dating."

Deena laughed and then stood once the estitician walked into the room. She slid into the leather chair and laid her head back as the short woman went to work plying and coaxing her skin, her smooth fingers bringing her skin to life. She closed her eyes and let the feeling of floating take her away, thoughts of Charles and the last words he'd uttered this morning: *can't wait to see you*.

For three hours, the trio was massaged, rubbed and soothed, feet and hands pampered, hair trimmed and tamed. And during that time, Deena had gotten more than she paid for—she'd gotten to spend some quality time with two of the women she deemed close and dear to her and they'd offered her sound, sage advice—if Charles could handle the job she had to do without trying to change her or becoming angry because she gave her all then he was the man for her.

"Deena, you go and have a good time with Charles," Karen said as she hugged her. "And know that Charles is a strong man and isn't afraid of much. Besides, Gary is always bragging about him—always talking about how he was different even when they were in college."

"How so?"

"Gary said Charles was always the level-headed one and was never one to go along in order to get along; that he'd always been a strong brother with a clear and true sense of his-self. Shoot, we don't know too many like that. And what impressed me most was that Gary said he never shirked responsibility. If he did it, he owned up to it."

Deena thought about what she knew so far, that he instantly agreed with his ex-wife to allow his son to live with him, he disliked injustice and people who celebrated the downfall of others and he enjoyed quiet evenings listening to soft jazz.

"But the best thing, Deena, is that Charles isn't a womanizer. He's pretty much a one-woman-man."

Deena smiled at that statement. She was a one-man woman and wasn't interested in dalliances and sexual liaisons. She didn't play games. If she wasn't interested she wouldn't pretend to be—life was just too short and karma too strong to string folks along.

"Thank you for that, Karen." She looked at her soror. "And I'll try to go with the flow."

"Try." Karen implored. "You are a strong sister, but you don't have to be all of the time. I know the cape is heavy and you want someone who can hold you up and let you cry without judgment or thinking you're a weak woman."

"She needs a brother with a jack hammer and arms strong enough to break down that wall as well as hold her," Dionne stated.

Deena looked at them both. Their words rang true and a part of her so wanted to shed the whole strong black, superwoman thing. Each time she'd put on the cape and rescued someone, she found it hard to be rescued herself, to just be a woman with emotional needs and wants. She didn't want to wear the superwoman cape 24/7.

But men had accused Deena of being hard. Shoot, she thought to herself, if a sister didn't go for the ole' oke-doke, or played along with the D and C game, dumb and crazy, then she was labeled hard. Or if she took a brother at his word when he said he wasn't any good in relationships what was she supposed to do? Spend countless days and weeks trying to convince him otherwise. Hell no. She wanted and needed a man to bring his "A" game—his *all* that!

Deena slowed her footsteps as they stepped outside of the spa after paying for their afternoon of beauty. Her thoughts flittered about and as she looked down at her watch, she suddenly became nervous.

"So, are you going to try to hang with Charles? I mean give him a chance."

Deena nodded her head.

"Good, sis. I'm glad to hear it," she said as she looped her arm around Deena's waist. "You need a strong man who isn't intimidated by you or us." She leaned her head on Deena's shoulder. "And I understand from Dad, that this brother is pretty cool peeps."

"Yes, he is." Deena blushed.

"And I'm glad you're going out. I was getting worried about you, Sis. I don't want you to be the only one at my wedding without a date on your arm."

Deena stepped back and looked at Dionne. Karen stopped in her tracks. "You guys have finally set a date?"

Dionne nodded her head as her smile stretched across her face. "Yes, we have. We're going to Paradise Island the end of August."

Deena's eyes widened. "That's about two months from now."

"Sure is."

She looked her sister up and down, her eyes settling on her abdomen.

"Don't you even go there," Dionne said as she placed her hands on her hips. "I am not pregnant."

Karen exchanged knowing glances with Deena—their heads bent slightly with their lips pursed together. Deena was the first to crack as her laughter bubbled up and out, followed by sounds of laughter from Karen. They surrounded Dionne, placing their arms around her for a group hug and then began jumping up and down.

"Finally," Deena said once they stopped jumping. "Have you told mom and dad so they can have the villa in Nassau aired out and well stocked for the Walls clan?"

"No, and please don't tell them. Steve and I are going to tell them at Sunday dinner. But I do want to ask you to be my Matron of Honor?"

Karen squealed loudly as she hugged the sisters again. Deena laughed, thinking of how her Sorority sister was a diehard romantic and loved mushy moments just like the one they were having.

"And Karen, I'd like for you to be in the wedding as well. I'll be having a small wedding with you and Deena as my attendants."

Deena took Dionne's hand in hers. "You know I'm here for you, but I would like to know what the rush is."

"Steve and I have been engaged for nearly two and a half years and about a month ago we really sat down and discussed marriage; I mean how we'd like to live, how we view marriage; what are the deal breakers."

"Wow, that's kind of deep. I'm not sure many people do that." Karen responded. "So, what are your deal breakers?"

Deena looked at Dionne and knew that if Steve ever laid a hand on Dionne like Seth had laid a hand on her, he'd be toast. Whereas Deena had defended herself, Dionne was more vengeful and she didn't doubt that Steve would end up appearing on a milk carton.

"My two are infidelity and physical and emotional abuse. I just won't have it."

Deena had been infatuated with the good-looking law student who seemed to have eyes only for her. And after they graduated at the top of their class, Seth had asked her to marry him. Deena was so in love with the idea of being married she'd never talked to him about deal breakers. In truth, she didn't really think she had any—until he'd begun verbally assaulting her, insulting her cooking, cleaning, personal attire and even how she'd made love to him. And when he'd hit her.

"Deena," Dionne called out her name. She looked at her sister and prayed that Steve would always love and care for her. "You okay?" She took her hand in hers as Deena nodded; her eyes glistened with unshed tears.

Karen looked at her watch. "Girl, it's four-thirty. What time is Charles coming by to get you?"

Deena shook her head. She needed to grab a cab and get home so that she could dress for her date. She held up her hand. "Shoot, ya'll. He's going to be at my place at six. I have to get going," she said as she hugged and then kissed Dionne, followed by Karen on their cheeks right as a taxi cab arrived.

"Call me when you get home," Dionne said as she shut the cab door and stood on the sidewalk. She thought of the excitement she'd seen in her sister's eyes and the breathless way she'd spoken about Charles. Her eyes became misty as she thought about how her big sister deserved boundless of love. She just hoped that this Charles wouldn't hurt her—for Dionne hadn't been this excited about Seth.

Chapter 10

"Dad, where are you going?" Corbin asked as he stood in his bedroom doorway.

"I'm going to Grant Park."

Corbin folded his arms across his chest. "Okay, for what?"

"For the movies in the park."

Corbin sucked his teeth. "What's playing?"

"*Cabin in the Sky,*" Charles replied as he pulled a shirt over his head, looked at his reflection in the mirror, tugged the shirt off and walked over to his closet. He dragged the hangers to and fro until he found another shirt.

Corbin huffed loudly. "Why am I pulling teeth? Dad, who are you going with?"

Charles laughed, pausing to look at his son. The questions he was asking were the same ones Charles would be asking if the roles were reversed. No way would he lie to his son. "I'm going to Grant Park with Ms. Deena Walls. She's an attorney working on a case that I've been involved in. We are going to the Movies in the Park to see the classic *Cabin in the Sky* and I should be home around midnight or so. Her father is the retired judge we golfed with. And her brother, David is the one I told you about who's a Sensei—you'll be in his class come September." Charles motioned his son closer. He picked up the new bottle of cologne he purchased earlier and handed it to him. "What do you think of this?" He watched as Corbin unscrewed the top and took a sniff.

"That's hot, dad. Yeah, wear that."

Charles picked up another bottle of cologne, one he wore daily. "Or should I go with this one?" he handed the bottle over.

"Nah," Corbin sniffed and then placed the bottle on the armoire. "You wear this one all the time. This is a first date—you've got to go all out."

Charles looked at his son and shook his head. *Out of the mouths of babes*. He wanted to ask him what he knew about first dates, but changed his mind. He'd save that question for another time.

Corbin walked over to Charles's bed and sat down. Charles went back to dressing, glancing at his son. He remembered when Corbin had been a little boy and he'd sit and watch as Charles readied for work. Charles would always end the ritual by applying a smidge of cologne on the side of Corbin's neck. And later, when Charles would come home, he'd pick Corbin up out of his crib and nuzzle the side of his neck.

"What time are you picking up Ms. Walls?"

"Six o'clock. What time is it?"

"It's five," Corbin responded. Charles looked at Corbin reflection in the mirror as he lounged on the bed.

"Are you trying to rush me?" Charles faced his son. "Do you have some plans I need to be clued into?"

"No, daddy," Corbin responded quickly. "It's just that this is the same person you got Uncle Gary to hook you up at that awards dinner. And besides, you're always telling me not to be late."

Corbin was a good kid and wasn't one for foolishness, but he was at that age where he'd try a few things just because. Charles thought of how he'd been at Corbin's age and remembered the first time his parents left him home alone. Charles had called a few girls and guys from school over. And though nothing more than a few bags of chips disappearing and the soda noticeably low, he had been too shy to try anything other than holding one of the girls by the hand.

"I'm going to call one of your uncles to come over while I'm gone."

Corbin jumped up from the bed. "Dad, don't you trust me?"

Charles picked up the cordless phone. "Sure I do. I just don't trust everyone else." He began dialing his brother, Christopher's number. After being sent to voice mail, he tried two other numbers to no avail. Charles tossed the phone onto the bed and then sat near Corbin. "Look, I know you and a few of your buddies want to hang. But just remember this: make them treat your home as if they owned it and make sure that no girls are in this house." Charles looked Corbin in the eye. "Are we clear on that last point?"

"Yes, sir."

"Good, now go and call your buddies and tell them to come on over. I'll spring for some pizza."

Corbin rushed out of the room, taking the cordless phone with him. Charles chuckled and shook his head as the sound of excitement peppered his son's deepening voice. He looked at his watch. "I've got to get out of here."

Finally satisfied, Charles searched for his son for a final good-bye and found Corbin in the basement. Charles hugged him and reminded him of what time he'd be back.

"Have a good time, Dad. I'll be right here and we won't tear up the joint."

"Sweetie," Charles called out to their dog that was lying on an old couch in the corner of the basement. "Make sure you watch them tonight, okay girl?" He squatted down, rubbing the dog behind her ears, her short, stumpy tail wagging quickly from side to side.

"Wait, Dad." Corbin pointed to Charles's head. "You forgot something."

Charles looked down. His sandals were clean, the cream colored slacks pressed and creased just so, and the matching, short sleeve pullover was clean and fit just right. "What?" His hands open.

"Where's your hoop?"

Charles's hand went to his right ear. He rushed back up the stairs, taking them three at a time, and headed to his bedroom. Once there, he rummaged quickly through his jewelry. Upon finding his small gold hoop, he tried to put the piece into the lobe of his ear. His hands shook. He sat down on the edge of his bed. He was both excited and nervous. Like Lee had said, this sister is different and Charles had gotten the feeling that she didn't play games, didn't suffer fools and wanted a man to mean what he said, and say what he meant. No games.

Charles inhaled deeply, willed his hands to be still and then placed the hoop into the pierced lobe. He looked up to see Corbin standing in the doorway.

"You're going to be late, Dad," Corbin said then stood to one side as Charles rushed past him.

Charles pressed several bills into his son's hand, hugged him again and then headed out the rear door to the garage to retrieve his SUV.

Late was the last thing Charles wanted to be after he'd slow walked Deena all week in an attempt to get her to agree to a date. He thought about her as he headed to her place. He knew the price tag to live on the penthouse floor was high, so if Deena was living on the top, then to him it stood to reason that her place cost a small fortune. Way too pricy for his blood.

He shook his head not wanting to go there—not wanting to allow the demon of self-doubt creep into his mind and sabotage something that hadn't even begun. He knew she was far from broke and probably cleared five times what he bought home in two weeks. Yet, he was both fascinated and perplexed by her. His frat brother, Gary, had said she was single, no dates, and had divorced a real "piece of work" some years ago. At the end of one of their many hour long conversations, he'd found that Ms. Deena Walls was a fiercely independent woman who didn't hesitate in speaking her mind. But Charles knew people—knew that there was something much deeper to Deena Walls and he was itching to go below the surface to find out.

Deena sat on the chaise lounge. She looked at her watch and wondered where Charles was. It was already ten minutes past six and he was late. She inhaled deeply as she closed her eyes. Her temples were trying to throb, but she forced the negative thoughts from her mind as she rose from the chaise and headed to the kitchen. Opening the refrigerator, she took out a pitcher of iced tea. Retrieving a glass from one of the many cupboards' in the gourmet kitchen, she poured herself a generous helping. Just as she began to drink from the glass, her phone rang.

"Hello," she responded into the receiver. "Yes, I'm expecting him. Please send him up." She placed the receiver on its base and then rushed to her bedroom. She looked at her reflection in the mirror and hoped that what she had on was just right. He'd told her to dress casual. She jumped at the sound of her doorbell. It was rarely rung and the sound was somewhat foreign.

Deena rushed down the foyer toward the door. She paused and inhaled deeply. There would be no turning back now. She opened the door and wanted to pass out from the wondrous scent of the too fine man standing just across the threshold. She looked up into the dark eyes that had held hers. And when he opened his arms, she automatically went into them; and rested her head on his wide chest as his arms engulfed her in a sensuous, yet protective embrace. She didn't want to let go.

"You smell good," he whispered in her ear as he kissed her on the cheek right before releasing her. He leaned his body on the door jam and watched her. Deena blushed as she stepped to one side.

"Please come in."

Charles picked up large shopping bag and stepped inside. "Wow, that's some view." He said as he looked ahead toward the living room.

"How about the ten-cent tour." Deena asked. She wanted to get this out of the way, see how he reacted to her living in a two-story penthouse.

Charles followed behind her, trying to keep his eyes focused on the curls about her head and not the hypnotic sway of her hips as she showed him three of four bedrooms, one on the main level, and two on the upper level, two bathrooms, a powder room, a den and a kitchen so large it would dwarf his three times over, with room to spare. He actually liked her living space.

"Well, that's *casa* Walls."

"Nice digs," he replied. "I could hang out here. With a little Coltrane or some Miles playing in the background and me sitting in the window. Oh, yeah, I could do this." He walked over to the window, his hands in his pockets as he looked out onto Lake Michigan.

Deena joined him at the window. He placed his arm around her waist and pulled her close. She looked up just as he looked down into her eyes. She wanted to know who he was, was he there to try to conquer her or to compliment her?

"I'd love to stand here with you all night, you know that," he said as he turned his body then hers to face him. "But I guess we should get going."

Deena nodded and allowed him to take her by the hand as they headed to the door. So far he'd passed a few tests, one being that while he seemed to like her place, she didn't get the impression he was intimidated.

"Where's your purse and keys, baby?"

She looked around, her mind everywhere but on the purse as she thought of the feelings he was awakening, the scent he was wearing and the way he looked in his slacks and shirt, the sleeves straining against the muscles in his arms. It was getting warm. "Probably in my room. I'll be right back."

Moments later she returned. "Ready." She said as she came to stand next to him.

"I should have brought my other gun."

Deena looked up at him.

Charles chuckled. "I'm going to have to shoot someone, baby. That dress is talking." He blew out an exaggerated breath. "And you smell so good." He closed his eyes briefly.

She blushed and then giggled—glad she had chosen to wear the turquoise blue halter dress with the beaded u-shaped, shirred neckline; her feet encased in a pair of low-heeled jewel strapped sandals. And her cologne, Chanel's Chance, was just what she wanted: a chance to see if this man was for real.

Charles took Deena's hand in his as they headed out the door. They began to engage in small talk as they walked slowly to the elevator.

"Wait," Charles stopped. "You got me vexed, woman. I've forgotten about the stuff I brought with me to add to the picnic basket."

They both laughed as they headed back to Deena's place. She worked alongside Charles, placing several covered items into the basket. He topped it off with pulling his iPod and two mini speakers and a blanket from the bottom of the bag.

"Now, we can leave."

"But, you still haven't told me where we're going."

Charles slung the blanket over his forearm, grabbed the basket and then her hand and headed out the door again. He stood at the elevator and began whistling. "I thought I told you."

"No, you didn't. You just said we we're going out."

"Well, at least you know we're going on a picnic."

They rode the elevator, both chatting nervously. Deena hadn't felt this giddy, if ever about a date. A part of her wanted to pull back, take it slow, and slip into the safe zone. But it had been that safe zone which had left her dateless many a night. She glanced up at Charles. A part of her said she didn't want safe—she wanted to peel this brother back and have him do the same to her, to go below the surface, be at a place where she'd never been before. She wanted pure passion. She wanted to know how it felt to have her cup 'runneth' over.

Outside, Charles took Deena's hand in his again and they began walking down Michigan Avenue. A warm June breeze blew around them as they talked about their respective day. At Balbo, Charles headed across the bridge and then over near Buckingham Fountain. Once Deena could saw they were heading toward the Petrillo band shell, she began to smile broadly—they were going to the Movies in the Park.

Deena smiled up at him. "I love this part of Grant Park and the movies." She wrapped her hand around his bicep. "*You* heard me."

"I'm a good listener." He slowed his steps as he thought about the conversation they'd had surrounding old movies. So when he saw this one playing in the park, he knew it would be perfect for a first date.

"Pick a spot, milady." He bowed slightly and watched as Deena moved across the lawn, side stepping a few people who had already staked their claim. Deena walked a little further and then over to the right. She stopped and waved Charles to her.

"Looks good," he said as he laid the large blanket in Deena's outstretched arms. He placed the basket on top of the blanket she'd just spread out on the lawn. Deena sat down and then looked up at him.

Charles swallowed hard. He thought she looked so beautiful sitting there, the setting sun framing the back of her head, the brown smoothness of her shoulders, her toned arms. He wanted to run his fingers through her hair, down her arms, across her entire body—have the tips of his fingers memorize every inch of her. And the broad smiled she gave him had lit up her beautiful honey-colored eyes. They seemed to dance and change colors as she looked up at him. He liked that—liked seeing that this simple act had brought her such joy and happiness. Truth be told, the way she was looking at him made him want to do more for her, to be that man she'd obviously been looking for, otherwise she'd have a boyfriend.

He continued to watch her closely as she took off her shoes; her toes painted a wild, wicked red, and tucked them under her. He sat beside her when she patted the spot next to her on the blanket.

Charles and Deena removed the containers from the basket, with Charles pulling out his IPod and the mini speakers. He hooked the speakers to the iPod and then nodded as the easy sounds of smooth jazz seeped out as they began their feast.

For nearly an hour they ate and talked, waiting for the sun to set before the organizers could begin the feature movie. Deena was impressed with the types of picnic food Charles had brought along. In one container was a seafood salad, another contained chicken Caesar salad, and yet another contained tropical fruit salad. The bottle of wine he'd sent with the basket had been chilled all week in the refrigerator and the crackers were still fresh in their air-proof cellophane. The picnic meal had been topped off with decadent walnut brownies, laced with a hint of bourbon liqueur.

"I am too full, Charles." Deena patted her stomach. "And the salads were great."

"I'm glad you've enjoyed the food." He lay back on the blanket and looked up at her. "It's getting darker so the movie should be starting soon."

Deena looked down at Charles as he folded his hands behind his head. The fabric of his shirt stretched around his large arms. Her eyes traveled down the length of him, getting a good look at him. His dark eyes were surrounded by long eyelashes, so long she'd become envious and his eyebrows were a smooth black atop a flat forehead that moved into a aquiline nose right above his full lips perfectly shaped for kissing. She thought he had the most beautiful pair of lips—if that could be such a thing for a man.

The pleasant visual trip continued across his chest, the hairs again peeking from the top of his shirt, past his waist to his muscular thighs, his legs crossed one over the other ended at a pair of leather sandals. And the gold hoop in his right ear didn't escape her. Deena thought it added to his handsomeness—not detracted from it. She wondered how he'd look minus all the accoutrements.

Suddenly, Deena became warm, even though a nice comfortable breeze blew off of Lake Michigan. Admiring his muscular physic had heat rolling up and down her entire body. The sensation was so heated she swore her skin was hot to the touch. She looked into his eyes and saw them grow darker—the look of desire.

The sound of the music announcing one of her favorite movies could be heard. She twisted around so she could face the screen. Moments later she felt Charles's nearness as he sat up and shut off the iPod, his body moving closer to Deena's. Instinctively, she rested her back against his chest feeling the rise and fall of it against her back as Charles rubbed her arm lightly.

The movie, *Cabin in the Sky*, released in 1943, featured some of the race's best actors and actresses, like Ethel Waters, Lena Horne and Eddie Anderson, who was best known as Rochester, Jack Benny's valet on the TV show. A Black film classic, the movie had great music and was the directorial debut of Vincente Minnelli, ex-husband of Judy Garland and father to the incomparable and talented Liza Minnelli.

For forty five minutes, Deena and Charles laughed, hummed and in a few cases, sang along with the movie. And Deena couldn't remember the last time she'd had so much fun.

Once the show was over, they packed up the basket and folded the blanket, then headed back to Deena's place. She wasn't sure if she should invite him up or just steal a kiss from him and then rush up to her penthouse to spend the rest of the evening fantasizing about him.

Wrapping his arm around Deena's waist, Charles walked slowly with her through the park toward Michigan Avenue, again their conversation flowing easy, her laughter, which he'd enjoyed hearing, made him smile.

Yeah, he thought, the date had gone really well and he wasn't quite sure he was ready for the night to end. He'd been on enough dates to know when they went well and when they hadn't—this one, in his estimation, had gone super well and he couldn't recall the last time he'd truly enjoyed the simple company and conversation of a woman. And he knew one thing—seeing more of Deena Walls was number one on his list.

Chapter 11

Deena could see her apartment building in the distance. And while she really enjoyed her home, considered herself sort of a homebody, for the first time since purchasing her penthouse digs, she wasn't quite ready to go home.

It had been a long time since she'd gone out on a date and even longer since she'd just been able to be herself—not an attorney to some of Chicago's rich and famous. Charles hadn't laughed at her or made fun of the fact that her taste in music and movies was eclectic—she'd admitted to loving show tunes and foreign movies with subtitles. And he admitted to owning some of the same proclivities. When she told him that she enjoys watching history and animal shows on cable, with her favorite show the British program "*It's Me or the Dog*," he'd laughed, stating they he too loved watching history and animal shows, along with the typical sports events. They'd talked a little bit about everything except the one thing that had brought them to this point—Kasha Bentley.

She looked up at him, admiring the side profile of his handsome face. Her mind tried to find a reason to prolong the date—for him to hang out with her just a little while longer, to hear his laughter and listen to his deep voice as he told one story after another of his family, including his son Corbin, and the people he encountered every day.

Shoot, she fussed inwardly; she just wanted to be around him.

As they reached the front of her building, Charles paused,

looking down at her. "Are you tired?"

"No, you?"

He shook his head. "Hey, where's the popcorn shop?" Charles asked.

"I know you aren't talking about Garrett's?"

"Sure am. Isn't there one over near State Street?"

"Man that stuff is like crack."

Charles laughed and pulled her into his arms, kissing her on her forehead. "Then sweetheart, let's go get high on some popcorn."

Charles placed the picnic basket and blanket in the rear of his SUV, then grasped Deena's hand. "Lead the way."

They walked over a mile to the famed shop, their conversation turning serious as they discussed crime, politics and current social issues.

He asked Deena how she got into law.

"My parent's first firm was in the basement of the house I grew up in," she said as they walked slowly down Michigan Avenue. "We'd have all kinds of folks in there. From politicians to civil rights leaders, folks came and went and my parents turned down very few clients. They even defended a prostitute once who had brought charges against her pimp for cruel and unusual punishment that was thrown out of court. They sued him in civil court and won. We learned early on to dislike injustice of any type and to never be afraid to speak up."

They came to a crosswalk. Deena looked up and saw the deep thought of concentration on his face. Most of her dates wanted to hear the stories of who she represented and how much the family firm brought in annually. This man standing next to her, with the cute dimple in his chin, was asking her questions that would lead to her soul. And Deena wasn't quite sure she wanted him to touch her soul.

"Okay, enough of me."

"Wait, not yet. Tell me about your family."

Deena smiled broadly as she told her him all about her three siblings and how she felt growing up with a full house. When she was finished, Charles nodded his head.

"Enough about me, please tell me about you? What made you want to be a cop?"

Their conversation was briefly interrupted when a homeless man approached them. At first he begged for money then stopped abruptly.

"Yes, Tommy, it's me. And you know it's against the law to

panhandle."

"Sure, sure, I know. Arrest any innocent folks lately?"

"Nope, but here's a little something for you to use to head over to the new shelter in Uptown." Charles pressed a twenty dollar bill into the man's hand. "And I don't want to see you asking folks for money."

"Sure, Charles. Thanks, man. Take care." Willie walked away the then turned back. "And she sure is pretty." Willie then went on his way.

"I take it you know him well."

Charles nodded. "Can you believe he's just forty? He got strung out on drugs. I got him to go into treatment, but he also has some mental health issues. The shelter deals with mental illness."

Deena was surprised, but then thought again. Charles was a detective and she knew that detectives got to know a long list of folks from all walks of life.

Charles took her hand in his and they continued toward the popcorn shop.

"You asked me what made me want to be a cop," he began. "Well, there's a legacy of black cops in my family. My great grandfather integrated the Chicago Police Department. My dad is a retired cop, my mom was an evidence technician for the department and two of my four brothers are cops, as well as a few other relatives."

"Four brothers? Any sisters?" The awe in her voice matched her wide eyed expression.

Charles laughed at her expression. "No sisters. My mother said each time she was pregnant she hoped for a girl, but instead she ended up with five sons. But my sisters-in-laws are her daughters and she's really close to each of them."

She thought of the last thing he'd said—his brothers. "Wow, five boys. What number are you?"

"I'm the youngest. There's three years between each of us."

"How in the world did your mom handle you guys?"

"We were a handful, I'll admit. But mom was the disciplinarian in the household, of course backed by dad. Plus my maternal grandparents lived with us and they were quick to step in when they weren't around. Even that didn't always stop us from getting into mischief."

While they stood in the long line, Charles entertained Deena with stories of antics he and his brothers would find themselves in. At one point during one of his stories, Deena found herself laughing so hard she had tears in her eyes.

"I'm telling you, the dive my brother, Aaron, made across that room onto our parents bed remains as one of our classics. We tell his kids the story all the time."

"What happened to the bed?"

"Of course it broke, but we propped it up and prayed that it would hold. And for about three nights it did. Then one night, mom and dad got into that bed and it broke again. We laughed so hard that my mom knew we had done something to their bed, but we wouldn't talk."

"You guys were too much."

"That's what my mom use to say. But we weren't bad kids, maybe just a bit too inquisitive and curious. We've redeemed ourselves—we're all college grads with three of us attending on full academic and athletic scholarships."

Charles went on to tell Deena how he felt being the youngest of five boys, he loved all of the attention, and how having his grandparents live on the first floor of a two-flat family home, which was still in the family and occupied by his parents and one of his brothers and his own family. He continued with how his grandmother had doted on him.

"Grandma Eliza was something else."

"How long has she been deceased?"

Charles looked up and met her eyes. "About five years now. She was 100-years-old when she died peacefully in her sleep. My grandfather, Charles, died when he was seventy. He was fifteen years her junior."

She saw the quick flash of sadness in his dark eyes. She decided to change the subject, for she hadn't liked the look, hadn't liked seeing the change in his kind eyes, regardless of whether it was warranted or not.

"Did I hear you tell my father that you have a son?" She watched the light return to his eyes. *His emotions run deep*, she thought to herself.

"His name is Corbin. And he came to live with me two years ago. His mother felt he needed to be with a man once puberty hit."

Again, Deena found herself laughing as he continued with more stories of his family. She couldn't recall ever laughing so much on a date before or having conversations flow so easily. Deena felt free to just be herself, not the high-powered attorney using twenty dollar words with two vowels each. No, she found this date much different from any she'd been on and knew, without question, it was because of the man standing next to her—making her smile, causing heat to suffuse her entire body, making her pulse and everything in between race and skitter across her entire being.

She didn't want to fall so fast—couldn't believe she could be so enamored. But she felt it and knew she was falling for Charles and couldn't think of a thing to do to slow it down.

Having gotten their bags of popcorn, they began the long walk back to Deena's place. Once out front, Charles retrieved the picnic basket and blanket from his SUV.

"Thanks for agreeing to go out with me, Deena."

"Thank you for asking. I had a great time."

Charles placed the picnic basket on the ground and put the blanket on top of it. He smiled and tilted his head to the side, his right eyebrow raised. "Did you have enough of a great time to agree to go out with me again?"

Deena had hoped he'd ask her out again. She looked up into his dark eyes and saw the question in them. She'd be a fool if she'd said 'no,' and her momma hadn't raised any fools. "I'd really like that, Charles."

She watched as a smile appeared, his eyes lowered. He seemed to be looking at her lips and knew that if he wanted a kiss she'd gladly give him one, for she had wondered how his lips would feel upon her own. She heard him clear his throat.

"Would I be out of line if I asked to kiss you?"

Deena shook her head and then watched as his face got closer to hers. Finally, she felt his lips upon hers the smooth fullness of them touched her lightly just as his arms reached out and pulled her to him. He started out with small pecks each one lingered longer than the other. Deena almost slid from his arms when she felt his tongue outline hers, commanding her to open and receive. She closed her eyes and turned her head, opening her mouth to allow the sensuous onslaught to take over. The heated core began to stream down her body and she reached out to him, slipping her hands up and around the nape of his neck. She wasn't sure who the deep, throaty moan came from.

She moved closer, the feel of his chest against her; the solid feel of his need pressed against her abdomen. She didn't want him to stop kissing her as he began to languidly lavish her tongue with his own while his hands traveled lower, holding tightly to the sides of her hips. It had been a long time—too long—since she'd made love and the message Charles was sending just in his kiss, the way he captured her lips with his—her hips in his large hands stated he was not only in command but that his passion could quite possibly match, maybe even exceed, her own. Deena could barely concentrate; the feel of his powerful erection pressed against her, his hands, his full lips, snatched her reasoning as she began to slowly grind her hips into his.

Deena stopped and hid her face in his chest. Charles took the tips of his fingers and gently raised her chin upward until her eyes met his.

"My full apologies, Deena. I got a little carried away." He rested his forehead on hers and held her by her arms. "You're a really beautiful temptress."

An odd feeling crept over Deena—she had never been this attracted to a man so suddenly before. In some ways it scared her, for she wanted to throw all caution to the wind and take this man into her, let him love her until the end of time; and then love her some more.

She looked into his eyes and was startled to see the searing desire plainly displayed. She wanted to drink of what he was offering without hesitation, without thinking about what the next day would bear.

"I think it's time I walked you to your door," Charles picked up the basket and blanket, then took her hand in his as they walked into the foyer, stepped on the elevator and headed up to her penthouse.

Charles stood near her, but didn't dare touch her, for each time he had, he'd felt as if he'd gotten a shock. He liked the way she felt in his arms, the response she'd given him when he'd intensified the kiss, the way her body molded itself to his. The painful fullness in his groin stood as a reminder that not only had it been a long time, but that his attraction to her was immediate. He knew that once he had her, branded her his, filled her with his essence, he couldn't see himself without her and that was a scary proposition. He'd thought he had been in love before and didn't tend to believe in love at first sight, but something about this woman had crept under his skin and taken permanent residence.

As the elevator opened to Deena's floor, he followed her down the corridor then took her keys from her hand, opening her door. "Deena, if you have no plans for next Friday, I'd like to take you out to dinner."

Deena smiled. "Sure. That sounds great."

"And can I keep calling you every day?" He smiled at her.

She nodded and then took his free hand in hers. "As many times as you like, Charles." She rose on the tips of her toes and kissed his lips. "Honestly, I'd be disappointed if I didn't hear from you at least twice a day," she responded as she took the picnic basket and blanket from him. "And again, thank you for tonight. I had a great time."

"So did I. I'll talk to you tomorrow." He pulled her to him and kissed her again, his tongue now seemingly at home. He knew it was her response to him that pushed him forward, but he wouldn't move on her—not yet. He needed to know that what he wanted was what she wanted as well and that the passion he felt she kept bottled up would be solely his, for he wasn't a man into sharing. Period.

Slowly breaking apart, Deena touched her lips—the tingling sensation was only matched by the heady feeling she got from being held in his arms.

"Good night, sweetheart," he quickly kissed her again, then headed down the hall way.

Deena watched and waved as he disappeared into the elevator. Closing her door, she looked over at the large window, a place where she'd spent countless evenings looking out and wishing on stars she'd seen in the east. The electricity was real, the emotion he was coaxing out of her intoxicating, and the feel of him against her promised fulfillment. But even more than that, she found Charles seemed to be the kind of man she'd wanted in her life. He was strong without being overbearing or brutish; kind without being a pushover; and, warm without being too mushy.

Deena headed upstairs to her master suite. Deciding on taking a shower, she removed he shoes and dress, placing them in the large walk-in closet before going into the master bathroom to begin her nightly ritual. After showering and applying her favorite scented lotion, Deena grabbed her book and climbed into her queen-sized canopy bed. She tried to read, but the words on the pages seemed to blur as thoughts of Charles invaded her mind, the feel of him seared into her memory bank.

The sound of her phone broke into her thoughts.

"Hello," she said into the cordless phone and smiled as his deep voice filled the receiver. Deena closed her book and rolled over on her side as she and Charles launched into yet another deep conversation, this time about relationships.

When they finally hung up the phone, having decided on meeting up at the golf range to hit a few golf balls, Deena blushed, her smile wide as she thought of the man who'd just insinuated himself into her life.

Chapter 12

Charles had arrived home with two thoughts on his mind: his son Corbin and Deena Walls. He hoped Corbin and his friends had a good time and that his house was still intact. And he hoped like hell Deena wouldn't run like demon dogs were at her heels when she met Corbin and Sweetie. He knew he wanted her around, wanted to get to know all about her. And his fierce sexual attraction to her was no mistake—he wanted her and he intended on having her.

Stepping into the house, Charles paused, training his ear to hear sounds in the house. Sweetie came up to him.

"Hey, girl." He rubbed and scratched behind her ears. "Was Corbin a good boy?" He asked as he headed toward the basement, sounds from the television met him as he descended the stairs. Charles chuckled softly to himself when he saw Corbin and his two buddies, Leonard and Nate, along with Charles' nephew, Willie, sprawled out all over the basement—Corbin and Willie on opposite ends of the couch, Nate on the floor and Leonard on, of all things, the couch Sweetie slept on.

Charles looked at his watch and noted the hour. It was ten minutes to midnight and he wondered had the boys called their parents to let them know they were spending the night. He walked over to the bar and grabbed the receiver from the wall phone. He called both boys parents, apologizing for the late night, to let them know their respective sons were passed out and that he would be bringing them home later the next day. Once completed, he turned off the television, went to retrieve blankets, returned, covering each boy up and then headed to his bedroom. Sweetie's low whine stopped him.

"Bet you haven't been outside," Charles said as the dog rushed up the stairs. Charles followed behind her, opening the door to the yard. He stood in the doorway, the light from the full moon allowed him to see Sweetie without turning on the bright yard lights. After several moments, Sweetie returned to the house.

"Come on girl, seems as if your bed is taken."

Sweetie followed Charles into his room then lay out on the floor near the foot of the bed. He stepped over her and began disrobing, beginning with the removal of his small caliber hand gun attached to the ankle strap. Once finished, he put on a pair of shorts and a tank shirt, and headed to the washroom. He looked at his reflection in the bathroom mirror and thought of Deena. He wondered what she was doing. He wanted to hear her voice.

Charles headed back to his room, taking the cordless phone with him. He dialed her number, having committed it to memory. As he listened to her extension ring, he looked at the clock—it was after one in the morning.

"I just had to call," he said once she answered the phone.

He lay back on the bed and settled down to talk to the woman who made his blood simmer, his fingers twitch and his body taut just thinking about her. And he knew that it would be hard to get her from under his skin—if ever.

True to Charles's words, they began talking to each other more than twice a day and seeing each other nearly every other day, learning those nuances couples do to see if they fit. Between working on the case, making sure Kasha was safe and her dates with Charles, Deena kept busy. But the daunting work during the day was eased with the lunches and evenings spent with Charles. And each time she saw him, felt his lips on hers and wrapped her arms about him, she knew that this man was consistently chipping away her wall—breaking through to her—making her feel the emotions deep inside, which often warred with the fears she carried. Yet, during the nearly three weeks of their getting to know each other, he'd been one way—gracious and kind—and she wondered when the other shoe would drop and he'd change. They always did, Deena thought as she headed into her parent's house for Sunday dinner.

She thought back to the night of their first date. She and Charles had talked for hours following their date and then met up a few hours later for breakfast followed by hitting a few buckets of balls at the golf range. She had stood back and watched his form and was amazed that a brother his size was so fluid. He'd worn white shorts and a matching polo shirt. The beautiful color of his skin was accentuated by the white fabric. *And those legs. Mercy.* Deena thought she'd never seen a more muscular pair, cut in all the right places, his thighs looked like granite and the way his arms were formed. Jack LaLane had nothing on Charles. She could tell that he worked out regularly.

She'd hit poorly. He was a distraction as he stood off to the side. Her whole body was on fire for she knew he was soaking her up. She only hoped her full behind didn't look too big in the pastel blue golf pants and sleeveless top. At one time as she prepared to swing, she stopped midstride and looked back just as Charles's eyes motioned upward just as they met her eyes. He was busted. He'd been looking at her behind.

Once they'd finished, he took her hand in his and escorted her to her car. He had pulled her into his arms and kissed her again, this time with a little more reserve than he had the night before; but it's result was still the same—Deena's head swam, her body heated up and her core throbbed rapidly. All she could do was go with the onslaught, hoping that one day he'd either extinguish the fire or soothe it. *Something*. Deena wasn't sure she could take much more of his expert ministrations.

Again, they'd talked for hours once she arrived home from doing some work at the office. She couldn't believe it—she hadn't talk to any male that much since she was a teen. It was a good feeling. During that conversation, he had admitted what she'd thought: they wanted to see each other again. And that's just what they had been doing.

"Hey ya'll," Deena said as she stepped into the kitchen and saw her mother, Dionne and her sisters-in-laws, Lorene, David's wife, and Olivia, Darius's wife. Deena hugged and kissed everyone then looked around for her nieces and nephews. "Where's my monsters?" Deena called and smiled broadly as her brother's children, three girls and two boys, rushed out to hug her.

"Come on everyone, let's get the food on the table and eat," Deena's mother ordered as everyone took up a dish and headed out to the large dining room, which Deena's father had extended years ago to accommodate a large table that sat twelve comfortably.

After the food had been placed on the table and blessed, the conversation began, with Dionne stealing glances at Steve. Deena watched them, knowing that Steve was great for Dionne—her weaknesses seemed to be his strengths and vice versus. They complimented each other well and she knew he'd be a welcomed addition to the family.

"Ya'll, Deena been dating."

She looked up at her sister, her mouth open and her eyes wide. She felt like a teenager again, with Dionne and Darius telling all of she and David's business.

"I hope it was with Mr. Harris," Deena's father said as he peered at her from the tops of his glasses. "That young man is going places. I hear he's being considered for the FBI but I don't know if they told him yet or not, so mum's the word."

"Daddy, how do you know all of that?" Deena asked, somewhat miffed at why he hadn't mentioned ever applying with the FBI. She ignored the crazy emotion and listened as her father went on to tell of how his good friend at the department mentioned it when they ran into each other.

"And you just happened to mention Charles's name?" Deena twisted her mouth in a smirk. Bless her father's heart—he was trying to be a matchmaker. She laughed at the thought.

"So, have you been dating Charles?"

"Yes, daddy, I have been dating Charles."

Deena's mother put her fork down and looked at her. Out of all of the kids, Deena was most like her mother, whom she'd been named after, in temperament. "Well, your father sure spoke highly of him. And David has agreed to teach his son karate, but all that doesn't matter, what do you think of him and when will we meet him?"

"Mom, how about I bring him over next Sunday?"

"Why am I just now hearing about all of this?" Darius, the oldest, asked as he looked at his younger sister.

Deena knew that the inquisition had officially begun. She rolled her eyes at Dionne and began telling her family about Charles, what he does, where they've been going, and his love of golf.

"Well, that's a definite brownie point here," Darius said. "Got to get him out on the golf course with me."

Deena frowned. She knew Darius was going to grill Charles. None of them had been the same following Seth's little foray into madness.

After dinner, Deena and her mother headed into the kitchen, followed by her oldest niece, Stephanie who seemed to love helping her aunt and grandmother clean up the kitchen. This was their time together and they often took it to discuss day-to-day stuff like boys, fashion and school. Stephanie's mom, Olivia welcomed their assistance in raising the teen. Though she wasn't Darius' natural child, no one could tell, for they treated the child as if she was, with them having come into their lives when she was five-years old. At sixteen, Stephanie needed all the guidance the entire family could give and they gave her their all.

"How's the job at the conservatory?" Deena asked Stephanie as they stood next to each other at the double sink. She arranged for her niece to work at the Chicago Music Conservatory for the summer. During the school year, her niece went to a magnet school for gifted students. Stephanie was an honors student with a photographic memory and a love for classical music. Deena's father had brought Stephanie a baby grand piano when she was ten-years-old.

"It's okay." Stephanie began washing the dishes, her eyes focused on the plates. Deena thought this odd. She had been excited about her job at the conservatory.

"Anything special going on this summer?"

Stephanie shook her head.

Okay, Deena thought to herself, this was not her niece. Something was wrong and Deena was going to get to the bottom of it.

After they finished the dishes and cleaning up the dining room, Deena suggested the family go to Rainbow for ice cream. The entire family piled into several vehicles, with Stephanie riding along with Deena.

Once the car doors shut, Deena started. "Okay, what's wrong, baby?"

"Auntie Deena, there's going to be a party thrown by some kids and I want to go."

Deena exhaled. She thought the worse, but then again, with teenagers, everything is the worse. "When is the party and where is it going to be at?"

"Friday. It's at this one kid's house. Or should I say mansion, they live in the Highlands. But I know mom isn't going to let me go."

"Why won't she let you go?"

"She'll want to know who the chaperones are."

Deena glanced at her. "I'd want to know that myself. What's

wrong with that?"

"If she don't know the people, then I can't go and Auntie Deena, all the kids are going to be there."

Deena smiled in spite of the frantic sounds in her niece's voice. "Well, how about I talk to your mom as well as agree to take you and pick you up." Deena asked as they pulled up to the ice cream parlor and got out of the vehicle. Stephanie ran around to the driver's side and hugged Deena tightly. "I love you too, baby. Let's see what your mother has to say, okay?"

She took the teen by the hand and walked into the shop. The vibration of her Blackberry let her know that either someone was calling or she had a text message. Deena looked at the screen and blushed. It was from Charles, who, according to the message, was just saying *hi*. She would call him once she headed home.

The entire family filed out of the parlor and headed to the rows of picnic tables at the rear. They laughed and talked and Deena couldn't imagine not having them in her life. This was how her parents had been with them and as she looked at her nieces and nephews, she could see that they were just as close. Deena looked up just as Dionne and Steve stood, rounding to stand near the head of the table where their parent's sat. Finally, Deena thought, they're going to announce the wedding.

"Mom, Dad, Steve and I have set a wedding date."

Deena watched as her parents looked at each other, their hands entwined. That's what I want; Deena said to herself, I want to be in love forty-five years after I marry. *Marry?* Deena wondered where that came from. She had no intention of ever walking down that lane again.

Jedidiah nodded his head.

"We're going to get married the last Saturday in August at Paradise Island. We want a really small ceremony, at sunset, with just the family and of course Karen and Gary."

Deena's mother's eyebrows knitted together. She knew her mother was having the same thought Deena had had the day Dionne told her of the wedding.

"No, mother," Dionne said in exasperation, "I'm not having a baby."

Deena's mother flashed a serious look at her five grandchildren who had begun to snicker. All quieted as she turned her attention back to her youngest child. "That's good to hear. I'm glad you two have decided on a date. We don't have much time. That's a little over a month away."

Jedidiah rose from his seat and stood in between Dionne and

Steve. He inhaled deeply. Deena had no idea what her father was about to say.

"I feel the need to say this to you Steve. You've been around this family enough to know that we're close and have very few secrets. I will give you my daughter, my baby girl, as long as you understand that I raised her, we raised her," he pointed to his wife, his voice barely above a whisper. Her brothers nodded their heads looking directly at Steve. "And she doesn't need raising." He then looked over at Deena and she instantly knew what he'd meant. He hadn't had this conversation with Seth—hadn't thought he needed to—but when Seth put his hands on Deena, Jedidiah was willing to risk his life to make sure Seth never did it again. "So if you ever think she needs to be re-raised, you bring her back to me. Understand me, son?" Steve nodded his head tentatively. Deena assumed he was too stunned to speak or too afraid, for he looked petrified.

"Good. Then congratulations and welcome to the family." He hugged him. The entire family took turns hugging him.

Deena and her family returned to their conversations. After an hour the entire clan went back to her parent's house. She kissed her mother and father goodbye, promising her mother that she would call her tomorrow.

Climbing into her two-seater, she headed home, her thoughts on what her father had said. She wondered if it would have made any difference with Seth. *Probably not.*

Arriving at her penthouse, Deena went to her den which doubled as her home office, checked her email and then headed to her master bathroom, where she showered then dressed for bed. Taking the cordless phone, she called Charles. She was taken aback when she heard the voice.

"Umm, may I speak to Charles?"

"Yes, ma'am, may, I tell him who is calling?"

Deena smiled. Someone had instilled some manners in this child. "Sure, you can tell him Deena is calling."

"Thank you. Please hold on for a moment while I get him."

She heard him yell out and began laughing—teenagers. And she laughed harder when she heard Charles pick up the extension and tell his son to hang up—twice.

"Hey, baby," Charles said into the phone.

Deena melted at the sound of his voice, the deep smoothness. He should be on the radio.

"Hi you—how're you doing?"

"Better now that I'm talking to you."

"You're too kind. I wonder when Mr. Hyde will appear." Deena voiced aloud before she could catch himself. She knew that the insecurities had been kept at bay, but the more he talked to her, showing her the sweet side of him, the more she wondered where the ugly side of him was at.

"Wow, baby," he responded, his voice full of awe. "There is no Mr. Hyde here. Now, I'm no mean brother, but I don't take no stuff either. You can't in my line of work, especially when you're going up against folks who think so little of life. And I don't like to have my emotions toyed with, Deena so I don't make it a habit of doing the same to anyone. But if I'm coming on a little too strong for you, then tell me, 'cause that's how I am. A little intense, but I mean you no harm. I like you, Deena, I'm not going to lie to you, but I want you to take whatever time you need to get to know me, 'cause to tell it straight, I like you and I think you like me, too. And this attraction isn't easing up."

Damn! Deena didn't know how to respond. Once again, he had put her in a place where she couldn't readily respond. How should she respond to a person who had shown her kindness, but then again, so had Seth—at first. She shook loose the thoughts. Charles was not Seth—she felt it in her gut, but she didn't always trust her gut, which was what her mother had always told her to do. She was an attorney, trained to get into the nooks and crannies and find the loop holes, find the thing that could give her the edge up. But Charles wasn't on trial and she really shouldn't be looking for the loop holes.

"So, how was your day?" he asked her, saving her from having to respond. She was grateful and began telling him about her family's Sunday dinners and how he was invited to the next one.

For an hour they spoke, with Deena doing most of the talking. She knew she was rambling, for Charles had caught her short with his words. But she would do as he asked her and continue getting to know him—really know him.

"Are we still on for Friday?" he asked.

Shoot, she thought. She'd agreed to take Stephanie to the party after talking to her mother, Olivia. "Oh, Charles about Friday," she said. "I promised my niece I'd take her to a party at some kid's mansion in the Highlands—someone she goes to school with." Deena had told Olivia, based on the start time and end time Stephanie had provided concerning the party, she would drop her off and have her home no later than eleven. "Can you forgive me? We can hang out on Saturday."

"I can forgive you only if you promise to allow me, Corbin and his two buddies to tag along."

Deena chuckled. "Why would you guys want to go?"

"Well, now that you mentioned it, Corbin asked me about some party and it seems as if it's the same one you'll be taking your niece to. So, how about we roll together?"

"That sounds good to me."

"I'll pick you and your niece up then we'll head to the party. What do you think?"

"Sounds good," Deena responded.

They spoke for several more minutes. When they finally signed off, Charles promised to call her at work the next day.

"Sleep tight Ms. Deena."

"Thank you, Charles, same to you." She pressed the off button on the cordless phone and climbed out of bed to stand in front of the floor to ceiling window in her bedroom. She thought about what he'd said and felt the need to run this whole thing past someone. Deena was afraid—she really liked this guy but thought it too soon to be having such strong feelings. She grabbed the phone and dialed the one person she knew could help her. Her mother.

"Hey dad, is mom still awake?"

"She is. You okay?"

"I'm great dad and that was some speech you gave."

"Well, I meant it and I wish I'd…"

Deena interrupted him for she knew where he was about to go and right now she had one thing on her mind and didn't want the past craziness of Seth to interfere. "Don't worry about it, Daddy. None of us knew."

"Well, here's your mother. Goodnight, child of mine."

Deena chuckled. "Nite-nite, Daddy."

"Your father is something else," Deena's mother said. "I thought poor Steve was going to have a coronary." She laughed before she turned serious. "But I hope he knows we meant every word. So, anyway, what's wrong, baby?"

Deena closed her eyes. Her mother knew he so well. She began telling her the whole story, from how she met Charles to his words that night.

"And now you are frightened, not quite sure; and rightfully so, but does he know why, Deena?"

"No," she responded absently shaking her head.

"I think you need to tell him your story, sweetheart. He doesn't know what he's up against if you don't tell him. Are you ashamed of it?"

"Yes and no. I mean, I never gave Seth any reason to hit me, mom, so in that respect, no. But I should have known."

"How could you? Not one person in this family knew Seth lived with those demons. He hid them well." Her mother paused and then inhaled deeply. "Oh, my baby, you think that Charles may be like Seth."

Tears began to stream down Deena's cheeks, her mother understood. And even though she didn't believe that Charles would ever intentionally hurt her, her fears still were very much real. "One part of me knows, Mom that he's nowhere near like Seth. I mean, when I'm with him I feel protected. But the other part of me, the one on the defense, just isn't sure."

"Deena, you need to continue taking the time to get to know Charles, but you also need to follow your instincts. Remember, you had doubts about Seth after dating him for six months, and I was surprised when you accepted his proposal. This time, follow your instincts which will work in concert with your heart."

"I will, mom; thank you. What would I do without you?"

"I wonder what I'd do without all of my babies," she asked. "Between your father and all of you guys, ya'll keep me going."

Deena and her mother spoke for another half an hour.

She'd felt better, got clarity on her feelings and her fear. Now, if she could keep her fear to a minimum, she'd be able to move forward. But one thing she did know: she had to tell Charles her story—and he couldn't have her without it.

Chapter 13

Deena awoke early, her dreams full of Charles and his arms, lips and legs. She had to laugh, for the wicked thoughts had gotten more nefarious each time she'd seen him.

She looked at her reflection in the mirror. She had on a pair of jeans, high-heeled sandals, and a blue silk blouse. Looking at the clock, she yelled out to her niece to make sure she was dressing.

"Charles will be here in 20 minutes, Stephanie."

Deena finished her attire with a gold watch, a tennis bracelet and simple diamond stud earrings. One last look in the mirror and she was satisfied with her appearance. When she heard the land line ring, she rushed down the stairs to answer the phone. Once the doorman informed her Charles was in the lobby, she requested he inform Charles she was on her way down.

"Come on Stephanie," she yelled again as she gathered her purse and keys. "You are going to end up staying here." Deena said right as her niece appeared.

"This is so funny looking," the teen fussed crossing her arms over her chest.

"Child, what is wrong with what you have on?" Deena looked at her niece and thought her outfit was just fine, even though she felt her jeans were a tad too tight. When Stephanie didn't respond, she shook her head and took her by the hand. "Come on, let's go."

She wanted to laugh, for she had told Stephanie who was

going, adding that Corbin, her classmate and Charles's son, thought she was cute. That did it. Stephanie had brought over a suitcase full of different outfits, just in case, and she was only spending the night, not the week.

Finally reaching the lobby, Deena saw Charles leaning against a silver mini-van. He pushed away from it when he saw her come outside.

"Hey there, beautiful," he said as he kissed her on her cheek.

"Hi, how are you?"

"Great," he responded then leaned close and whispered, "I'll be even better when you and I get to be alone."

Deena looked up at him and smiled as he pulled back. She needed to change the focus, so she introduced Stephanie to Charles, who in turn introduced her to Corbin and his friends and his nephew, Willie. Stephanie nodded at them then climbed inside of the van, sitting next to Corbin. Deena noticed that she had barely looked at Corbin.

Charles closed the side door once Stephanie was seated, and then closed the passenger door after Deena slid onto the seat. He started up the vehicle and headed to the party.

Pulling up to a large wrought iron fence surrounding the property, Charles spoke his name into the intercom then waited for the gates to open. He whistled loudly as the winding driveway ended at an imposing brick mansion with two large columns, one on each side. The front seemed yard four times the size of his own.

Heck, he thought, these folks got some loot. He glanced over at Deena and thought about her penthouse. She could buy this.

Charles rolled down the window when a valet appeared. He shot his son a "yeah right," when he overheard him tell Stephanie how he could have driven.

"I'm dropping them off," he said as he stepped out of the mini-van, followed by Deena and the teens. "Where are the parents?" he looked at the valet who pointed to the door. "Thank you. Just pull it over there, I'm not staying." Charles came around the van to stand next to Deena.

"Dad, Mikel's cool." Corbin looked expectantly.

"I didn't say he wasn't. I just want to meet his people, is that okay with you?"

Deena stifled a smile as she watched Corbin's face turn sullen. She understood and thought maybe they should just walk to the door and then head on back to the van. She touched Charles on the arm.

"Let's just see them to the door, Charles." Deena whispered stepping forward.

The door to the mansion swung open and out stepped a small-framed, freckled-faced boy with red hair. He gripped Corbin by the hand and hugged him the way she'd seen men do. The red-headed boy did the same to Nate and Leonard, before taking Stephanie's hand in his and held it. Deena tried not to show the surprised expression on her face.

The teens were talking in their usual code when they were joined by a man and woman Deena assumed were his parents. The woman was a bleached blonde with a wide smile and beautiful green eyes, and the man, who stood as tall as Charles, but not as well-built, had warm brown eyes.

"Welcome, Corbin. I finally get to meet your father," the bleach blonde reached out and grabbed Charles by the hands, pulling him toward her.

Deena wanted to laugh when Charles looked back at her, an expression of "help me," on his face. She had recalled Stephanie saying that Mikel's parents were a bit eccentric, especially his mom who refused to grow old gracefully. Deena observed the woman's demeanor and the smoothness of her creamy skin. Uncharitably she thought, Botox does wonders, then felt ashamed of her unkind thought.

Charles pried Mikel's mother's hands from his and then stepped back next to Deena. He quickly introduced everyone, then told to Corbin, Stephanie, Nate and Leonard to be on their best behavior.

"We'll be back by eleven," Charles said, adding that he had no intention of coming inside to find folks—he wanted them outside waiting when he pulled up. Deena hugged Stephanie and reminded her to call her if she was ready to leave at any time.

Charles and Deena headed to where the valet had parked the minivan. He glanced back at the imposing mansion—its white columns reminded him of the pictures he'd seen of plantation houses.

"From the looks of it, they're going to have a lot of fun." Deena voiced as she sat in the van. "And where did you get this van from?"

"It belongs to my brother Chris." Charles explained as he drove down the driveway, the gates swinging open.

"Hungry?"

"A little bit, how about you?"

"Yeah, I can go for something to eat," He responded as his cell phone began to ring. Charles removed it from the clip at his waist, looked at the caller-id and smiled. "It's my mother," he explained to Deena. "Yes, mother," he said into the phone. "I'm good and you?"

Deena watched as he absently nodded his head up and down, his eyes focused on the road as he drove toward the main road.

"No, I just dropped Corbin and his friends, along with Deena's niece at Mikel Henderson's house."

Charles smiled and looked over at Deena. "Yeah, mom, she's nice." He winked. "And she's pretty, too." He rubbed her hand with his.

"I'll ask her, hold on." Charles pulled over to the side of the road. He depressed the mute button as he faced Deena. "My mom has done her usual and cooked up a mess of cat fish and spaghetti. My brothers are over at my parents. Would you like to go? I know its short notice and all."

Deena became nervous. She hadn't thought she'd meet his family so soon. She looked at the excitement in his eyes and knew that she couldn't tell him no. She inhaled deeply and thought of how her mother had always taught them to be prepared for the unknown. She was prepared and hoped that meeting Charles's mother would not be like her first meeting with Seth's mother—who took an instant dislike to her and never got over it. Even more so when she'd had him arrested and she called to curse Deena out. Deena had taken that opportunity to tell the woman what she'd thought of her as well. Needless to say, Deena hadn't been proud of some of the language she'd used, but she had finally gotten an opportunity to say what she thought.

"Sure, Charles, I'd love to meet your folks. Let's go."

Charles leaned over and kissed her quickly on the lips. He knew his family was going to just eat her up—they loved people and loved to entertain. He picked up the cell phone, released the mute button and placed it to his ear.

"Mom, we're on our way," he said. "Ask her what?" He nodded then looked at Deena. "My mom wants to know are you allergic to any foods?"

Deena shook her head a smile on her face. "No, I have no food allergies. But do ask her can I bring something."

"Deena wants to bring something." He listened and then shook his head no as he ended the call telling his mother they'd be there in twenty minutes.

Deena shut her eyes momentarily and said a silent prayer, her hands wrung nervously over each other. She opened her eyes when she felt Charles's hands on hers. When she looked up into his face, he was smiling at her.

"Don't worry, baby, they're going to love you as much as I do." He paused. What had he just said to her? Had he really said the "L" word? Was he that gone? He looked at her and didn't notice any change in her nervous state, guessing maybe she hadn't heard what he'd said.

Charles pulled off from the side of the road and headed to the home he'd grown up in and to the people who meant the world to him. He wasn't worried. He glanced at Deena and could see she was.

❧

Deena watched the landscape change as they turned onto the residential street. The single family homes of various sizes were neat and the lawns green and lush. Charles stopped in front of a three story, beige brick structure. He appeared at the passenger side of the van, opened the door and held out his hand. She placed her hand in his and held it as they strolled up the walk.

"Where's everybody," Charles yelled as he opened the service door with a key. "We're here." Charles shut the door, looking down at Deena. "You look good and you're going to be okay. Trust?" He nuzzled her nose with his.

"Trust," she replied and then noticed a woman standing at the top of the stairs looking down at them, dressed in a pair of denim crop pants and a white sleeveless button down blouse, white flip-flops on her feet. Deena noticed her smooth face accentuated by a short cut of curls about her head.

"Deena, welcome." The woman began walking down the stairs, her arms opened wide. Deena could see where Charles had gotten his coloring and his beautiful eyes from—he favored his mother a lot. "I'm so glad to meet you. I'm Charles's mother, Winnie." She embraced Deena warmly.

"Thank you, Mrs. Harris, it's nice to meet you, too." Deena returned the embrace.

"Tsk, tsk, Deena, please do not call me Mrs. Harris. You can call me what my daughters-in-law call me, Ma Winnie."

She looked over at Charles, a look of satisfaction etched on his handsome face. She looked back at his mother. "Okay, Ma Winnie." Deena was rewarded with a kiss to her check. "Oh, and this is for you." Deena took the colorful bag from Charles and handed it to his mother.

"Deena, I thought I told you I don't need a thing," she beamed as she opened the bag and pulled out the case that contained two bottles of wine.

"It's just a little something I insisted on picking up. My mother would hide me if she knew I came over for dinner empty handed. Charles said you like Merlot and I know a wine shop that has some of the best."

"Thank you. I'm going to put one out and keep one for myself." She grabbed Deena by the hand. "Come on, the fish is just about done."

Deena followed Ma Winnie up the stairs and was taken aback at the number of people gathered. Charles stepped forward and took Deena's hand in his as he took her around and introduced her to his family. There were so many folks, she was sure she'd forget someone's name before the night was over.

"And this is my father, Charles."

Deena put her hand out to him as he stood from the Lazy Boy he was sitting in. "Baby, we don't shake hands around here, we hug." He pulled her into a bear hug. "Welcome to the Harris home. I know it's a lot of us, but stick around, you'll get used to it."

She offered to assist in the kitchen, but was told that since it was her first time she wasn't allowed in the kitchen, but when she came back, she would find herself with the kitchen crew, which was made up of two of Charles's brothers, Chris, the oldest and William, third born, and their wives, Lorna and Robin. Deena laughed as Ma Winnie told of how she taught her sons how to cook, with Chris and William, Willie for short, were the two who seemed to enjoy cooking the most after nearly burning down the kitchen learning how to.

Hours passed as they sat in the rear yard at two large picnic tables. Deena was

being entertained with stories of Charles as a kid growing up, his mechanical acumen and his quirks, so much like his fathers.

Charles looked at his watch. They had 45-minutes to get the teens from the party. He rose from the bench and tapped Deena on the shoulder. She had been embroiled in a deep conversation with Willie, a cop, and his wife, a doctor, who specialized in trauma medicine. He had listened to them banter back and forth and had been proud of Deena as she held her own in the spirited conversation. *Yeah*, he thought, *that's my woman.*

"Ma Winnie, thank you for inviting me," Deena held her hands in hers. "I had a great time."

"Glad you came. And feel free to come back. As you can see, we love company and this house is never empty, especially with

Randall and his wife living downstairs and the kids over after they get out of school." She hugged Deena. "So you come on back anytime. Hear me? Besides, I'm saving that bottle of wine." She laughed.

Deena nodded as she headed back to the van, followed by the entire family. She counted Charles's five brothers, their wives and children, which totaled fourteen and that didn't include Aaron's wife, Louise, and Randall's wife, Krista, who were both expecting in early autumn. And here Deena thought she had a large family.

She waved as she slid into the van, rolling down the window. William stepped up the side of the van.

"Make sure he doesn't wreck this baby. I just got it. And he's got my boy." He leaned in and kissed Deena on the cheek. "Welcome to the family," he whispered before stepping back and joining the family.

Deena blinked her eyes rapidly—she wanted to cry. Her own family was a lot like Charles's—very warm and welcoming, with few strangers, if any. His family, which was much like hers, didn't believe in airs or shows of superiority; they were just plain ole folks who just happened to be working professionals.

"Thank you," Deena said and waved as Charles pulled away from the curb. He looked over at her. His heart flopped in his chest as he looked at the woman he had such strong feelings for he had used the "L" word earlier. And to add to it, his mother had taken to Deena immediately and that pleased him. He felt his mother had great instincts and he often felt he should have listened to her when she asked him to wait another year before marrying the first time. The sound of his cell phone ringing broke him out his reflection.

"Yes," he answered. "Umm, ugh. Yeah, mmm, yes. Umm, sure. I'll ask her. Thanks again, mom." He paused, then "love you, too." He paused again. "Okay, I'll have him come over tomorrow. Talk to you later. Bye, mom."

Charles glanced at Deena as he placed his cell phone back on the waist clip. "My mom says you are beautiful and I agree." He took her hand and kissed it. "And she loves to shop and has invited you to her annual shopping extravaganza in two weeks."

"Give me the date and I'll see."

"Sure, I'll give you her number and you can take it from there. But let me warn you, my mom can shop. Aaron's the only one in the family who can hang. And all of my sister's-in-laws go, as well as a few of their own family members. It's some serious shopping. They rent a bus."

Deena laughed heartily thinking of her own mother, sister, sister-in-law and their extended family who loved to shop. If she was free, she'd be sure to invite her clan as well as Karen.

They arrived at the Henderson's home right at eleven. They picked up their brood and laughed as they listened to each of them tell stories of the party. Even Stephanie added to the mix and Deena could see that she had gotten along with Corbin and Willie, with her gravitating toward the two teen cousins. She was the oldest grandchild and had no cousin's close in age.

Charles dropped the boys off at his home then headed to Deena's. Deena instructed her niece to go on up, handing her the keys, stating she'd be up momentarily. Once Stephanie disappeared into the building, Charles pulled Deena in his arms, his lips captured hers in a heated rush, his tongue demanded its due, his hands held her firmly against him. He drank of what she offered, took it without question. This woman was under his skin and he would be remiss in not taking what she offered.

They pulled apart when a car rolled by and someone yelled for them to get a room. Deena rested her head on his chest, listening to the sound of his heart beating as fast as felt her own. *This man*, she sighed, was turning her into mush, making her head swim and her body ache with a need she'd never experienced before. Each time she was with him, heard his smooth, deep voice, felt his lips on hers, she wanted to curl up into his arms and just stay indefinitely. He made her want in ways that were foreign to her and a little scary.

She looked up at him and smiled. It was time to head in. "Thank you Charles for taking us with you and for the dinner at your parents. You have to give me their address so I can send a thank you note."

"I'll email it," he whispered as his head lowered, his eyes fastened on her lips. She knew it was coming and she was powerless to stop it—the kiss that always ignited the fire she knew he was the only one to put out.

He took her face gently in his hands and kissed her lightly, his lips barely touching hers, several times before he captured her lips with his and began to make love to her mouth, his tongue lapping and lightly circling her own. He knew they were making out in front of her building, but he didn't care. He had to sample her lips before he left, had to feel her in his arms one more time.

"Woman of mine," he breathed out heavily as he released her and playfully pushed her away from him. He looked down at her kiss swollen lips and her chest as it rose and fell in unsteady breaths. He wanted to be with her, had to see her again and next week wasn't good enough. "Go out with me tomorrow?" he asked as he began to stroke her face, his thumb outlining her lips. When she nodded yes he released her and turned her toward the building. "Go on up, now, woman." He chuckled as she turned her head to face him, her eyelashes batted exaggeratedly.

Deena waved at him as she headed toward the glass double doors. She inhaled deeply in an attempt to steel her runaway heart beat. Once inside, she waved one last time as she stepped onto the elevator. On the ride up, she knew that it would be a long time, if ever, before she'd gotten her fill of Charles Henry Harris, the third.

Chapter 14

She knew where they were heading was a path of no return and she also knew that once she told Charles what she had been through, he would either understand, willing to stay the course or he'd skip it and she'd be on her own again. Either way, she had to unload her story.

"Good morning, Kimmie," she said as she walked into the office. Kimmie always arrived early in order to make sure the office was set up for the day and this Saturday was no different from the rest with the exception that they didn't work eight hours.

"Morning, Deena, how was the party? Or more specifically, all the time you've been spending with the super fine detective? I know ya'll getting awfully chummy. Flowers, lunches, and whispers on the phone."

"My aren't we nosey," Deena laughed as she sat behind her desk, the calla lilies sitting in the vase, were slightly drooping. They were the latest flowers Charles had sent her. Every Friday, she received flowers from him. She pulled one from the vase and sat it to the side intending on saving it.

Kimmie sat in the chair closet to Deena's desk, her arms and legs folded. Deena could see she would be unmoved until Deena at least gave her a tidbit.

"Okay, on our first date he took me on a picnic and to the

Movies in the Park."

Kimmie clapped her hands together. "That's so romantic. Did ya'll?" She tilted her head to one side, her eyes wide.

"Kimmie!"

"Well, that's so romantic I would find it hard not to." She lowered her eyes.

The women looked at each other and then burst out laughing.

"Kimmie, you sound like Karen," Deena said. "Every day she insists on my calling her or she calls me so she can get a Charles update. I'm surprised she hasn't called me by now."

The phone on Kimmie's desk rang. "Yes, Ms. Karen, Deena's right here. Hold on,"

"Thanks, I'll take it in my office." Deena walked into her office, shutting the door behind her. She picked up the phone and began laughing the minute Karen heard her voice.

"So, what did ya'll do yesterday?"

Deena told Karen all about taking the teens to the party in the Highlands, followed by the impromptu dinner at his parent's home. She then thought about the last Saturday they had gone out and wondered how, if she even would, she was going to tell Karen how close she and Charles had come to that next step.

The whole incident thing had started out so innocently and then escalated.

They had met up that morning, their ritual now breakfast first, followed by either eight rounds of golf or hitting a few buckets at the driving range. Charles had insisted on them going to the show, some Italian foreign film with subtitles. Following the movie, they had returned to Deena's for a night cap.

"Where's your CD player, Deena," Charles had asked as they entered the penthouse.

"In the office," she replied and watched as he walked down the hallway to her office. She had speakers built into the walls, so that music played over the entire unit that she controlled with a remote. Deena smiled when Charles returned and heard the strings of the smooth Jazz. She hadn't been a huge fan of Jazz, but since meeting Charles, he had introduced her to both modern, fusion and smooth Jazz.

"Come dance with me, baby," Charles held out his hands to her.

Deena walked into them and began to sway with him, the smooth melodic sounds of the Crusaders. She laid her head on his chest, listening to the sound of his heart beating. Today she had finally spent some time getting to know Corbin, who had gone to breakfast and golfing with them. In speaking with the young man, she found that he attended the same school as her niece and he talked about how smart and pretty she was. He also mentioned the same party Stephanie had. Deena had smiled at the compliment he'd paid to her niece—she couldn't wait to tell her what Corbin had said. She was sure that would make her day, for Corbin was nearly the spitting image of his father—only a few inches shorter and not as built, but he had the same intense dark eyes and beautiful dark coloring.

At the end of their golfing, Deena didn't get the feeling as if he disliked her or was putting up with her for his father's sake, so she was pleased with how the day had gone. After they dropped Corbin off at one of Charles's brother's homes, they headed to the movies and then to Deena's.

The sun was setting as they swayed to the music.

"Aren't you hungry, baby? You didn't each much today."

"I'm fine, Charles. But I'm a little hungry now."

"What do you have a taste for?" he asked as they continued to dance.

"How about some seafood?"

"Goose Island?" He leaned back and looked at her.

"You know that's my favorite," she gushed. "Man, you keep this up and you'll never be able to get rid of me."

He slowed his motions, his eyes bore into hers as he covered her mouth with his, his tongue doing that dance she was so fond of, the heat of her body reminding her that this virile man was hers for the taking. She had to tell him her whole story first before they went there, but she sure was enjoying the journey.

She moved closer, her body molded to his, their lips locked in the passionate dance of foreplay. She began stroking his face, loving the feel of his smooth cheeks and the neatness of his trimmed beard. Her nipples hardened as he began lightly rubbing his hands up and down her sides, his palms dangerously close. Deena moaned loudly as he began moving his hands across her behind. She arched her back, and Charles's lips left hers and began kissing down her chest, the tops of her breasts and then finally the engorged nipples though the fabric of her sun dress.

Placing one hand around her waist, Charles put the other up her dress and down into the waistband of her lace panties. Deena moaned again as he awakened her bud with light, persistent strokes, her hips twirled against his hand, as the orgasm sat right at the base of her, ready to burst forth.

Slowly, Charles backed Deena over to the couch and laid her

on it. He pulled the dress from her and looked down at the wonder which lay waiting, clad only in a pair of panties and a bra that barely hid the darkness of her beautiful, large nipples. Charles dropped to his knees and began kissing her, beginning with her eyelids and ending several agonizing minutes at the tips of her toes. As he began his travels back up, he removed her panties with his teeth, rubbing his nose on her mound, inhaling her sweet, unique womanly fragrance. He was heady, wanting to sink his entire soul into this woman. But he could feel a part of her was still holding something back. Well, tonight he'd up the stakes just a little.

"Raise up," he ordered her and then removed her bra. "Damn, baby you are too beautiful. Tonight I just want to explore. Okay?"

Deena nodded her head. She'd agree to anything just so long as he kept worshiping her body.

Charles sat next to the couch and began circling her nipples with the tips of his fingers followed by his mouth. He kept this up for what seemed like an agonizing forever, but he wasn't finished and showed her he meant what he said when he trailed his tongue south, pausing at her navel before he slid onto the foot of the couch and lowed his head to sample her valley.

Deena moaned loudly as he inhaled, rubbing his face across her hair. When he flicked his tongue across her bud several times, she gripped the side of the cushions.

Charles stopped and then looked up at her. "Ready, baby."

Deena nodded and felt his tongue began the wickedest dance she had ever felt. He held her hips in his large, strong hands as he lavished her, lapped her with such a purpose and force, her eyes became crossed and she swore she saw stars. And then she felt it—the beginning of the orgasm as it snaked its way from her mind, down her chest, and finally to her core as she let out a long hissing moan, her hips undulated against his face, the feeling so exquisite she thought she would pass out from the force of it all. And that's just what she did. She had fallen asleep in his arms and didn't even awake when he'd carried her to her bed, placed her in it and covered her up. Outside of her body wanting more, the only other thing he'd left behind was a note saying he'd talk to her later.

Coming back to the present, her body humming hard, the thoughts of what Charles had so selflessly given engrained in her mind and now her heart. She was falling for this man and she hadn't even made love to him.

"Karen, I'm falling," she admitted. "But I haven't told him all about Seth yet."

"You need to and soon."

The two talked for several more moments. Once she hung up from speaking with Karen, she called Kimmie into the office.

"I haven't heard from Kasha in a couple of days. I tried to call her several times. See if you can get Brad from the half-way house on the line."

Deena and David had finished gathering as much information as possible to use

in Kasha's defense. The bench trial was next week and she needed to move Kasha back into the state, even though she was just across the border in Indiana. She had seen Kasha several times and had prepared her for jail, for that was the only thing she could do because of her refusal to speak. And coupled with her brother still in a coma, the outcome didn't look good. Heck, they couldn't even get her to go for a plea bargain.

Dionne had found out that a man by the name of Winston Barnett was somehow involved in the whole scheme of things, which explained why Kasha wasn't talking. Winston Barnett was the number one gangster in the city and it had been rumored, but not proven, that he was responsible for several murders and a cartel of illegal activity that ran the gamut.

And though she and Charles didn't speak about the case or Kasha, she wondered if he knew all about this Barnett guy who had the audacity to go by the name of Brother Barnett. *Some brother*.

She picked up the daily paper and began reading. Her eyes scanned the Metro section before moving on to the other sections of the paper. She stood suddenly when she read about the murder of one Juan-Carlos Valdez. The story went on to state that his body had been found floating in the Little Calumet River, his hands tied behind his back, his neck slashed. She covered her mouth. No, she hadn't liked him, hadn't liked the way he seemingly did business and knew that the firm's decision to refuse any further business with him was a sound one, but she didn't think he deserved to die. She had to get in touch with Kasha.

Moments later Kimmie interrupted her. "Deena, Brad is on line one."

"Thanks, Kimmie," she said as she picked up the phone. "Good morning, Brad.

How's Kasha? I've been trying to call her all weekend."

Brad blew out his breath. "You're going to have a brick, Deena.

Kasha's gone."

Deena pounded her fist on the desk. "What the hell do you mean, gone? Gone

where? I trusted you with her!"

She listened as he told her how Kasha had seemed more sullen and withdrawn and he and the youngsters at the group home had gone out last night to the movies. When the movie ended and they were ready to return, Kasha was nowhere to be found.

"Damn it, Brad. Her agent was found floating in the Little Calumet. I've got to find her. Call me if she comes back." She hung up the phone and rushed to David's office.

"We've got a problem. Kasha's disappeared."

"Yeah, and your boyfriend is on his way up here."

"Why?"

"He just called, said something about this case being more than what either of us thought. Let's go to the conference room."

Deena looked up just as Charles and his partner, Lee, stepped across the threshold of Walls and Associates. She hadn't heard from him this morning and therefore didn't know he was working.

She watched him as he strolled up to her, his grey suit hung on him as if it was made just for him, accentuating his broad shoulders. Their eyes met and she could tell from them that what he was about to say or do wasn't something he was looking forward to. Shoot, the hell with her fears, this damn case was going to be their undoing.

"Good morning, David and Deena," he said his eyes on Deena.

"Detectives, good morning to you both. Let's go to the conference room." David led the way. They remained silent until after Kimmie had brought in a carafe of coffee, sweet rolls and condiments for the coffee and then left the room, closing the door behind her. Charles and Lee sat across from David and Deena at the large conference table.

"As you may now know, Kasha Bentley's agent was found dead last night," Charles began, looking from David to Deena. "And we know that you guys had her up in Indiana at that halfway house and she's now missing. You both know that's obstruction, but we won't say anything about that. Our issue now is her brother." He looked directly at Deena. "Someone tried to suffocate him with a pillow last night."

"My God," David uttered, shaking his head. "Detectives, what's really going on here?"

Lee began speaking. "This case is taking some really

unpleasant twists and turns and unfortunately, we have to ask where you both were over the past 48-hours." He looked at David as he removed a small notebook from the breast pocket of his suit.

Deena and Charles glanced at each other and she wondered what he was thinking. She had spent a lot of her past 48-hours either with him or talking to him, with the last time she'd been with him he'd taken her to the edge. Now she knew for sure, she wanted to fall over that edge with him.

And she now had one of the answers to her initial concern about Charles—he could separate the business from the pleasure. But that led to another question: would he be really hard on her and could she take it?

"Ms. Walls, where were you?"

Deena wanted to ask him if he was serious, but decided against it and began to tell Lee all about her series of dates over the weekend with Charles.

The look on Lee's face was priceless as he tried to retain the professional look he'd come in with. It was evident Lee had no idea they'd hung out that weekend. She knew Charles had told Lee about them dating, but she guessed Lee wasn't nearly as nosey as Karen.

"Well, if either of you hear from Kasha, please contact one of us immediately. Her life may be in danger and we'd like to get to her." Lee rose, shaking hands first with David and then Deena, who he winked at.

Charles rose from his seat. "Hey, Lee, give me a minute. I need to talk to Deena," Charles said, looking at Deena.

David huffed lightly. "I guess that means I'm dismissed." He smiled at them. "Deena come to my office when you're done. Charles, will I see you on Sunday?"

"You sure will, David. See you then."

Deena waved at Lee and watched as he followed David out of the conference room. Charles walked over to Deena. He stood over her, his eyes clouded with what looked like uncertainty. He put his hand out to her. Deena placed her hand in his and rose from the seat. He pulled her to him and wrapped her into his arms.

"Good morning, sweetheart. Sorry to have to see you under these circumstances."

"Same here," she hugged him, laying her head on his chest. She wasn't too sure if they'd be able to do this once all the factors surrounding the case came out. Already he knew that not only were Kasha and Eric siblings, but also knew she had Kasha moved to a half-way house in Indiana. She'd done it for her protection. Surely he'd understand that.

"Charles, I only did it to protect her."

"Shhh, baby, I don't want to deal with that right now."

Deena pulled back slightly and looked into the handsome face with worry lines etched across it. She too had some things she needed to tell him, to see if they could move forward, to tell him her story and then let the chips rest where they may.

"We still on for tonight?"

"Sure are—your place or mine?" Deena asked.

"How about mine? Corbin's going to my parents to help with some yard work and other household stuff and he'll be over there the entire week."

"Okay, I'll call you when I get home."

He pulled her closer to him, his heart raced. She knew that this evening would be the time for her to tell him all about Seth. So far he knew that she'd been married and divorced, but that was about the extent of it.

"And if you don't mind, pack a bag. I'd like for you to spend the night with me."

Deena nodded in agreement. He kissed her on the lips, promised to call her later, and left the conference room. She sat down on the chair and twirled around in the seat just in time to see him and Lee climb into their department-issued Sedan.

This night would either signal the next step, or nothing. Deena wrung her hands over each other. She wouldn't worry about Charles. Plus she had to find Kasha—fast. She picked up the phone on the conference table and dialed Dionne. After telling Dionne all that had occurred, including the visit from Charles and Lee, she ended with telling her what her gut instinct was telling her: find Kasha before Brother Barnett does, otherwise she would end up like Juan-Carlos.

Chapter 15

Seth tossed the newspaper onto the floor. He'd read about Juan-Carlos's untimely demise and knew he only had two weeks to finish gathering all of the evidence against Brother Barnett and his cartel of nasty-assed thieves. He'd already moved his mother, telling Brother Barnett that her health was failing. As for his two brothers and one sister, they each worked for Brother and he knew they would be the first ones to tattle, so not even they knew where their mother was. So far he had been able to keep that and a few other secrets from them. Besides, they were surely to go down with the cartel for they too had been seduced by the financial largesse of it all. His sister was the financial wizard and his two brothers were a part of the goon squad—Brother's enforcers. Seth didn't want to think of the types of crimes his brothers had committed. They just hadn't been caught doing anything, yet.

Seth looked around the oversized room, the walls painted a rich, blood red, the décor of ancient Asia, large Chinese symbols of wealth, prosperity and health were boldly painted in black on each wall. His black lacquer furniture with gold accents added to the décor. He turned on the flat screen television mounted on the wall. Daily, Seth read several newspapers, including the *New York Times* and the *Washington Post,* as well as several foreign presses and never went more than a couple of days without watching the local and national news.

Seth climbed out of bed. He looked over at the latest piece of the month and thought about all that he had, yet he was an empty man. The one woman he had truly loved, the one woman he should have given his best, couldn't stand the sight of him and knew that if he'd ever looked like he was going to call her, much less approach her, she'd have him tossed in a jail cell—the restraining order was miraculously renewed every year like clockwork.

He walked over to the window and pulled back the dark, heavy drapes. The car sitting in the alley behind his house he knew contained two of his own men and one of Brother Barnett's.

He shook his head at the thought of Brother Barnett. When he'd ordered the hit on Juan-Carlos Valdez, he hadn't counted on the slimy attorney being a life-time, undercover, card carrying member of a street gang. With his death, Brother had inadvertently started a gang war. And all for what? Some chick who sang, her brother who was a greedy gangster wannabe, and Juan-Carlos's penchant for the young trade. What a mess. But this was one mess that he wasn't going to go for, one he would not do all in his power to get Brother out of but he would use all his powers to make sure Brother would never see light of day.

Seth had tried to get Brother to understand that getting into a business that had enough hoodlums and rough necks in it already wasn't advisable and not overly profitable. But he had been hell bent on getting into the recording business and saw Kasha as his means. And then he learned about Eric being related to the young singer and brought him into the fold. Best laid plans can quickly go to hell in a hand basket, especially if it's carried by someone like Brother who has on gasoline draws. And that's just what happened.

Eric turned out to be a loose cannon—not easily impressed with the peanuts Brother was shelling his way, especially if he could cut Brother out and deal direct, which was what he had started doing. Seth knew that the final stand between the two would be over Kasha—he just didn't know how or when. So, when she showed up at the spot unexpectedly, the whole plan went awry once Brother's goon squad showed up and began shooting, with the singer being shielded from the bullets by her brother.

"Damn," Seth rubbed his hands down his face. The last thing he wanted was this, but Brother had once again ignored his advice and tried to have Eric snuffed out—the two offenders had been caught and were currently being held for attempted murder. Then to add to the injury of it all, Deena turned out to be Kasha's attorney.

"Deena," he whispered her name. He'd watched the surveillance of her with Kasha as they headed to and from the courthouse. She looked so beautiful and had been dressed smartly—something she'd always done. He wondered if she still wore that intoxicating perfume. He'd once bought it for a woman, but it just didn't smell the same on her as it had Deena. *Deena.* She'd been the one, he was sure, that could have cured him, could slay the monster that had taken residence in his soul.

He shook his head and decided that he was going to keep that tail on her, even though she'd been spending a lot of time with that detective. Seth was jealous, but also relived, for in the video he saw them embrace, the detective's arms wrapped around her waist. He knew that Brother would keep his distance with the cop so close to her. Therefore, the detective would buy him some much needed time, for he'd kill Brother with his bare hands if he tried to move on her. And then there was Kasha. Deena always was smart and moving her to Indiana wasn't a bad move—she just didn't know the girl's movements were being monitored by Brother. But when they'd approached her at the movie theatre she'd smartly escaped from his infamous goon squad.

So far the only saving grace to this whole nightmare was that Kasha wasn't talking and he'd hoped, for her sake, she stayed that way—even if she had to do time. He could keep her safe in prison.

He chuckled ruefully at that last thought—he couldn't protect her on the outside, but he knew enough women in prison who he'd helped that Kasha would want for nothing but her freedom. Now, if he could find her before Brother, the detective *and* Deena, so that he could convince her jail would actually be her safest place then he'd be able to move on to the next phase of his plan. If not…he shrugged his shoulders.

"This shit is getting out of hand." Seth walked back to his king-sized bed and sat down on the edge. He pushed away the hand of the woman who continually reached out and tried to soothe him. He didn't dare look at her—he didn't want to see the accusing, sad, hurt look in her eyes. Why did she make me hit her? He wondered and then knew it wasn't her, it was him. He had tried to get some help. Tried to stay away from women outside of an occasional fling to satisfy his needs, but he'd always craved the closeness in hopes of filling the emptiness in his soul and hoped someone would help kill the monster. He was a monster and knew it, so what he had planned was just what he needed to shut down the monster he had become.

"Harris," the voice called out. "Come into my office."

Charles rose from his desk and headed to his commander's office. He knocked on the door as he poked his head into the office.

"Come on in, Harris."

He walked into the office and sat down across from the man who had mentored him and made sure he was always at the right places at the right time. Schoop's tan face had aged badly thanks to the tanning salons he loved to frequent. He was the only person he knew who kept a tan year around. Charles's eyes met his green ones.

"What's up?"

"The FBI," he responded then pushed a stack of file folders over toward Charles.

Charles looked at the stack and picked up the file folder on top of the stack and noticed Barnett's name on it. He'd gotten the case because he knew Brother Barnett and had wanted to arrest the man as badly as anyone.

Charles frowned and looked around the office at the numerous awards and citations. Schoop was a thirty-year, highly decorated cop—a cop's cop, with a twist: he didn't stand for misconduct of any kind. The Blue code of silence didn't exist in his mind—bad was bad and he'd go after a bad cop with the same vigor as an offender. But as a cop, he understood the erosion and infestation it had on the force. And to him that was never to happen on his watch.

"I got the call today from the FBI," Schoop said.

Charles sat back in the chair. He had heard the rumors, but wasn't sure if they were true. He knew one thing for sure though, once the Feds came into a case, all others took a back seat and orders from them. He'd worked with the Feds once, and though the undercover experience was something he had added to his law enforcement resume, he wasn't interested in working with them again. They hadn't been big fans of the way he'd collected information from informants. He hadn't laid a hand on any of them, but he used what his mother gave him: old fashioned patience. Charles had a way of just leaning on them and waiting them out, sometimes just showing up at times and places they least expected it. Once, Charles had showed up at one of his informant's mother's house. The look on his face when he arrived and saw Charles sitting in the living room, sipping coffee with his legs crossed was priceless.

"Yeah, so the rumors are true?"

"What did you hear?"

"That they were sniffing around looking for a few good men to assist with this investigation into Brother Barnett. And they are looking at me and Lee."

Schoop nodded his head. "Well, the rumors are true and they do want you and Lee to assist with this case. They said they want your help in taking down Brother Barnett."

Charles shook his head. "Aww, man Schoop, you know how I feel about the Feds. Besides, if the connection between Eric Williams, Kasha Bentley and Brother Barnett is what I think it is, he's going to go down anyway with or without their help."

"That may be true, but apparently he's taken a few things out of the country and way over the top. Hear he's doing a slave trade kind of thing."

Charles raised his eyebrows. *A black man selling his people into slavery? Unreal.* "And this is in addition to all of the other stuff, drugs, prostitution, and murder?"

"Seems that way. So, you are to report to the FBI."

Charles shook his head. "Do I have a say in this, Commander?" he asked even though he knew the answer.

His latest informant dropped several names, even mentioned something about an attorney who was somehow mixed up in this whole thing. And when the informant mentioned Kasha, he knew the young girl was in serious trouble—her life was in danger, which could put Deena in harm's way as well. Unfortunately, for her she was defending a client who had an unknown connection to Brother Barnett and the Feds weren't above using a few innocent people for the greater good of the entire cause.

"Well, unfortunately, this time, you don't. They called the chief first."

Charles rose from the seat and walked over to the wall of pictures. He spotted the picture of the two of them the day Charles graduated from the academy. He looked so young.

"Dang, why me?"

"Actually, they spoke highly of you. Said they liked your tactics."

"Yeah right, I bet." Charles huffed as he resigned to his position. "Okay, seeing as how I have no choice, when do I go over to the dark side?"

Schoop began laughing. "They're the good guys, just not as laid back as you are." He rolled his chair over to a box of files. "Here's the rest of what they've been gathering. And who is this Deena Walls you've been seen with?"

Charles's head snapped up and his eyebrows knitted together. "How do you know about Deena?"

Schoop inhaled deeply and leaned over the desk. "Barnett has someone following her and you know the FBI is following them, so that's how I know." He sat back and waited.

"She's a..."

"I know she's Kasha Bentley's attorney, she and her brother David run the family firm, her father is a former judge and her sister, Dionne is one hell of a bail bondsman. I want to know what she is to you."

Charles knew he had to be straight with his commander, mentor and friend. He told him how they met, ending with the fact that he was dating her.

"You've got you to keep your head on with this one, Charles."

He nodded, knowing exactly what he meant. But that still didn't ease what he had heard: Brother Barnett was watching his woman, had someone possibly scoping her for God knows what; and that tidbit settled in his stomach like gut rot.

"I know you and I know you're going to do the right thing, but also go ahead and have a guy or two keep an eye on her." Schoop said then switched gears. "Now, what the Feds need at this juncture in the case is the local connect and that's where you come in. And there is a strange twist to this entire case. The Feds say they are being fed bits and pieces of information from an anonymous source inside of Brother's cartel. And they need you to find out who's doing it."

Charles was somewhat relieve as he stated, "Find the mole"

Schoop nodded his head. "Correct. And what do you know about this murder of Juan-Carlos Valdez?"

"Hell, man, this dude is tied to a major drug cartel in LA with uglier ties to a cartel in Vietnam. And this dude's death is going to unleash an all out war."

"Shit," Schoop dragged his fingers through his sparse grey hair. "We need to get to the players first and fast." Schoop laced his fingers together. "Starting Monday, you and Lee are to report to the FBI's Chicago field office."

Charles rose from the seat. "I'll be there and we'll take along the serious leads we've uncovered this past month, see if the FBI has something to add. Who knows, we may be able to bring this crap to a close sooner versus later."

"Oh, and you and Lee cannot discuss this with anyone."

Charles shook his head. He had planned on telling her she was being followed and that he had been chosen by the FBI for some undercover work. Now, he was bound to silence. Heck, he just hoped that when all of this came out she'd understand. If not, he knew his heart would never quite be the same.

Charles leaned against the car and waited for Deena to step out of her penthouse. He had gone home early and wanted to make sure not only that the house was clean, but that Sweetie had been bathed thoroughly and that he'd had a enough food to last them the weekend just in case they decided to stay in.

He smiled broadly when he saw her, dressed in a pair of jean crop pants and a off-white, oversized tunic, a gold belt around her small waist, and a pair of strappy, high heeled sandals on her feet.

Charles reached out and removed the large tote bag from her hand and then pulled her close into his arms as she stepped up to him. He kissed her deeply, needing to feel her, impart on her just how special she was to him. Heck, if he didn't know any better he'd say he was in love.

"Hey beautiful," he said as he broke the kiss. "You look too good, woman." He nuzzled his nose in her hair. "I like that outfit on you."

Deena smiled back and then looked around his large frame. "Wait, is that yours?" She pointed to the car behind him.

"Yes, it's mine."

Deena paused and let out a low whistle at the vintage automobile. Without prompt, Deena released Charles's hand and began to walk around the vehicle. She looked at him as she began to recite, from memory, the ins and outs of the car.

"The year of make is 1965, manufactured by Pontiac. The GTO was Pontiac's answer to a fast vehicle in a compact model—the beginning of the muscle cars," she said as she circled the car. "Able to reach 60 in 22.2 seconds, the GTO is considered a classic muscle car by aficionados." She then paused before she continued her assessment. "It looks like you've installed twin cams, which means you must have a V-8, 400 with 3 deuces under the hood," she said and then came to stand in front of Charles. "How fast does she go?"

"One-eighty," he said as he blinked his eyes. "Wow, woman, why are you just now letting it be known you are an automobile aficionado?" He asked, his eyes round in awe. He had never met a woman who knew so much about cars other than park and drive.

"I thought I told you I tinker a little bit here and there. Can I test drive it later?"

Charles looked at her as he shook his head, his eyebrows raised. If she knew this much about cars, and she did own a two-seater sports Mercedes then she was a demon for speed and probably had a passion for it.

For nearly three weeks, he'd learned a lot about Deena, but each day that he spoke to her, spent time with her, he found out more and was intent on making her all his. But there was something that continued to hold her back and he'd hoped after their weekend together, the final obstacle would be torn down.

He rubbed a hand down his face and looked down at Deena, her light eyes bore into his, her smooth, makeup free face beamed up at him. God, he thought, she's beautiful.

"So how about it, Charles?" She asked and nodded her head toward the vintage vehicle.

"Can you drive a stick?"

"Don't make excuses, Charles, I'm a great driver and I'd love to drive this," she responded as she pointed to the classic black-on-black, drop-top vehicle.

"We shall see," he stepped up to the passenger door and opened it. He watched as Deena's eyes never left his when she sat on the seat and then swung her legs around into the car. He found the simple move highly erotic and swallowed a thick lump that had lodged in his throat.

He slid into the seat beside her and started up the engine, the vehicle roared to life before the engine began purring. Charles easily moved out into traffic and headed to his home.

The twenty minute ride was made longer as Charles cruised down the street, Deena sitting next to him, the wind blowing through her hair, which she had a head full of long, ringlet curls. She seemed to love the way the wind tossed her hair about her head. Most women would have long asked for the top to be put up. She had her head laid back a sweet smile on her face.

He tapped her on her thigh once they came to a light.

"Hey, you feel like going to dinner and maybe a little dancing afterward?"

"Sure, what do you have in mind?"

Charles started up from the light. "How about some Ethiopian food at Mama Desta's and then a little dancing at this club I know?"

"Sure, I haven't been dancing in years. I'm game. Let's go dancing, darling," she replied and then blushed as Charles took her hand in his and kissed the back of it. She watched his profile, the strong jaw and chin, the smooth dark skin.

Deena was in love and she didn't know how to do anything but to try and not let her fears get the best of her. She was going to tell him all about Seth at dinner and then go from there.

Chapter 16

Deena stepped into the house and was immediately greeted by a rather large dog that she identified as a Rottweiler. She stepped backward, her back met Charles's hard chest.

"Sweetie isn't a vicious dog, but she is a guard dog. Put your hand out to her. Let her sniff your hand."

Deena did as instructed and watched as the large animal came to her and began sniffing her hand before the dog pushed her head under Deena's hand.

"Sweetie likes you. She wants you to rub her head. I think you've got a friend."

Deena squatted down and met the face of the dog. She laughed loudly when Sweetie began licking her face. "That's all I needed. My face washed by a dog's tongue."

"Let me give you a tour." Charles took Deena by the hand and with Sweetie close on their heels, he showed Deena his home.

"You have a really nice house, Charles." She asked when they arrived in the basement. "How long have you been here?"

"About ten years now." He took her hand in his as they sat on the couch. He examined her small hands, her nails painted a pale peach color.

"Are you ready to go?"

"Actually, I'd like to change if you don't mind."

"No, I don't mind. Come on, I'll show you where you can change." He showed her to the bathroom and then the spare bedroom where he had placed her tote bag. Upon making sure she needed nothing, he left her in the bathroom.

For a half an hour, Charles waited for Deena to change. He had liked what she had on and wondered what she would step out in next. This woman had so many sides to her, and so far he liked each one.

Deena tried to hurry, deciding on a white cotton peasant top and matching, flowing skirt, her feet covered in cloth espadrilles. She took one last glance at herself in the full-length mirror on the closet door and smiled. The outfit was just right without being overstated.

He watched Deena's smile widen as he whistled when she stepped out of the room. The peasant blouse showed off enough of her cleavage to make him salivate, and the long skirt flowed around her ankles, with the right ankle adorned in a gold anklet and her curly hair hung loosely about her shoulders.

"You look great," Charles said as he stepped forward to meet her. He reached out and pulled her gently into an embrace, the perfume she wore seeped into his olfactory, once again reminding him that he was glad he was a man. He held her in his arms and rested his head on top of hers as he deeply inhaled her scent. He didn't want to let her go, had the overwhelming need to take her right here and now. He'd teased her, letting her know that not only did he want and desire her, but that he was willing to give unselfishly of himself.

Deena wanted to sigh aloud when he released her from his strong embrace. She'd felt the warmth he emitted and loved the protective feel of his arms around her—she always felt protected and wanted; emotions she hadn't experienced in a long time and it scared her. The emotions made her want to do as she'd done so many times in the past—run.

She looked up into the dark obsidian eyes and saw the certainty in them, the blunt desire, which was the one thing she couldn't deny, the one thing she had fought successfully for years to bridle, and here he was, awakening all of her senses. The pull of the arousal between them was making her forget why she had been fighting it for so long. The sexual attraction between them was fierce and was so the day she first laid eyes on him at the police station and even now as he stood in front of her dressed in a pair of black jeans and a black silk t-shirt that hugged nearly every mouth-watering, eye pleasing muscle in his upper body. And his eyes—the depth and darkness bore into hers and commanded all of her attention.

"Are you ready?" he whispered close to her ear, the blatant double entendre was quite clear to her and Deena wondered was she truly ready. She nodded her head, not sure she wanted to trust her voice at this point, for the heated gaze he cast upon her and the blaze rolling in her core spoke of his completing what he had started on her couch.

"Whenever you are," she replied and looked up into his dark eyes. She knew the night would end as she had dreamed—in his bed.

Momma Desta's Red Sea restaurant sat nestled between two buildings located along a busy North side street. Its interior décor was dimly lit with pictures of landscapes of Ethiopia and Halle Selaise decorating its walls.

Deena waited as Charles held open the door. He requested a table for two, then placed his arm around Deena's waist as the waitress escorted them to a waiting booth.

Deena inhaled deeply the inviting aroma from the kitchen as they got closer to their seating near the rear of the restaurant. She smiled up at Charles as he stood to one side and allowed her to slide into the booth.

Charles slid in next to her and then picked up the menu. All the way to the restaurant, he listened as Deena talked about city architecture. And though he knew she was an admitted history buff, especially the history of Chicago, he also knew the sexual tension between them was like a volcano—waiting to blow. On the way over, he found himself enjoying her company to the point that he'd been caught several times lingering too long at traffic lights. And now here he was trying, almost in vain, to get his runaway emotions under control.

"This was a good selection, Charles," Deena said as she looked around the restaurant.

"Thank you. Think you know what you want?"

"How about you order for me?"

He nodded his head before holding up his hand for the waiter. He started with an appetizer of Asmara Foole, followed by an entree for two of vegetable soup, Dora Tibs, Atkilt Kilkil served with Tej honey wine. After placing their orders, he put his arm around her, his fingers gazing against her shoulder.

"I know we haven't really talked about Kasha or the case."

"Does that bother you?"

Charles shook his head. "No, not really. You?"

"I just thought the less said the better. Plus, we are technically on the opposite sides of the fence. I don't want you or I to get into any trouble."

"Are you sure that's all?" he asked, tracing a lone finger across her cheek.

Deena blinked rapidly. "Actually, no," she said her voice low. "I don't want this case to come between us."

"Baby, I have no intentions of letting this case come between us." He looked her in the eyes. "I told you, when we go to court in two weeks, you do your thing. I'm a big boy." He looked away. He hadn't lied to her in the nearly month they'd been talking and hanging out, but right now he had no choice. "But on a serious tip, this whole case is about to get real ugly and its going to call for me to work serious overtime the next two weeks." He said then watched her expression. He saw the uncertainty flash across her face. What he didn't tell her and couldn't, was that he was going under cover, that she was under surveillance by someone in Brother Barnett's camp, and he was going to put a tail on the tail, for he'd be damned if they were going to lay a hand on her.

Deena nodded. "I understand. I have to finish Kasha's defense. We're just about done."

"Have you found her yet?" He knew they hadn't. And when she shook her head "no", the worry plain in her eyes, his heart flopped in his chest. He wished he knew her whereabouts, but he also was well aware that as long as no one knew where she was, not even the Feds, then Kasha was safe.

"I have something I want to tell you," she said and looked into his eyes and loved the way he looked at her, the smoothness of his handsome face, the sweet fullness of his lips, that touched hers and made her heart race at a break neck pace. "Charles, I need to tell you about Seth," she looked down at her hands. This was the one thing she needed to get off her chest if they were to move forward. As her mother had said she needed to tell him her story.

For the first time since her divorce, Deena spoke of the man who'd hurt her both physically and emotionally.

She inhaled deeply and began telling him how she met Seth, when they married and the first time he emotionally abused her, followed by the first time he hit her, blacking her eye, bruising her arms and wrists, and splitting her lip. When she ended her story with how he ended up in the hospital, she became quiet. Her mind wondered what he thought of her, did he see her as weak. A lone tear rolled down her cheek. She tried to will the tear to stay, but it wouldn't be helped. She felt Charles's finger entwine in hers.

"Baby, look at me." He commanded softly. "Look at me."

She raised her head and met his eyes. She really wanted to cry, for what she saw was not pity or indifference, but a man filled with compassion and respect.

"That's really deep, Deena. And now I totally understand your trepidation. I'm not into battering. My father never hit my mother, much less ever raised his voice at her or us. He loves his wife and protects her with his life; and that's what the Harris men were taught in our household. Your ex was a very sick man and you did right. Thank God for your family." He kissed her gently on the cheek, wiping the remnants of the tear from her face.

Now, more than ever, Charles wanted to hold and protect her, making sure no man harmed her. He knew he'd lay his life for her making sure that she was always safe. And though he knew she was no shrinking violet, the fact that she had put her ex-husband in the hospital attested to that, she would never, as long as he was breathing, have to fight a man again.

He felt the need to tell her about his own failed marriage, how his ex-wife had gotten pregnant and he did what he thought at the time was the right thing. After Corbin's birth, he realized they had made a mistake.

They became quiet once the food arrived. Charles broke off a piece of injera, the spongy, crepe-like bread and scooped up some dota and vegetables and then handed the portion over to Deena who admitted to never stepping foot in an Ethiopian restaurant. Charles smiled as she opened her mouth to sample the fare.

"Good?" he asked and watched as her tongue darted across his finger. He'd

never been shot, but the electric shock he'd gotten from the innocent act shot straight to his groin.

"Thank you for showing me how this is done," she replied as she tore off a piece of injera and mimicked Charles' actions. She held out her portion to him and watched as he leaned over and took the offering from her fingers, his tongue lapped lightly at her fingers. Deena pulled her fingers back, her mind twirled, trying to think of something to say, to ease the sensual attraction, the growing emotions.

Once they completed their meal and their plates had been cleared, both passed on desert, the check arrived. Deena and Charles reached for it at the same time. Charles playfully removed her hand from the bill.

"No way, Deena," he said then pulled his wallet from his back pocket.

"Charles, you either let me treat or I won't speak to you for the rest of the night." She batted her eyes and pursed her lips together. He pulled his hand back and sat back as she removed a credit card from her wallet and laid it on the table.

"Thank you, Charles for picking this restaurant. This was a great choice."

"You are most welcome. You feel like dancing?"

"I need to, I'm stuffed."

Charles smiled. In the weeks he had grown so accustomed to hearing her voice, her laugh, her slight sigh she gave him whenever he'd done something that pleased her, like when he'd just fed her. He watched the way her eyes absorbed him as he did so. This woman was too much, he thought to himself.

The bill settled, Charles slid out of the booth and held his hand out to Deena. She looked up at him and reached out, placing her hand in his. He held onto her as she slid from the booth. Once on the edge, he pulled her to her feet, the darkness of his eyes rested upon hers.

"Deena, has anyone ever told you that you are a gorgeous woman?" He watched her expressions go from surprise to doubt to finally acceptance. "And I sure am glad you didn't have a boyfriend when I first asked you out, 'cause I'da hated to have to tell him he's got to go." He smiled at the sound of Deena's soft laugh.

"Where'd you like to go dancing? Reggae, Salsa, House?"

Deena smiled up at him. "You decide."

"You're my kind of woman," he replied as he leaned closer to her, his face inches from hers. He looked at her lips and almost shrugged his shoulders as his mind screamed for him to just skip the whole dancing and take this woman home and make love to her. But he wanted to continue as he had—making love to mind and soul.

Chapter 17

The bouncer seemed to know him and waved them past the long line of hopefuls waiting to get into the reggae club. The dance floor was packed with moving, gyrating bodies as the music blared from the large speakers situated around the room with a few suspended along the exposed brick walls. Charles held onto Deena's hand as they stepped into the large dance club and headed toward the rear where small tables for two were arranged close to each other.

Now, they were being ushered up a flight of stairs by some guy dressed in a white dashiki and jeans. Once at the booth, Charles and their escort shook hands and embraced before the door to the booth was shut.

Deena looked around the booth its walls decorated a loud, garish green. A black leather couch and two matching chairs, end tables and a cocktail table were situated in a semi-circle and actually gave the place a homey feel. Large, leafy plants were dotted around the booth. She guessed the decorator was trying to create some type of suite reminiscent of Jamaica. Deena wanted to laugh out loud—this wasn't it.

The booth could easily fit a party of ten and gave an unobstructed view of the dance floor below and the bars that lined both sides of the room. Though the music could still be heard, it wasn't as loud as on the dance floor.

A woman, dressed in the tightest pair of leather pants and matching bustier, entered their booth just as they sat on the couch.

"Hey there, Detective, long time, handsome," she said and then smiled a little too broadly at Charles.

"How've you been, Tina?"

"Good. I'll tell Nino I saw you. You know he'd be glad to hear that." She chuckled.

"I'm sure he will be."

"What are you having tonight?" she asked as she glanced at Deena. Deena knew the drill—knew that this skinny chick was trying to size her up and dis her, but there would be none of that, Deena mused to herself as she felt Charles's arm encircle her just as he turned to face her.

"Baby, what would you like to have?"

Deena pursed her lips together as the woman glared at her. She wanted to lick her tongue out at the waitress. "I'll take a cosmopolitan with Stoli's."

Charles smiled and then leaned over close and whispered in her ear, "good choice."

"Tina, please bring my lady what she requested and I'll take a Ting beer. Thanks," he said moving closer to Deena before he turned his body to face hers.

Deena wanted to melt. He had staked his claim and wasn't above letting anyone know it.

Where was this man when I needed him? She wondered to herself as she looked at the man sitting so close to her that she could see shadows of herself in his pupils.

"Okay, detective, how do you know all these folks? I didn't peg you for a lounge lizard."

"Being a detective has its perks. A little pay here, a little take there." He looked at her trying to keep a straight face as he watched her eyes widen.

"I'm joking." Charles threw his head back and laughed.

Deena swatted at him. "You're crazy."

"You go out with crazy men?" He turned his head to one side and then made a face at her. Deena swatted at him again. "Okay, for real. The owner, Tommy, and I went to high school together. The bouncer, Big Lou, is a moonlighting cop who I mentor—he's about to take the exam for detective. Tina is the owner's baby sister. And Nino is her husband, who I arrested years ago when I first became a detective. He's been clean and out of trouble for some time now, but it's a standing joke between us—Nino doesn't ever want to lay eyes on me again."

Deena crossed her legs and set back further on the couch. She listened to Charles as he talked, his face inches from her own.

Deena had come to know that Charles was like her—afraid of the unknown; but, he had one thing over her, he wasn't willing to allow the fear to debilitate him. She had.

He hasn't been what I've been through.

"Hey, man," a voice was heard and Deena glanced around Charles's large, broad shoulders to see a beefy man step into the booth. "We don't want no trouble tonight."

Charles faced the voice and then stood, laughing as he took the man's hand in his and then embraced him. "Don't start none, won't be none."

"Who's the beautiful woman?"

Charles narrowed his eyes and shook his head. "She's too smart for the likes of you. But my momma taught me manners. Deena, this is Tommy, the owner. Tommy, this is my girl, Deena."

"Dude, she must be hard up to go out with a clown like you," Tommy said as he stepped around Charles. He took Deena's hand in his and attempted to kiss it, but was cut off when Deena smoothly removed her hand from his.

"Nice to meet you,too," she said dryly and looked up into the man's sky blue eyes, her head tilted to the side.

"Miss Deena, I meant no harm. I've known him since we were scared little boys in high school. I love this man like family and I would do anything for him." He bowed at the waist.

Deena looked into his eyes and could see the sincerity in them. She figured he was actually harmless and smiled at him.

"Tell me how he's looking at this moment. Is his right eyebrow is raised?"

Deena looked past Tommy and then frowned. "I'm afraid it is. What does it mean?"

"I've got one hell of a cussing-out coming my way."

Deena laughed at Tommy who had the most contrite look stretched across his tan face. She felt sorry for him even though she thought his words had been a little mean. "I'll try and put in a good word for you." She nodded her head and pursed her lips. "But I can't make you any promises. The detective here doesn't take no stuff."

He straightened and headed to the chair closest to Deena. He sat down and then looked at Charles as he reclaimed his position near Deena on the couch. "I'd be forever grateful. And to show you how much, your drinks are on me for the rest of the night."

For a half an hour, Tommy regaled Deena with stories of he

and Charles growing up. She had laughed at Tommy, who she finally surmised that though he had a big mouth and was a little impetuous, she found him likeable and harmless.

The drinks had relaxed Deena and she found herself laughing more than usual. She knew how to hold her liquor, but the closeness of Charles, his hip flush with hers, his cologne and the way his hand was lazily drawing circles and rubbing her shoulder was adding to the effects of the alcohol.

Once Tommy left the booth, Deena turned her attention to the crowd, the music now reaching a frenetic crescendo, the crowded dance floor of bodies close and gyrating to the infectious beat. The music's beat reverberated through her and she began to nod her head to the beat.

"Want to dance?" Charles asked.

Deena stood and placed her hands on her hips as she looked down at Charles sitting on the couch. "Sure. Think you can hang?" She challenged.

"Aww, now girl, you looking at the Dancehall King," he said in a false patios then stood up. "Come here and let me show you me moves." He pulled Deena close to him. He could see the dare dance in her honey-brown eyes.

Deena smiled broadly as she allowed Charles to take her hand in his and lead her out of the private booth, down the stairs and onto the dance floor. Charles made a path through the middle of the crowd as he bobbed his head to the island music. He let go of Deena's hand and then faced her, his hips swayed slowly, his finger motioning Deena forward. Deena swayed toward him, trying to keep her eyes on his, the sway of his hips pulled at her like a hypnotic spell. When the music reached fever pitch, Charles pulled Deena close, their hips swayed in unison as the bass line seeped into them, his hands hung loose around her hips as he pulled her even closer. Deena closed her eyes and she could feel the strength in his hands as they held her, the muscles in his thighs as they nestled against her. She felt heady, almost light headed as the now all too familiar heat crept from the top of her head to her toes, resting longingly at her core.

"Let yourself go," Charles whispered into her ear. "I promise not to tell a soul that Deena Walls has a wild side."

Deena moved closer, her thighs now dueling with Charles' as the music hit a peak, the heavy bass line thumped with the patois laden voice of Sean Paul. The beat moved her, caused her to gyrate with heated intensity. She looked up at Charles as she draped one arm over his shoulder and moved in syncopated rhythm. She thought about something her sister once said: if a man can move his hips then he's good in bed. Deena looked up in the dark obsidian eyes of pure flaming desire. Her mind told her to put a little space between them, to move back; but the look he possessed, mixed with the heated music had her lost and she allowed the music to carry her closer to him. She felt his arousal pressed against her abdomen. *Oh my goodness,* was all she could muster to herself as the beat continued to add to their erotic tangle, drawing their bodies even closer.

Charles wanted to move, wanted to put a respectable space between them, but when she'd moved closer, his body instantly reacted. She was doing something to him, pulling the emotions and the need out of him. And when she pressed her chest against him, he wanted to pick her up, carry her out of that place and bury himself deep.

He looked down at her and saw the fire in her eyes. They had one more hurdle, but he knew he wouldn't be able to share it with her—his upcoming undercover work with the FBI and why.

"Enough," he whispered in her ear, took her hand in his and led her out of the club. He stopped long enough to ask Big Lou to tell Tommy he'd left.

Deena nodded and followed, thinking that this heat, the reaction to his body, her attraction to him had come to a peak.

Charles drove home quickly. His mind swirled with the possibilities of where they were about to take this relationship—one he had become accustomed to, used to, and wanted to see it go further. She had told him about her ex, and at first he wanted to find this Seth guy and beat the hell out of him, but he also saw Deena as a woman who'd gambled and lost, but hadn't completely shut down. With the right man—him—she would completely flourish.

The garage door opened and Charles backed the vintage vehicle into the spot next to his SUV. Stepping out, he came around to the passenger side, opened the door and put his hand out to Deena. She placed her hand in his and rose out of the car, her body close to his. Charles's groin tightened to steel and he fought the need to take her right there.

He took her hand in his and led her to the house. Once inside he stopped, turned to face her, captured her face in his hands and began placing kisses about her eyelids, nose and lips. Her arms snaked around his neck, pulling him closer to her, melding her body to his. She felt so good in his arms, he thought as his lips met hers, the feel of them opening to receive his tongue as it played havoc with her own. He moaned when she began trailing her small hands up and down his back, pausing at the top of his behind. She bypassed his butt and began feeling his thighs. He wanted to howl—her hands were dangerously close.

The sounds of whining from Sweetie interrupted him. Without missing a beat, Charles opened the rear door and let the dog out then shut the door. He looked down at Deena.

"Deena, if we go there, there's no turning back, baby. They'll be no one between us and I'll have no other man lay a hand on you, in anger or love." He looked at her. He knew it may have been an inopportune time, but he needed her to know that he played for keeps—wasn't sharing what he was considering his. "Are you okay with that?"

Deena nodded her head. "Charles, I only want you. Please, make love to me."

Charles smiled as he began slowly raining kisses across her face, taking time to allow his lips make its own path around her face, down her neck, up and around her ears, then back down her neck, nibbling and suckling. He knew that she'd have passion marks all over her when he finished. And that's what he wanted. He wanted her to look in the mirror and see the marks as a sign of the passion they'd shared.

He slid the sleeves of the peasant blouse down her shoulders to rest right at the tops of her breasts. He lavished them, alternating between licks and kisses. Her felt her chest rise and knew he was close—close to sending her to her first orgasm for the night. Charles slid the blouse further down, the sight of her bare breasts caused his already engorged member to become painfully harder. He didn't think such a thing could happen, but they had been leading up to this for over a month.

"Beautiful, baby, just beautiful," he said as he reached out and lightly fingered her nipples, the tips of his fingers traced lazily, short circles around the areola. When she tossed her head back, he latched on to one nipple with his lips, pulling the hard bud in and out of his mouth several moments before moving to the other for equal treatment.

Charles inhaled the womanly fragrance wafting up from her core. The scent, mixed with her perfume, was an intoxicating mix. He knew she was probably soaking wet, but he wanted to hear her say his name and tell him just what it was that she wanted from him.

"Charles," she breathed out.

"Yes, baby, talk to me," he responded as he continued the erotic assault of her nipples, his hands now holding them possessively, slightly kneading the fullness of them.

He slid the blouse and the skirt down her hips, his eyes followed the garments as they pooled at her feet, her mound covered by lace, with skinny strings attached. Charles stepped back and soaked in his angel, this woman who made his pulse race so fast he thought he was having a coronary. Slowly, he lowered to his knees and brought her hips close to his nose. He inhaled deeply before he buried his face into her mound. Deena's hips thrust forward as his tongue flicked across her bud.

Charles felt her fingers grab his head as he let his tongue make wicked love to her bud, coaxing, plying, playing, teasing, tasting—this was his. He knew she was close as she gyrated her hips against his lips and tongue and he increased the tempo, the beat, to bring that song to its first crescendo before beginning again.

Her body stiffened as she climaxed and Charles reached his hand around to hold her close to his face by her behind. He wanted to drop her to her knees when he found her behind bare.

"Charles, may goodness, what are you doing to me?" she looked down at him. He could see her eyes dark with desire. He wasn't through with her.

Scratching at the rear door reminded him that Sweetie was outside. He rose slowly, his lips captured hers, sharing the unique taste of her essence with her. He admitted to himself that he loved her taste.

Feeling around for the door knob, Charles opened the door and said one word to the dog: basement. He listened as his dog padded down across the kitchen and headed down the stairs to the basement.

"Now," he kissed her again as he took her hand and placed it on his erection. Deena's hand stiffened at first and then relaxed as he guided her hand up and over his erection. "See what you do to me woman of mine?"

He picked her up, wrapping her legs around his waist and carried her, holding onto her bountiful bottom, to his bedroom. He felt her lips as they kissed his face and then began nipping his neck. He found the tentative action highly charged.

Reaching his king-sized bed, he hooked his fingers around the flimsy string of her panties and pulled them off of her as he sat her on the bed. He tossed them behind him and watched as she scooted backward.

"Stop me, now, baby."

Deena shook her head and watched as Charles removed his shirt. Her eyes soaked in the cut planes of his muscular chest, the hairs on it smooth and curly, his sculpted pecs. He unzipped his pants, rolled them down his hips along with his briefs. She had felt his erection, had been marveled at the hardness, but she had no idea of the girth. Suddenly, she became nervous. It had been years since she'd been intimate and she wasn't sure she was ready for what he was bringing to her.

Charles saw the uncertainty in her eyes. He recognized it for what it was and he crawled onto the bed and began kissing her, taking his time, letting her feel through his ministrations that he found her deliciously sexy.

Deena lay back as his kisses rained upon her, moving down her body, taking his time. She wanted to feel him and did so as she reached out and touched him, first the muscles in his back, then around to the pectorals, returning to his back. She massaged his back, liking the feel of the smooth, hard planes of his body. And when he began suckling her nipples again, her body reacted, arching up to meet his mouth. She thought he had to have the most talented tongue and lips she'd ever experience.

Her scent began to seep into his nose. He placed his fingers between her legs, slipping one and then another into her vagina. He moaned loudly. She was not only incredibly wet, but she was also maddeningly tight, her internal muscles grabbing his fingers. He knew that if he entered her now, he wouldn't last a minute. He began to ply her bud once again, this time with his thumb. He leaned back slightly. He wanted to see her soar this time.

"Come, for me baby," he said as his thumb played its instrument, coaxing the sound from her, plucking the tune he wanted to hear.

She placed her hand on his as if she were trying to get him to remove it. He shook his hand and continued, watching her beautiful face contort into masks of passion, her eyes slanted, her chest rising and falling, her large nipples hard and peaked. He was enjoying watching her come apart in his hands—literally. Her passion was ripe and he knew that once he sunk inside of her, their passion would enrapture them both. This, he mused to himself, was what he had been looking for.

"Charles!" she screamed his name as her groin hit his hand time and time again, her light eyes now so dark he thought they'd literally had turned as dark as his.

"That's it, baby, come for me." He held his hand to her groin and let her ride his hand. When she finally came down, she had a wild look in her eyes, like a tigress. He was somewhat taken aback. He'd awoken her passion and now he wasn't sure if he could quench it. He reached over to his night stand, opened it, and retrieved a condom. Deena took the packet from him, ripped it open and then slid the latex sheath over him slowly, her fingers grasping his member tightly. He gritted his teeth as her warm hands pumped him up and down, her finger sliding over the head on the upstroke.

He'd had enough play.

Charles pulled Deena under him and positioned his member at her opening. He noticed her eyes had closed.

"Open your eyes," he ordered. And when she did he sank inside of her in one smooth, fluid push. "Oh, my God."

He was still, the feel of her muscles contracting around him. If she kept that up, he'd be lost and he wanted to savor this moment, this feeling to last as long as he could. He began to slowly slide in and out of her, pulling her legs around his lower back, then placing his hand under her bottom, allowing him to sink further inside of her.

They found their rhythm, their bodies in sync, the motions fluid and sensual. Deena wanted to cry. Charles was filling her with a passion, with a love, she had never experienced and she didn't know if she'd ever want to go back. The feel of all of him, from his fingers, to his tongue, to his fantastic member, she was a goner. And she was loving every moment of it.

Deena almost protested loudly when he pulled out of her. She quickly recovered when he positioned her on her knees with her behind up in the air. She knew he was strong, handling her body almost as if she were weightless. Admittedly, she loved it.

Tears pricked her eyes at the scrumptious feel of him sinking inside of her, his fingers once again playing with her bud, while his other hand held onto her breasts, two of his fingers rolling her nipples around. She matched his stroke as she ground her behind into his groin, his member sliding delightfully inside and out. She was so wet that she felt her own juices roll down her thigh. All of this was a first and she found it so satisfying she didn't want to stop.

Again, Charles changed positions, having Deena lie on her side. He smacked her gently on her bottom as he lay behind her, pulled her leg up to rest on his and then entered her. She pushed back against him and reached back to hold onto his bicep, the feeling creeping up her spine, the orgasm right there. She began to buck against him, calling out his name as the orgasm rocked into her, her eyes rolled back, her muscles contracted viciously. After she had come down, Charles yet again switched their positions. He sat up and pulled her onto his lap, sinking once again into her tight wetness.

"Baby, I can't get enough of you." He began pumping into her, his mouth attached to her nipple, his hands held her hips. His movements became more reckless, harder. Deena twirled her hips in a circular motion, which had proved to be the undoing, for Charles pumped wildly into her, calling his name as he exploded into the sheath, his member throbbed like a jack hammer as she squeezed him, milking his member.

He placed his head against her chest, his face nuzzled in between her full breasts, his arms wrapped tightly around her. He didn't want to move, didn't want to come from inside her warmth. He just wanted to stay inside of her.

Without uncoupling, Deena managed to lay on top of him. Charles placed the comforter over their bodies and held her as their breathing normalized. And when her muscles involuntarily clenched around him, he responded by getting hard again. Deena raised and looked down at him.

"Man, I am going to become addicted," she said and then laughed. "Can you see me in group therapy? Hi, my name is Deena and I'm addicted to…"

He interrupted her. "Don't you say it," he laughed. "But I will say that you, baby, are some type of hypnotic—girl, you move." He rolled his eyes.

Deena laughed and laid her head on his chest, twirling her fingers in his chest full of hair. She liked what she saw and felt; and knew that she would never get enough of him. And when they began again, this time achingly slow, a tear rolled down her face as she loved the man who had stepped into her life and brought with him the type of healing she needed to soothe her soul and love again.

Chapter 18

Once Charles dropped Deena at home, he lingered long, kissing her lips and speaking of how he'd miss waking up and making love to her. She felt the loss. And by the time she had unpacked her bag, taken a shower and readied for bed, she felt a profound sense of aloneness. She too had enjoyed her weekend with Charles, his jokes, his attention and his body.

Dinner at her parents went even better than expected, with her mother and father fawning over Charles and her nieces and nephews enthralled with the fact that he was a detective. The only time she worried was when Darius had asked Charles to follow him outside.

Deena had watched her oldest brother and the man she had fallen in love with stand face to face, their heights matched, but Charles had Darius by at least fifty pounds. She could see Darius pointing toward the house and then thump his chest. Charles had nodded. And when Charles put his hand in Darius's for a shake, she knew that this man who had awakened her body with a passion she'd never experienced was in it for the long haul.

And then he had surprise her even more when he had let her drive his GTO from her parents to her home. She smiled broadly at that thought, for she hadn't thought he would.

"Deena, catch," he had said as he tossed his car keys to her.

He almost laughed aloud at the shocked then mischievous grin that swept across her face. That was what he wanted—wanted to see her smiling and he hadn't seen her smile this much since he'd met her. He liked to see her happy and knew he'd move heaven and earth to see to it that she was.

Charles held the driver's side door to the GTO open and watched as she slid behind the wheel. He crossed himself as he walked around to the passenger side and joined her. He put on seat belt.

"Good idea," she patted his hand as she raised her skirt up her thighs. The fitted skirt was a little too restrictive. She looked at Charles as he raised one eye brow and then looked down at her exposed thighs.

"Don't raise it any higher, baby." He said and then buckled his seat belt.

Deena laughed and then peeled away from the curb, taking the corner with precision handling. She glanced over at Charles one large hand gripped the door cushion, while the other held onto the dash board.

Deena slowed the vehicle as they entered Lake Shore Drive. She'd driven this stretch a million times in her Mercedes, opening the sports vehicle up to its top speed, but she didn't want to open up the GTO just yet and opted to cruise the speed limit. She looked over at Charles.

"What's the matter?"

"I guess I expected you to be flying down the Drive."

"Want to get a feel of the vehicle," she said. "Charles, this is a really nice car. You've done a great job restoring it and the added toys are a plus." Deena tinkered with the radio controls located on the steering wheel. She selected a station once she heard the rich voice of Barry White seep out of the car's speakers. She began to sing along.

"You've got a nice voice," Charles said as he settled back into the seat and watched her as the wind blew her hair around her head and face. He smiled as he watched her—contentment plastered on her face.

"Thank you. My parents are big into music of all kinds. I'm surprised they didn't show you their music collection. They've got an album collection to rival any DJ's. The only music they really never listened to was techno."

Deena looked over at Charles. It was time to stir him up.

"Hold on," she said and then pressed her foot onto the clutch, switched the gears and pumped the accelerator. The powerful vehicle lurched forward as the speedometer rose quickly from forty-five to seventy and climbing.

At eighty miles an hour, Deena weaved the vehicle expertly from one lane to another, passing slower vehicles. At one point a Dodge Charger rolled along side them. Deena looked past Charles to the occupant who pointed his finger forward. Deena nodded her head and punched the accelerator, pushing the vehicle to one-hundred and twenty miles an hour, the overhead street lights were a blurry whiz in the nighttime darkness.

Charles closed his eyes. Even he had never driven so fast. He knew the engine could hold it—could handle the speed. But he wasn't sure he could. As she came into a curve, Charles opened one eye and then shook his head holding onto the dash board. Over the soulful music, which should have soothed him, all he could hear was Deena's laugh as she raced the vehicle next to her, leaving it in the GTO's dust.

"Oh, oh. We've got company," Charles heard Deena say. He opened his eyes and looked behind them, the unmistakable blue lights belonging to the City's finest.

"Well, counselor, this is a fine mess you've gotten us into." Charles said, his voice mimicking Hardy from the comedic duo.

"Me? You let me drive. Why didn't you tell me to slow down," Deena looked over at Charles and laughed as she pulled the vehicle to the shoulder. "I hope you're going to use your special powers to get us out of this."

Charles folded his arms across his chest and stared forward. He shook his head. "You're on your own, woman." He peeked at her and resisted the urge to laugh at the incredulous look on her face.

"Fine. I've talked myself out of worse." She reached for her purse and retrieved her driver's license and a copy of her insurance card. Once the officer reached her side of the vehicle, she handed the items over without allowing him to begin his spiel. She sat with her hands firmly on the steering wheel. She refused to look at Charles, knowing he'd have an amused expression plastered on that fine face of his.

For several long moments the pair sat silently, the only sounds were that of the cars whizzing by them and the waves of Lake Michigan as they crashed upon the rocks.

"Ms. Walls, you really need to be more careful." The officer handed her documents back to her. "And have a good night Detective Harris. See you around."

"Sure thing, Billy, good night and you be careful out here."

Deena looked at Charles. "You know him?" She asked and watched in rapt amazement as he nodded his head. "And you let me go through all of that?" She watched as he nodded his head again. Two could play it that game, she thought as she sped away from the curb and headed toward his house. As she rolled along, she kept her eyes focused on the road and pretended to ignore him as he began apologizing. At one point during his apology, she tossed him an evil glare and then wanted to laugh out loud at the look of contrition on his face, his lips, and those talented lips, pressed into a frown.

Tired of her own game, Deena suddenly gunned the accelerator, crossed three lanes of traffic and then exited at Montrose Harbor where she pulled the vehicle into a metered stall. She laughed at Charles's expression as he gripped the armrest tightly.

"I'm sorry," he muttered.

"What did you say?" She leaned toward him.

"Baby, I'm sorry. I should have said something. Next time I will; just promise me.

you will never make a move like that one again." He opened the door and slid out of the car.

Deena watched him as he walked away from the car and headed toward the beach. She jumped out of the vehicle and rushed to catch up with him.

Charles smiled when he heard the hurried steps of her small feet. When she finally caught up with him, he twirled on her, swept her up into his arms and began carrying her toward the water. "Say you sorry." He laughed as he swung her toward the water, his grip around her strong. "Say it, woman. You was wrong for that last move." He swung her again and began laughing harder as she squealed, her arms tightened around his neck.

"No, Charles," she screamed out his name with spurts of laughter intercepted.

"Apologize, woman of mine, or it's the lake for you." He began to walk further down the dark beach, the waves lapped at the hem of his trousers. Charles pretended to drop Deena, laughing as she gripped him tighter, her chest pressed against him. He waded further into the water. "Well, if you're not going to apologize, at least tell me you have a crowbar to pry loose my heart from my throat."

"Oh, Sweetheart, you have my full apologies. Can you forgive me?" She batted her eyes playfully as she began stroking the side of his face.

He stilled and looked down at the woman in his arms as she looked up into his eyes. His mind refused to acknowledge that they were outside as he moved his face closer to hers, their lips centimeters apart. "Ever make love outside, baby?"

She shook her head and closed her eyes, gently pulling his face toward hers and then moaned loudly when she felt the smooth fullness of his lips upon hers, followed by the movement of his tongue outlining hers before it masterfully slipped between her lips to play and tease with her own. This was what got them started.

She felt her nipples harden to pebbles as his hands roamed a slow descent across her stomach to her round behind before he began lightly kneading her butt.

She felt herself lowered, her body sliding slowly and wickedly down the length of his. The rock hard erection she felt pressed against her reminded her of the type of pleasure it was capable of providing.

Charles's hands made a wicked path up under her blouse to rest right under her breasts, his mouth still mating with hers. Deena tilted her head to the side to get more of him, to have his tongue continue mating with hers as she felt his hands slide further upward, across her breasts covered by the thin material of her bra. His thumbs expertly began to caressed her nipples into hardened pebbles. Deena moaned loudly as she felt him free her breasts from their confines via the front clasp. He broke the kiss long enough to lower his head to feast on the nipple that had become hard and ripe under his ministrations.

Deena pushed his head closer as he suckled her nipple in and out of his mouth; the quick motion caused her knees to buckle and her panties to become moist. She threw her head back, which gave him more access as he plied her nipples to life suckling each one before he took his large hands and gently pushed her breasts together in order to lap greedily at both of her nipples. Deena cried out at the exquisite feel of his mouth and tongue.

His lips returned to her mouth and he began to mate with hers, his tongue was insinuating and gyrating in and out with the most sensuous movements, the most erotic and alluring act she'd ever experience just kissing. Her head spun slightly as she tried to match him, to convey to him just what he was doing to her body, her mind, her senses.

It was not her imagination and at that moment, when her feet touched the cool water, she had decided she wanted this man right then. She pulled the skirt up and her thong panties to one side as he lifted her effortlessly, holding her with one hand as the other freed his hard member. She moaned loudly when she felt him slide inside of her, his strong arms held her as he began to pump inside of her, his girth stretched her, filled her with a glorious fulfillment. She felt her muscles contract, her body signal that she was about to have an orgasm. Sensing this, Charles held her again with one hand as the other began to toy with her bud, making it twitch as the orgasm washed over her, causing her to scream out his name, her voice bouncing over the waves. And when she felt him throb his release with a deep, husky groan, she squeezed him causing him to pump inside of her harder. The aftershock was too glorious to describe.

"Woman, you're going to kill me." He kissed her and then placed her on the ground, straightening her clothes. He took her by the hand and led her back to the car. One they arrived at the car, he held out his free hand.

"What?" Deena replied, putting her hand behind her back. "Why do you have your hand held out?"

"Keys, woman," he replied as he motioned for her to hand over the car keys. He had already experienced her driving and while she handled the vehicle like a race car driver, he wasn't quite up to experiencing her turning Lake Shore Drive into the Autobahn.

"Spoil sport. I wasn't going to drive fast." She looked up at him as she handed over the keys. She stood to one side as he opened the passenger door. He watched as she slid onto the seat, doing that swing movement with her legs. He leaned down and kissed her before shutting the door. He walked around the front of the car and then slid behind the wheel, starting the vehicle. He turned and faced her.

"Thank you, Deena, for giving me you. This has been a great weekend."

Deena reached out and gently stroked his cheek. "You are too welcome, Charles. And I really mean it, I enjoyed every minute of you." She smiled slyly at him as she leaned over and kissed him on the lips.

Her eyes became darker as the thoughts of his skillful fingers plying her along with his wicked lips and tongue invaded her mind. *Oh, my gosh, yes,* they had just made love and here she wanted to make love again.

Charles looked at her and saw the tell-tale sign in her eyes. He knew just how she felt, but he had to be up early and needed to get some sleep. Besides, if he touched her one more time, he'd be spending his night making love to her. That wouldn't be so bad, he mused to himself.

"Let me get you home, temptress." She watched his face as he backed the car out of the space and headed to Deena's penthouse.

Deena's thoughts were brought back to the present with the sound of her phone ringing. She answered it and then smiled when she heard his voice. This was it. And she knew that no matter what, she would never love a man like this again. It would be her secret, she thought, as to she wasn't sure how Charles felt about her. But no matter, she knew that this was a one in a million for her.

Chapter 19

Charles rolled lazily home. He yawned, but knew sleep for him wouldn't come easy—and it wasn't because he wasn't tired, but because he had Deena on his mind. He'd met plenty of women, had had enough in his forty years on earth to know what to do with one, but he truly had wanted this one like he'd wanted no other. And when she came apart in his arms, the way her body responded to him—matched him, the bridled passion in her kiss, the way she held on to him—he was lost.

Shoot, he rubbed his hand down his face; they'd just made love without a condom. Damn. But if she got pregnant, she'd just have to marry him. *I've got it bad, I'm over here talking marriage.*

Several minutes later, Charles pulled into his garage. He took his time as he climbed out of the car, closed the garage door and then headed into his home. Inside, he sat in the kitchen as Sweetie came and sat next to him. He rubbed her head.

"I bet you need to go outside." Charles rose as Sweetie whined loudly. "How about I do one better?" He bent over and looked her in the eyes while cradling her large head in his hands. "Let's go for a walk. I'm too wound up to sleep."

Charles watched as Sweetie rushed to retrieve her leash. He went into his room and removed his clothes. Changing into a pair of sweat pants, he removed the ankle holster and the small pistol. He examined it, making sure that water hadn't gotten into the chamber then placed the revolver in the safe. He removed his Glock from the safe and placed the weapon in his shoulder holster and then put the holster on. He pulled a sweat shirt over it. He needed to feel the night air on him—to help him make sense of what he was feeling. Everything he'd ever known said it was too soon to have deep feelings; to be enamored to the point of wanting to spend every waking moment with a person. That's for kids like Corbin, the right side of his brain reasoned. But the left said something altogether different.

"Let's go, girl," Charles said as he took Sweetie's leash, placed it on her collar and then headed outside. They jogged for several blocks, the late night sounds of crickets and cicadas could be heard as he thought about Deena and one of the last times he couldn't sleep. That had been fifteen years ago following Corbin's birth. Back then he'd wondered and worried what kind of father he would make. His own father had been great, spending lots of time with Charles and his brothers, both collectively and one-on-one. Now, here he was jogging with a eighty pound Rot lobbing along with him as his mind wondered about the woman who had invaded his thoughts, and gave her body to him unselfishly and uninhibitedly.

He allowed his thoughts to continue thinking of Deena, her initial reluctance and final acceptance, and then her admission that she had once been a victim of domestic violence. He couldn't fathom why a man thought he had to control a woman, period; much less try to by hitting her. He knew that whoever the dude was, he'd sure hate to come into contact with him.

Charles headed back to his house. He had called her, making sure she was safely in bed, loving the sound of her soft voice when she was relaxed, the thought of how she had looked when he held her in his arms and allowed her to be the woman she was by not mentioning the lone tear that rolled down her beautiful face when he made love to her. As he sat in the darkness of his bedroom on the edge of his king-sized bed, the smell of her all over the room, and thought about the woman, his woman, who had come into his life, he came to the stark and unmistakable realization he was deeply in love with Deena Walls.

❧

Charles and Lee walked into the office of the FBI. They had met earlier and gone over several of the files. He filled Lee in on what Schoop had told him about Brother Barnett having a tail on Deena.

"That's bastard won't get a chance, man." Lee pounded

Charles fist with his.

"Don't we know it."

Handing over their ID's and service weapons, they were escorted to the third floor and shown a room. They both sat at the lone desk with four chairs lining one wall, and two facing them. Charles shook his head. The FBI always made a statement.

The door to the room opened and in walked Schoop, followed by two men dressed like the characters from *Men In Black*. Charles wanted to laugh out loud at the absurdity of it all, but refrained from doing so. Besides, he thought, he needed to get this case wrapped up, for he had no intentions of Deena ripping him a new one on the witness stand. He told her he could take it, but that was before he found himself madly in love with her.

"Detectives Lee and Harris, thank you for joining us. I'm Special Agent Knight. And this is my partner, Special Agent Johns. You will be working with us for the next two weeks on the Brother Barnett case," Agent Knight said as he walked into the room.

Charles sized the agent up, figured him to be no older than 30, his fresh face made his seem even younger, his deep blue eyes darted nervously from one side to the next. Charles knew he was nervous. He looked over at his partner, a brother who stood about 6 feet even. His demeanor was cool, almost aloof as he entered the room, nodded his head and then sat across from Lee. They sized each other up and Charles wanted to tell them to take the pissing match elsewhere.

"Agents."

He nodded. "Detective Harris, we've asked the Chicago Police Department for your assistance for a lot of reasons. You're respected, your contacts are impeccable and you have a way with..."

Charles stood to his feet and stood face to face with the agent. He had the agent by at least four inches and forty pounds. "Stop blowing smoke up my ass and tell me what else you got, what's the game plan and when do we start." He stepped back an inch and crossed his arms over his chest. He hated to be patronized.

Johns stood and walked over to Charles. The agent held out his hand to Charles. "Welcome to the FBI."

Deena arrived at the office two hours before it opened. She awoke early, thoughts of Charles embedded in her mind, his fingers branded on her body, the places where his mouth and tongue had traveled still tingled. She wished he would have spent the night, for she enjoyed waking up and making love with him.

She stepped into the building, disarmed the alarm and then picked up the bundle of papers laying outside the door. She headed inside her office, setting down the cup of coffee and muffin she'd stopped and picked up on her way in. Her Blackberry vibrated and she pulled the contraption from her purse and spied the screen. She smiled as her eyes read the short noted from Charles. She sent a quick reply and then waited. She blushed wildly as his reply stated how much he loved being inside of her.

The sound of the ringing phone interrupted her morning electronic tryst with the man she loved.

"Good Morning, Walls and Associated."

"Girl, what are you doing there so early," Karen asked.

"How did you know I was here?"

"I didn't. I tried to call you at home, then your cell, which rolled directly into voicemail."

"I was just checking a text message from Charles."

"Ahh, texting sweet nothings, are we?"

Deena laughed and sat behind her desk, telling her soror and best friend all about the weekend she had spent with Charles and how her family had fawned and gushed over him during Sunday dinner.

"All I want to know is did ya'll get ya'll' groove cool on?"

"Karen! That's not any of your business," Deena responded and then remained quiet. She knew her response wasn't what Karen wanted to hear. "Girl, all I'm going to say to you is that man is truly talented." Deena gushed, her thoughts rolling around how he looked naked and how he had played her body like an instrument—he had coaxed all kinds of sounds out of her.

"Go on, girl. You deserve it."

"Thanks, sis. Now, why are you calling me this early in the morning?"

"Wanted to make sure you hadn't forgotten about today."

Deena looked down at her calendar and noticed she had written in a court date for Serena. "Thanks for reminding me. I'll be there and I've decided I'm going to defend Serena, pro bono."

"Thank you so much, Deena. She's going to be too excited to hear that. But I'll let you tell her. Your presence alone was going to give her hope."

Deena thought about the young teen she mentored and the last time she'd seen her. She'd had made a quick stop at the detention center to drop off the goodies she'd brought for Serena and two other female juveniles she mentored. Once she'd arrived, Serena had done something her counselors said she never did: she hugged Deena.

Deena had embraced the child back, rubbing her back and telling her that all would be okay. At that moment, she had made the decision to represent Serena in her upcoming trial.

"I hope so. I just hope her mom shows up. That would be the icing on the cake." Deena said a silent prayer, for much of Serena's problems stemmed from her mother's addiction. But her mother was in rehab and seemed to be doing much better.

"For real; so do I. But, I do need to need to switch subjects on you and right back to Charles."

Deena rolled her eyes and took a sip of her coffee. She wondered how long it would take for her to bring the conversation right back to Charles. But Deena didn't keep anything from Karen and told her about their dates.

"Wow, that brother is really romantic. And you sure you don't want to marry him?"

"Karen, who said anything about getting married. Okay, so we're going out, but that doesn't mean we have to get married. Besides, we've both been down that road before."

"So what. You know what to expect. Besides, you guys have a lot in common."

She inhaled deeply. She wasn't quite sure she wanted to remarry. Seth had been enough. But when she thought of Charles, she didn't see her future without him. As she thought more, it seemed as if he'd always been a part of her life, their connection was that strong.

"Look, Karen, marriage isn't something I want to think about right now. I just want to continue seeing Charles and not anticipate the next of it all."

"Just don't close yourself off to something permanent because of you know who. He wasn't right for you. You even said it yourself."

Deena knew her soror and best friend was talking about Seth. Since the day he'd laid a hand on Deena, Karen refused to say his name.

"Yeah, I know. Let me just enjoy Charles, okay."

"Okay," Karen said and Deena could hear the hesitation in her voice. She knew that if Karen had her way, she and Charles would be hitched by now and expecting twins. She loved her soror, thought the world of her, but she just didn't want to think too far ahead.

They spoke for another half of an hour, with Deena promising to see her following Serena's court case.

Deena began skimming through her papers, beginning with the *Law Review* and ending with the *Chicago Sun-Times*. She was surprised to see a small article on Kasha implying that maybe the star wasn't out of the country as first reported.

Deena looked at the clock sitting on her desk and wondered where the young woman was. She had been missing for three days and each day she was gone caused Deena more worry. At least the cops knew, thanks to Charles, but that would be added to her litany of charges, for Kasha was now considered a fugitive.

The phone on her desk rang interrupting her thoughts. She hoped that it was either Charles or Kasha. She really wanted to hear from both of them.

"Walls & Associates," she spoke into the receiver.

"Good morning, beautiful."

She smiled at the deep voice, his rich timbre. "Good morning to you, handsome. How are you?"

"Better. Much better, now that I'm talking to you. I only have a few minutes, but I want to know if you'd have dinner with me and Corbin next week."

"I thought he was in Florida for a few weeks."

"So did I, but he called me this morning and said something about coming home sooner. You know teens and I didn't press it. When I spoke with his mother she couldn't shed any light on his sudden wish to come home."

"Sure, Charles. That would be great." She knew Charles wanted the three of them to spend more time together. And in some ways she was honored, but on the other hand it so much like a little family and Deena wasn't sure she wanted to be a mother to anyone. Besides, the boy had a mother.

"But in the mean time, why don't you have breakfast with me in the morning. Say around five."

"Five? Man, that's an ugly hour."

"We could watch the sun rise," he replied. "Think on it. I've got to jet. I'll call you later tonight. Bye, baby."

"Bye," Deena replied and then hung up the phone. Five was awfully early, but she'd try and wake up for him if it meant seeing him for a few hours.

❧

"It looks like you two have gotten pretty chummy," Lee said as he lowered the binoculars he was peering into. "Five in the morning, ugh?"

Charles shrugged his shoulders and nodded his head. He didn't want to look soft, but he wanted to tell Lee how he enjoyed being with her, talking to her. He wanted to brag all about her, minus the intimate details.

"Hey, she's really great, man."

"And a demon for speed," Lee grinned. "Billy told me he stopped youl the other night. She must be special; you let her drive the GTO. Next thing you know you'll be asking for her hand in marriage."

"Whoa, we're just dating. Who said anything about marriage?"

"You the type," Lee said. "You don't go out much, don't drink much, ain't had a date since Moses was in diapers and you love to be at home."

"I'm safest at home. So that makes me marriage material?" Charles walked over to the desk set up in the room of a building across from Brother Barnett's main hangout. They'd arrived earlier that morning, before daybreak, dressed as thugs. So many folks rolled in and out of the building, they both knew illegal activity was going on.

"Yup, that makes you marriage material. You want a woman to be like you. Does Deena love old movies and to be at home?"

Charles nodded his head in the affirmative and then thought about what Lee was saying. If he was honest with himself he'd admit that what Lee was saying had much merit. He was the commitment, marrying kind; but he also was smart enough and intuitive enough to know that not every woman was marriage material for him. But Deena was. And his attraction to her and love for her was deeply entrenched and satisfying on so many levels it wasn't funny. And the weekend they had spent together, the way she came completely apart in his arms—Jeeze.

Lee's voice invaded his thoughts.

"Just be careful not to play the total knight in shining armor. She seems like a strong sister, so you can't just take over for her, you have to take cues."

Charles's thoughts were brought back to the fact that someone was watching Deena. And now the FBI had someone watching the ones watching Deena. He didn't like it one bit, but what choice did he have. All he knew at this point was that the guys watching Deena were some street level hoods supposedly working for Brother Barnett. But what no one could understand was why? Unless they were looking for Kasha. Charles knew Deena's sister, Dionne, was looking for the young woman. And knowing Dionne, if she was as smart as she seemed and Deena said she was, then she knew a lot of folks were looking for Kasha.

Charles brought the subject back to women.

"How you know what women need, Lee? You're on what? Girlfriend number five since the beginning of the year?" Charles sat at the desk and began making notations in a log book.

"So, sue me, I love the ladies, I do, but they all know I'm not the marrying kind. You on the other hand are looking for a wife and I think you've found her."

Charles shook his head and laughed. "How'd you figure that one out all by yourself?"

Charles looked at his partner as he returned to looking out of the binoculars. "What?" Lee asked.

"Nothing," Charles responded then went back to the log book. He looked at his watch and felt the day couldn't end soon enough so that he could see Deena. Commander Schoop insisted he continue seeing her as if nothing was wrong, but he was not to tell her he was working undercover for the feds, nor was he to reveal that folks were watching her. A small measure of relief came from knowing that some good guys had her back. But on second thought, he knew he'd have to really restrain himself from beating the crap out of whoever thought they were going to ever lay a hand on her. Not his woman—not his Deena.

Chapter 20

Seth stood outside the large building and looked up. He had followed Deena and needed to give her what he'd had. It was time to make so many things right in this life. He looked down at his hands, his knuckles were a little sore. He was ashamed at how they'd gotten that way.

He looked across the street at the building and noticed the guys he had hired were working as doormen, which meant she was home. He had another crew following her when she left. They had brought him a tape of her and the cop on the beach. He refused to watch for he had an idea what was going on. But he was also relieved to know she had really moved on with her life. Seth wanted to know who the cop was and had someone on the inside getting him the skinny.

Seth stepped into the shadows when he noticed Deena step from the building and hail a cab. He absorbed her beautiful face, remembering the last time he'd seen her. He closed his eyes and shook his head. What a monster.

He continued to watch her, with her smooth, warm complexion. His heart literally hurt. She was the one and only woman he had ever loved and yet he couldn't take care of her, much less cherish her. If she saw him he'd not only be hauled off to jail, but the information he held in his hands would fall into the wrong hands. He knew that Deena would do the right thing.

His cell phone vibrated. He didn't want to answer it, didn't want to have the one time he'd seen her in person since that fateful day interrupted. He absently raised the phone to his ear.

"Speak to me," he said in a low tone into the phone. He listened and nodded absently several times before speaking again. "Yes, follow her. And remember what I said." He hit the end button and placed the phone back into his suit's breast pocket. His eyes misted as he watched her climb into the cab, the tail lights finally disappearing into the warm night.

Deena looked back over her shoulder. When she stepped out of the building, she couldn't help but feel she was being watched—a feeling she'd been having lately. So, instead of driving to the 24-hour grocery store herself, she decided to hail a cab.

"Take the long way and see if you are being tailed."

The cab driver looked at her through the rear view mirror. She dismissed the look repeating her request. Finally, the cab driver nodded.

For nearly twenty minutes, Deena rolled around in the cab. Every few minutes, she looked at the driver in the mirror.

"No one is following us," he said.

Deena turned around in her seat. "Are you sure?"

The cab driver exhaled deeply. "Yes, ma'am, I am sure," he responded as he turned and headed to the grocery store.

She tried to dismiss the feeling, but couldn't and it stayed with her as she shopped for a few items to fix for breakfast. She would surprise Charles by making him a Denver Omelet, loaded with veggies and sausage and a stack of home-made pancakes. He had never really sampled her cooking for he was always taking her out to eat. She knew he would be surprised that she could cook. He'd never said it, but he probably thought as most men did; that professional women didn't cook, much less know how. She was the complete opposite. Deena's mother insisted they each knew how to cook, but Deena had also taken a couple of culinary classes in college and found that she actually loved to cook. She just didn't always have time to do so.

Deena stepped out of the grocery store. She noticed the woman standing near the door, her dirty hand held out. As she got closer, there was something oddly familiar about her.

Deena heard the soft sound behind her, the soft voice asking for a little change. She turned slowly and came face to face with Kasha. Her eyes became large.

"Kasha," she stepped closer, noting the dark circles under her eyes, her head minus the long weave and covered with a cap, her eyes void of the colored contacts she normally wore and her body covered in dirty, baggy clothes.

"Girl, where have you been?" Deena walked over to her. She noticed her shaking, her eyes darting all over the office. "I've been worried about you. You got everyone looking for you."

"Juan-Carlos is dead," she whispered.

"I know. How did you find out?"

"The guys who kidnapped me told me so, said they were going to make me join him." Kasha began shaking and crying. Deena wrapped her arms about her and moved her to the side out of the sight of the people heading in and out of the grocery store.

"Get it out, girl. Go ahead and cry."

She felt Kasha's tight embrace and felt her body shake. Through her sobs, she finally told Deena the entire story. When she finished, Deena was stunned. She had no idea her brother was so deeply entrenched in Brother Barnett's maze of illegal activity, or that Kasha had been witness to a drug deal gone bad in addition to the attempted murder of her brother.

"Why didn't you tell me this sooner?" Deena asked.

"Juan-Carlos told me Eric would die if I told the whole story."

"Well, Juan-Carlos is dead and according to Dionne, he was into a lot of shady, illegal activities. Juan-Carlos was close to being brought in by the authorities for additional questioning. Okay, so what changed your mind? Why talk now?"

"I went to the hospital to see Eric." She looked up at Deena. "He looked so peaceful lying there."

"How did you find him? I thought they had a guard around him?"

"A nurse's uniform and ID got me on every floor. Shoot, it took me nearly all night to find him and then twenty minutes to con the officer outside his door to let me in check his vitals."

"You do realize I need to contact the cops."

Kasha stood quickly. "No, Deena. They're only going to lock me up. You said so yourself. I can't do prison time. I've got some money and I want to head down to Mexico or somewhere."

"Girl, you can be extradited from Mexico. But if you tell the whole story and we can prove you knew nothing as well as fearing for your life, we can appeal to the mercy of the court and see if we can get you cleared. Or can get you off with maybe two years, six month served if you stay out of trouble."

Deena looked at Kasha. And though she seemed frightened, something in her gut stated that there was still more. Maybe she knew her brother was going to rob Brother Bennett and was in on it—standing to cash in.

Kasha backed away from Deena, shaking her head as she did. "I'll call you, Deena. I'll call you." She walked quickly toward the street. Deena ran out to find her, but the girl seemed to have disappeared into thin air.

Deena grabbed fists of her hair in her hands. This was infuriating, she thought, but she knew from the look in Kasha's eyes, she was really afraid. She needed to come up with a way to not only find her some protection, but to get her to turn herself in.

She didn't understand how these young women got themselves into so much trouble. Kasha was about to toss her entire career down the toilet. Her single had just hit the airwaves and instead of her basking in the success of it all, she was running from God knows who.

Well, she thought to herself as she hailed a cab, at least Serena's going to be okay. Deena had wanted to cry when the judge had decided to allow Serena to go home with her mother, who had showed up sober and clean. And though the teen was placed on house arrest for the next six months, at least she and her mother were together to start over.

Watching them embrace in court earlier, the relief and joy on both of their faces reaffirmed her decision. She would defend teens that were being adjudicated for crimes. She would keep a few of her clients, like Mr. Swift, but the majority of her legal expertise would be assisting teens in getting a fair trial.

Deena arrived at her place and noticed the same two guys standing outside the building she'd noticed the past several days. The odd thing was, they wore the winter uniform and not the summer ones.

Deena pushed it to the back of her mind as she headed up to her penthouse. Once inside, she called Dionne and told her she'd seen Kasha and where.

"Yup, and we have to find her a better place to hide until her bench trial next week. That is if she shows up."

Hanging up, she looked at the clock on her microwave. She hadn't thought it was that late, but given as how she had worked late, then worked out, followed by that crazy little trip to the grocery store, she shouldn't have been surprised that the dial read midnight. She thought of Charles. She hadn't heard from him since that morning and hoped that he was okay—he said he was going to call. Deena guessed he was just busy. She shrugged her shoulders and began to prepare the veggies for omelets by dicing several of the vegetables and placing them in the refrigerator.

She poured herself a glass of wine. She was too wired to really sleep—having seen Kasha and wondering about Charles had left her wired. Kasha had been missing for days and she'd worried about her, especially after Dionne hadn't been able to track her—and Deena didn't think anyone could hide from her. And then there was Charles. Since their first date, she had talked to him no less than three, sometimes four times a day, especially before she lay down for the night.

Deena shut off the lights and headed to her bedroom. She stood in the middle of her bedroom and looked around at the furniture. Her place was so different from Charles, she thought looked at the large canopy bed, with its sheer sheath, the matching night stand, a cushioned bench at the foot, her overstuffed chair and ottoman. She thought of all of the furniture in her place and felt none of it made the place feel like home. Charles's house had a real hominess to it. At one point during her weekend, they had sat in the basement, the large screen television in front of them, and cuddled on the large couch; even Sweetie joined them by placing her large head in Deena's lap. She had felt warm, protected, and safe. And Charles had promised her that as long as he was in her life, no one would ever hurt her again.

Deena decided on a bath. She undressed, replacing her clothes with a short robe as she waited for the water to fill the whirlpool tub, the fragrance of lotus petals and amber floated up from the hot water. She dimmed the overhead recessed lighting then went back to the kitchen to re-fill her glass when she heard her phone ring.

"Hello," she answered.

"Let me up, baby. I'm in the lobby."

Deena's body tingled at the sound of his voice, the term of endearment he'd started using when he spoke to her. She didn't respond. She just depressed the key on the phone receiver that would grant him entrance.

When she heard the knock on the door, she rushed to it, forgetting about what she was wearing. She opened the door and waited for him to step off the elevator. She watched his as he moved down the hallway toward her, his steps sure and stealth, his handsome face smiling. Without thought, Deena opened her arms to him and was rewarded with a tight hug from him, her body pressed against his.

"Umm, that's nice, baby." He met her lips with his, holding her face in his hands. He had truly missed her and hadn't realized it until his shift ended and it dawned on him that he hadn't really talked to her all day. His kisses became more urgent, almost desperate. He heard her moan.

"I know. I've missed you all day, woman of mine." He looked down and noticed that her robe had come undone. "Damn," he uttered then swept her up in his arms and carried her to her bedroom. He stopped at the foot of the bed when he heard the running water.

"I was about to take a bath," she said as she stroked the hair at the nape of his neck. "Want to join me?"

He nuzzled her neck and nodded his head as he walked where she pointed. Once inside the master bathroom, he sat her on her feet, her robe still open and exposing all that made her woman. And he loved every inch of it. He watched her expressions as he began disrobing, starting with his Bear's Jersey. Deena's eyes widened when she saw he was wearing a gun in a shoulder holster.

"If it bothers you, next time I'll leave it in the car."

Deena shook her head. "No, it doesn't bother me, it's just that I've never really seen it on you."

Charles stepped out of the bathroom, taking his jersey with him. He removed his weapon and shoulder holster and placed them in her spare bedroom. He returned moments later.

"Where was I?"

Deena was sitting on a small stool, her muscular legs crossed one over the other. "Taking off your clothes."

He pulled the t-shirt over his head followed by his baggy jeans, briefs, socks and designer gym shoes. He straightened and watched as Deena looked at him from head to toe, her eyes stopping at the erection he just couldn't control. It's all her fault, he thought as he watched her rise then slowly walk over to him. She reached out and stroked his face, staring into his eyes. He wanted to tell her, wanted to share how he felt, how she'd been on his mind non-stop, but he didn't want to scare her, thinking that maybe it was too soon.

He inhaled deeply as Deena began seducing him, letting her fingers trace circles around his male nipples and through the hair on his chest. Her hand roamed lower until she held him in her hand. She began massaging and gently pumping his engorged member. He didn't want her to stop, the sensation felt too good. She began her slow decent downward until she was kneeling in front of him. He couldn't believe what he was seeing. Was she really? And his question was answered when he saw the tip of his member disappear into her mouth; the moisture and feel of her tongue flicking across the tip caused him to grasp her shoulders. The simple ministration was driving him wild. But he thought he would lose his mind when he felt her pull him further into her mouth, while her hands pumped him. He wasn't going to last another minute if he didn't stop her. He pulled his body back and with a pop, his member was released from her wickedly delectable mouth.

Deena led Charles to the tub, pausing long enough to allow the robe to hit the floor. She loved the way his dark eyes narrowed, almost lowered to slits, the desire and lust plain. Once he sat in the tub, she settled behind him and took a sponge and began to bathe him, rubbing the sponge softly across his back. She kissed his neck when he leaned back, wrapping her arms around his shoulders. Deena loved this man and wanted to be with him for as long as he wanted her. He had promised to take care of her, protect her, and she trusted that he would do just that.

She continued washing his back, moving her hands lower to massage the top of his taunt behind. She loved his behind, the way it felt in her hands when he was on top of her. She reached around to his waist, allowing her hands to trace a path down his abdomen to stroke his member. She loved the feel of him—the power he possessed in both his mind and body. She loved this very man with her entire soul. And she had never loved like this before—not even Seth.

Charles inhaled deeply and flinched when he felt her nipples pressed against his back. He was so turned on, so heated, he was sure that the water had turned ten degrees hotter. And when her hands began exploring, moving across his stomach to fist his member. He felt he couldn't take it anymore, her hands was making his eyes cross, but he would try to hold out until she had gotten her feel of him; for he knew that once he began making love to her he wouldn't be able to stop. He felt like a randy teenager, he was so turned on and planned on making love to her until the sun rose.

He moved his body and faced her, taking the sponge from her hand and dropping it in the water. He reached out and began washing her with his hands, rubbing the bath gel he'd found on the ledge near the tub across her upper body. His hands rubbed and massaged up and down before dipping under the water to massage her bud.

Deena threw her head back as he began the now all too familiar coaxing of her first orgasm. But this time she wanted to feel him deeply inside of her while he awoke her bud.

She rose from the water, stepped out and grabbed an oversized bath towel. She held the towel out and watched as he stepped from the water. His body glistened and Deena wanted to faint. *Damn, he's sexy and all mine,* she thought to herself and watched as he stepped into her arms. She toweled him then herself, taking his hand and leading him into the bedroom. She pulled the canopy back and slid onto the bed. He came to her, lying in her arms, his face buried in her chest.

They remained embraced for long, lingering moments, the feeling of closeness enveloping them. He thought of the tails watching her and he wanted to go out and physically remove them all. If they were there, then he wasn't doing his job as her man and keeping her safe. He wanted to tell her what he knew but couldn't.

Deena was the first to move.

Charles lifted his head and began licking and sucking her nipples. Her back arched as he pulled the hardened peaks into his mouth, his fingers found their way south to ply and coax.

"Charles," she breathed out his name. "I want to feel you inside of me, now," she said as she had him roll over onto his back. She slowly worked her core onto his hard member and cried out at the sensation as he began moving and pumping in and out of her, his large hands holding her waist. She guided one of his hands to her bud. Deena became delirious as he stroked the bud while pumping furiously. She was nearly there, the threat of an orgasm close. As if he'd sensed it, he changed their position, lying her on his chest, her back to him. He entered her again and then began to finger her core at the same time as he tweaked her nipple.

Deena pushed her behind against his pelvis again and again, the orgasm so strong that she screamed out his name and was glad she had no next-door neighbors.

Chapter 21

Deena awoke to the feel of Charles's strong arms about her, his leg slung possessively over hers. They had made love nearly all night and when the sun rose, she had been laying in his arms as they watched the orb crest the beauty of Lake Michigan.

She slid out of the bed, trying not to wake him and tipped quietly to the bathroom where she quickly showered then covered in a black and gold robe. Once complete, she paused at the door and watched Charles sleep, his chest rose and fell steadily, his arms now around the pillow her head had vacated. He looked so peaceful.

She headed to the kitchen and began making breakfast. She turned on the small color television sitting on the counter top as the last of the morning news started. Deena knew that by the time the hour chimed ten minutes after nine in the morning Kimmie would be on the phone wondering where she was. Deena couldn't remember the last time she had just taken off without prior notice. She snickered and decided to beat Kimmie to the punch picking up the cordless phone from its base attached to the kitchen wall.

"Hey Kimmie, its Deena. I'm going to work from home today." Deena hid her smile behind her hand as she listened to the litany of questions Kimmie asked. "No, I'm not sick, I'm feeling just fine, I just wanted to stay in today. Is that okay with you?" Deena rolled her eyes at Kimmie's next question. "Yes, he is, but..."

Deena changed her mind about responding as to why he was at her place. "So, take messages and only contact me at home if it's urgent, like if Kasha calls," She instructs before ringing off.

Once she finished making breakfast, she arranged the feast on the bed tray and carried it into the bedroom. She noticed that Charles was still sleep, now turned over on his stomach with the sheet barely covering his butt. Deena sat the tray on the bedside stand and climbed on top of Charles, her body pressed into his strong back. He reached around him, his hands blindly roaming up and down her side. He flipped over almost causing Deena to fall out of the bed—he caught her around her waist.

"Where are you going?" He placed a kiss on her lips as he brought her to rest on his chest, his arms wrapping around her. "I smell food. Don't tell me, woman of mine, that you can cook?"

Deena nodded her head against his chest then laughed loudly at the sound of his growling stomach. She wrestled free from his embrace. "Well, I'll let you be the judge of that." She brought the tray over and almost tripped as he sat up in the bed, the sheet wrapped around his waist, but left his muscular legs and well formed chest exposed. An image of her rubbing her hands through his thick mass of hair and his legs between hers ran like a frenzied movie through her mind. She looked into his eyes.

"Wow, I've never been fed breakfast in bed," he said as she positioned the tray over his lap then sat next to him. "Girl, this smells good. And if it tastes as good as if looks, then baby I'm going to be in love with you forever."

Deena blinked. She wasn't sure she heard him right when he mentioned the word love. She laid a napkin across his chest. She didn't want to get her hopes up high, didn't want to make more out of a few simple words. Yet, she knew she was in love with him, had been for some time.

Charles cut into the fluffy omelet. He closed his eyes as he chewed, the deep moan started in his stomach and finally reached his mouth. "Baby, you have got to marry me. You can cook!"

She nodded her head. "And you didn't think I could. Probably let the whole attorney thing and living here fool you. Didn't you?"

Charles lowered his eyes. She was right, he had figured her to be one of those new eras, professional sisters who couldn't or wouldn't cook or clean. It didn't bother him though, for he knew how to do both and knew that whether or not she could cook or clean he was still in love with her. He looked at her, loving the way the sun peeked through the wooden slats at her window and shone on the beauty of her smooth skin, the way her honey-colored eyes looked at him with what looked like deep affection. He didn't think she loved him.

"Didn't you, Charles?" She stood, placed her hands on her hips and leaned close. "Well, let me tell you a little secret, Charles Henry Harris, I studied culinary arts in college." She wanted to laugh at surprised expression on his face. "I specialized in pastries, Italian and Meditation cuisines. And let me not forget Southern, down home cookin'—better known as Soul Food. Oh, and I do my own cleaning and ironing." She straightened, snapping her fingers at him.

Charles threw back his head and laughed. He loved this woman. There was no way he was ever going to let her make love, cook or clean for another man. He didn't want to say anything, but he knew that this was the woman he was going to spend the rest of his life with. He set the tray to the side and put his hand out to her, pulling her to sit on his lap. He traced her jaw line with his finger, and then placed his hands in the tresses of her hair, her face coming close to his. "Thank you for agreeing to go out with me, Deena." He captured her lips with his, moving her from his lap to the bed, slowly lying her down. He couldn't seem to get enough of the sweet elector, their bodies so in tuned, he felt like he was falling each and every time they made love.

As they began once again, Deena knew that this man filling her heart, mind, body and soul would be the last man she gave herself up to. The emotions and love she felt would never be replicated and she didn't want to either.

❧

"Don't you have to go to work?"

"Yup, later tonight," Charles responded as he read the newspaper, sitting up in bed next to Deena, soft jazz filtering through the speakers strategically placed around her penthouse. He actually liked the layout and wouldn't mind living in a place like this.

In the distance, Deena heard the sound of a cell phone ringing.

"That sounds like mine," he said as he slid out of bed.

Deena admired his taunt, muscular physic, eyeing him from head to toe as he walked naked out of her bedroom, heading to the spare room. Several long moments later, he returned, sitting on the side of the bed.

"Something's come up and I've got to head down to the station." He looked at her. "I'm sorry. I really wanted to spend the whole day in bed with you." He stood and headed to the bathroom.

Deena nodded her head, not sure if she could keep the disappointment out of her voice or off of her face. She had been enjoying his company, lying lazily around talking, laughing and snuggling. She wasn't quite ready for this time to end so soon.

"Look at me, baby," he ordered softly as walked back over to the bed and knelt in front of her. "I'll make it up to you?"

Deena straightened her back and squared her shoulders. She felt she was being silly—he had things to do and if she thought about it, so did she. Kasha's bench trial was Monday. "No, you don't have to make it up to me, I'm okay."

Charles placed his hands around her waist. "Yes, you're disappointed and so am I." He kissed her on the forehead.

"Go take your shower so you can go. I'll be alright." She smiled at him hoping that her smile would convince him.

He kissed her quickly on the lips and then rushed to the bathroom. Fifteen minutes later he emerged wearing boxer briefs. She watched as he dressed, his deep voice filled the room as he talked about nothing in particular. Once finished, he came over to the bed, kissed Deena again and then headed out.

Deena listened as he headed to the spare room and then to the front door, closing it behind him. Looking around the room, she felt a little disjointed. The last thing she wanted was to be was all gah-gah and dewy eyed over a man; yet, that's just what she was.

Climbing out of bed, Deena headed to the frosted glass encased shower to wash the wicked, intoxicating, scent of their love making from her body. The warm spray of the multiple shower heads as they drummed her body soothed her disappointment as her mind replayed the love they had made, like possessed individuals. She couldn't get enough of the man. Even now, she throbbed in a way that only Charles could calm.

Deena stepped out of the shower, dressed and decided to head out to do a little shopping for her mentees. With Serena back home with her mother, Deena had the two other mentees to support and check on, which included buying toiletries and other small incidentals they didn't receive at the detention center. Deena made a mental note to make sure Walls and Associates buy all the female detainees the necessities not provided.

Thinking of the day she stood in court next to Serena, the judge, whom Deena knew, gave her a slight nod of approval. Sometimes these kids need a break, especially after grown folks had dragged them into grown folk problems just because. Deena had argued successfully for the teen's release, submitting evidence of her attending all of the programs outlined for her. The last point, the fact that Serena's mother was there and had successfully kicked her addiction to alcohol, was the argument she used to ensure that the family remained together. Once the trial concluded, Deena promised to keep in touch, checking on the family to make sure Serena's stayed out of trouble.

Deena headed to the underground parking garage to retrieve her vehicle. Pulling out, she headed to the mall. As she cruised along she noticed a vehicle that seemed to be following her. Making several sudden turns, the vehicle made them. Deena opened up the sporty Mercedes, sifting into high gear as she rolled down the busy street heading to the highway. She looked in the rear view mirror and saw the black sports car still following.

Deena fished her cell phone from her purse and pressed one button.

"Dionne, someone is following me!"

"Where are you now?"

"I'm on the Dan Ryan, heading south, approaching the 31st Street exit."

"Get off and head to the Stock Yards you may be able to lose him in that maze of streets. Steve and I are on our way."

Deena tossed the phone onto the seat and jumped across three lanes of traffic to the exit. The vehicle did the same thing and was still behind her.

Driving down the sparse residential street, Deena reached a top speed of nearly 70 miles an hour, handling the wide street and slower cars like a pro. The black car was still with her.

At the stock yards, Deena whipped under the old archway and headed toward the maze of streets peppered by industrial sites.

The Mercedes hugged the corners, as Deena made each one, downshifting then shifting into high gear to increase her speed. She knew that one of these streets would lead to a dead end, but her mind was racing and she couldn't remember which one.

Deena took another right then screamed as the sound of gun shots could be heard. She lowered her head her eyes peering over the steering wheel, sweat began pouring down her face as if she had been submerged in a pool. Her breath came in short, heavy spurts as she dared to raise her head slightly to see out of the rear view mirror.

Another shot rang out. Her car began wobbling wildly. She fought to control the vehicle as she drove on the rim. When she heard yet another shot, she reached for her cell phone.

"Dionne, I don't know where you are but someone's shooting at me. I'm at 36th and Morgan, nearing the overpass, hurry!" Deena didn't wait for a response as drove on what she felt were two blown out tires on her car. She heard another shot and moments later her car finally came to a halt, steam sputtered and rose from under the hood.

Deena slid across the gearshift and opened the passenger door. She was not about to get shot sitting in the car and felt she had a better chance of surviving if she became a moving target.

"Miss Walls," the voice called out. "I'm not going to shoot you. I have a package from an old associate."

Deena paused and turned her head toward the voice. Sirens could be heard in the background.

"Please, Miss Walls. I don't have time, but I have to give you this package." She watched the lone figure began to rush toward her. Deena backed up as quick as her feet would allow her. "Here," he threw the package toward her, landing with a slight thump.

The hooded stranger ran back to the black vehicle with tinted windows. The loud screeching tires burned rubber and headed down the street. Deena sat down on the ground, her hands trembled as her mind tried to grapple with what had just happened. She looked over at the package still lying on the ground. Not trusting her legs, she crawled the short distance to it, grabbed it and sat back down. She looked down at what appeared to be a taped up brown expandable folder. The sounds of the sirens got closer. Something in Deena said to place the folder in her car.

Slowly standing, Deena walked on unsteady legs toward her car. She could see the two-seater sitting low on the ground. Damn, they shot out my tires she thought as she placed the folder on the rear floor of the car near her purse. She back down on the ground, too tired and exhausted to do anything else.

When she looked up and saw the police cars approaching, Deena started laughing; the sound of her own voice seemed odd. She thought, *now here comes the Cavalry.*

She could see Dionne running toward her. She smiled then remembered the strangest thought—Dionne had been the one to come to her rescue following Seth's attack. Tears rolled down her face and she held out her arms. The last thing she heard was the deep voice yelling for someone to call an ambulance.

Chapter 22

Charles paced the hallway outside of the emergency room. He looked over at Lee, Schoops and Deena's entire family joined by his two brothers, Willie and Aaron who were on the police force. And though he knew she hadn't been harmed, she was suffering from shock.

He had been sitting in Schoops office with the FBI going over the latest information they'd gathered. Lee had called earlier and informed him that the case had just taken a strange twist which was why he was needed at headquarters as soon as possible.

Once he arrived, Charles had sat with the assembled group and read, then re-read the file folder. He looked at the name several times, not wanting to believe what he was reading.

"How did you all find out Seth Scott placed the tail on Deena?"

Agent Johns responded. "From the informant you pointed out the other night. He was the one who told us Seth Scott put the surveillance on Kasha Bentley's attorney. He also said a hit had been placed on Kasha Bentley to the tune of a million dollars."

They each let out a long whistle.

"No wonder she's on the run. Luckily we still have Eric covered," Lee stated and then looked over at Charles. He moved his chair closer and whispered, "I know what you're thinking, but don't do anything crazy, okay. We'll find him."

Charles narrowed his eyes and looked his partner in the eye. "He hurt her once, man. I'll be damned to hell if I allow him to do it again."

Commander Schoops stood. "Seems as if that isn't all we've found out, Harris."

"Yeah, it seems as if your informant turned out to be the golden goose. He told

us Brother Burnett was going to be moving some major product in the next two days and that while Seth has been his lawyer, his *consigliore*, so to speak, for a number of years, he was the mastermind behind some cases we weren't able to solve. But it seems as if Seth has grown tired of it all. Yet, it still doesn't explain the tail of Deena Walls, though." Special Agent Johns looked at Lee then to Charles.

Charles hadn't wanted to tell them her business, but knew that they needed to know. Besides, he wanted them to find Seth before he did. When he finished telling them about Seth's connection to Deena, they agreed to put out an all points bulletin. As they were in the midst of planning their strategy on bringing in both Seth and Brother Barnett, Charles got a call from Deena's sister.

He jumped from his seat. "What? Where is she?" He asked. "I'm on my way." He placed the phone in his waist clip and rushed toward the door. "Come on, Lee, someone's following Deena through the Back of the Yards."

What seemed like an eternity to Charles, had only taken ten minutes to reach the old stock yards and pick up Deena's trail, thanks to Dionne's latest call. He didn't want to know how she got his cell phone number, he was just grateful she did. And when he arrived on the scene and saw Deena's car, the tires shot out, a bullet hole near the side, close to the engine block, he knew the FBI needed to catch up with Seth before he did, for Charles was going to lose his badge and catch a case.

Charles's attention was drawn to the sounds of Deena's family rushing toward the door as she stepped through it.

"I'm fine you guys, just a little shaken up. I'll be okay." She hugged her mother, followed by her father, then her brothers and sister. She looked up and smiled when she spotted Charles. "How'd you get here?" She walked over to him and hugged him tightly, feeling the warmth of his protection in his tight embrace. She could have sworn she heard his voice at the scene right before she fainted.

"Dionne called me while you were being chased." He looked down at her, his arms still around her. He didn't want to let her go and was not going to let her out of his sight for one minute, even if that called for him taking time off of work. Lee, Schoops and the agents were more than capable of making sure Seth was tailed. When asked, Charles had been informed their own surveillance team had been cut off in a traffic snarl while following Seth's men. He knew he needed to tell her what he'd found out.

"How about we all go to my house? There's a lot going on with this case surrounding Kasha." Charles stated and watched as Deena shook her head in agreement.

Charles took Deena by the hand and led her out of the hospital. Climbing into the sedan's rear seat, Charles sat next to her. He wasn't kidding when he said he had no intentions of leaving her side.

Arriving at his home, the entire crew stopped at the front door, with the exception of Charles's brothers, Lee and Deena—they were each used to Sweetie.

"She's a guard dog, not an attack dog," Deena said as she knelt down and began to stroke the dog's large head as the dog licked her face.

"Baby, you feel like putting Sweetie up?" he asked.

Deena took Sweetie by the collar and led the dog down a hallway.

"Looks as if she's been here enough times," Deena's mother whispered to Dionne, who only nodded in response.

Charles had everyone gather in his basement. Commander Schoops had told Charles that he knew Deena's father well, for Schoops had hired him a decade ago when his son had been accused of having drugs on his person with intent to sale and a weapons charge. Then Deena's father had defended his son, proving that his son was not only set up by his peers, but was completely innocent of all charges. He felt he owed it to Judge Walls to make sure he knew as much as possible to ensure his daughter's safety and he had told him such when they were at the hospital.

Schoops began, with Charles and Lee interjecting. Once they were complete, the Walls family sat near each other with stunned looks upon their faces. Charles looked at each of them. He couldn't imagine what they were thinking. He looked at Deena. She had turned ashen and her eyes held a sort of fear. He knelt before her.

"Deena, look at me," he said gently. "I will not let him hurt you, baby. I give you my word."

Deena reached out and touched Charles's face, nodding her head. She had never loved any man the way she loved Charles.

He was turning out to be all that she had wanted in a man and she believed that he would lay his life on the line for her; but she didn't want that, she didn't want him facing Seth. She thought about the folder and decided that she would get Dionne to bring the folder to her.

Once they were finished meeting, it had been decided that Deena would stay with Charles until Seth was found and brought in for questioning.

"Dionne, will you bring me some of your things to wear," Deena said as she rose and had her sister follow her upstairs. They entered the spare room. "Where is my car?" She asked once she closed the door.

"Why?"

"The guy chasing me gave me a large folder. I think there is something in the envelope that's key to this whole craziness. Get me the folder, Dionne."

"Okay, and I'll bring you enough clothes to last about a week." Dionne looked down at Deena sitting on the bed with Sweetie's head nestled in her lap. She had watched Charles, had seen the familiar emotion in his face, the way he'd looked when he arrived at the scene and carried Deena to the ambulance, her body nestled protectively in his arms. She knew that Charles loved her sister and she wondered if Deena knew it.

"Steve and I will be back. And we're going to spend the night, okay?"

Deena slid from under Sweetie's head and rose, hugging her sister to her.

"Girl, don't you worry about Seth, he knows better. Besides, I don't think he wants to meet any of us, especially Charles."

Deena stepped out of the room and embraced her parents, followed by David and Darius, then Aaron and Willie. She assured them she was okay. As they stood near the door, Charles came to stand by her side.

"I'm entrusting her in your capable hands," Jedidiah stepped forward and looked Charles in the eyes. "All of my children are important to me. When Seth laid a hand on her," he said as he pointed at Deena. "I thought I was going to lose my mind, for I wanted to hurt that boy badly. And then I had to hold my sons back—and we aren't even going to talk about that one." He nodded his head in Dionne's direction. "We thought we'd seen the last of Seth Simons." He inhaled deeply. "Make sure that we don't have to see him again, Charles." Jedidiah took his wife's hand in his and stepped out of Charles's home followed by his sons and daughter.

Charles watched as they each climbed into an SUV and left. He understood what Judge Walls meant, but he didn't have to say it—Charles had no intention of letting Seth within a stone's throw of Deena. He patted the weapon resting in his shoulder holster right under his arm. He'd never killed a man in the years he'd been on the force, but he knew in his heart that he'd fatally wound Seth Simons if it came to that.

Charles's cell phone rang and he looked at the caller ID.

"Hey mom," he spoke into the phone. "Yeah, she's okay. A little shook up. No, she's right here." He handed Deena his cell phone and went back to speaking with Schoops and Lee. Once she was finished, he spoke to his mother for a few moments then rang off.

After an hour, Schoops and Lee departed, followed by his brothers, leaving Charles and Deena by themselves.

"Hungry?" he asked as he shut the door and noticed that every move Deena made Sweetie followed close behind.

"No, I'm not very hungry right now. What I'd like to do is take a hot shower and go to bed."

"Sure, baby. Come on." He took her by the hand and led her to his bedroom. Fishing around in his chest of drawers, he removed a pair of shorts and a shirt for Deena to wear. "You can sleep in these."

He watched as she headed to the bathroom, Sweetie right behind her. Charles knew if he had to leave for any reason Sweetie would be her guard. He lay back on the bed and thought about the day's event. He thanked God that Deena hadn't been hurt or even worse.

Charles propped the pillows up, pulling the covers back, readying them for Deena then turned on the television. His face went slack when he saw Eric Williams' face on the screen. He turned up the volume and wanted to scream when he heard the news announcer state that Eric Williams and a man posing as a Chicago Police officer had been murdered in the hospital with no suspects in custody.

"Shit, this is getting out of hand," he swore loudly. It was just a matter of time before Kasha met the same fate—that is if she was found. So far, it seemed as if the young woman was well hidden. He picked up the phone on his bedside. As he dialed Lee's number, he thought about Corbin. Though he was glad his son was with his mother in Florida, this case was beginning to get too close to home and making him reconsider FBI's earlier offer to join them and head up the division on gathering and using informant information.

Charles had just wrapped up his call to Lee when Deena appeared in the doorway. Charles could see dark circles had formed under her beautiful eyes that shone with exhaustion, a part of it from the sedative she'd been given at the hospital.

Deena looked like a little girl, his shirt hung past her thighs. He patted the bed and watched as she padded silently over and lay down. He pulled the cover up over her, kissed her forehead and then rose from the bed. She grabbed his hand.

"Can you wait until I fall asleep?"

He nodded his head, removing his shoes, shirt and weapon, which he lay on the nightstand near the bed. Charles slid in between the covers and wrapped his arms around her as she snuggled close to him, his head on the pillow as she tucked her head into his chest as if she were hiding. He listened to her breathing, first semi-erratic as she fought the effects of the sedative then finally the steady breathing that signaled she had fallen asleep. He held her, lightly stroking her hair. Charles knew if he were to meet Seth now, the man's chances of living would be slim to none—and slim just left.

"She wouldn't stop, boss," the guard said as he moved to cover his face in an attempt to deflect yet another blow.

"You idiot!" Seth bellowed as he punched the man standing in front of him in the face. "I said get the package to her, not try to kill her!" He grabbed the man by the shirt and shook him, spittle flying from his face as he ranted and cursed. "Do you know what you've done?" He pushed the man from him and watched in anger as he fell to the floor. "Get the hell out of here before I kill you myself. It'd be preferred over what Brother Barnett's going to do to you."

He looked at the other man standing nearby. "And you probably just stood there, looking stupid." He shook his head. "Get out, but wait by the door. Now we've got to move fast."

Seth continued to fill the second large duffle bag with cash. Things had gotten so far out of hand it was crazy. He needed to get to Kasha, his daughter, for Barnett had already gotten to his son. He had no idea he was a father to either until his sister in one of her drunken, drug induced hazes, informed him he had fathered two children when he was a teen, right around the time Brother Barnett had taken a interest in him. At first he didn't believe her, knowing his sister was prone to lies and hysteria. But when he really looked at Eric and found out who his mother had been, he remembered. Eric and Kasha's mother had been his first love and they had spent many an hour dreaming of how they weren't going to be like the folks they lived around. Yet, here he was, he had become like them and in most cases, even worse. As for their mother, she had succumbed to the streets, leaving her kids to raise themselves for years before the state stepped in. No one had heard or seen her in over ten years.

By the time he had gathered the nerve to confront Eric to tell him who he was, he realized his son had been seduced by the streets and all it held. And when he had approached Brother Barnett about cutting his son loose, it was too late. His boy had already made a deal with the devil. But now Eric was dead. Seth felt no remorse for the things he had been putting in place—he was going to bring Winston Barnett down to nothing. Seth thought about Kasha. She had a one million dollar bounty on her head, put out by Barnett. In an odd way, he was glad no one, not even he, knew where she was hiding.

Now if Deena could only get that package, he would be assured Kasha would be free. He had already placed a quarter of a million dollars in an account in her name, that not even the feds could touch for it was the proceeds from an insurance policy her mother had taken out on his step-father. Though the man had been dead for over five years, the company was slow paying when the first death investigation was inconclusive. The second one stated that the man simply drowned.

Seth knew the payout wasn't much, but it would help her rebuild her life once she was exonerated of the charges against her.

Once he finished filling the bag, he shut down his computer, removed the picture of Deena from the desk drawer. Taking his lap top, he headed toward the door, looking back once more before he left. He knew in his gut that this was the last time he'd ever lay eyes on this office. That didn't bother him, for he knew his time was up—it was time for him to face the fact of bad karma.

He stepped out of his office carrying the two bags. He handed one to the lone guard he'd hired. Pulling weapons their waistbands, Seth and the guard stepped out into the darkness of the alley into the rented Towne Car. They placed the bags into the trunk of the car, then slid into the front seats. Seth informed his lone guard to drive him to Deena's place, though he knew it would possibly be guarded by now. But that was the chance he had to take as he had created another package just like the first one. He was going to deliver it himself, come hell or high water.

Chapter 23

"No, please don't," Deena yelled as she sat up suddenly in the bed.

Charles reached out to her, his hands wrapped around her. "Shhh, baby, I'm right here." He cooed, rubbing his hand up and down her bare arm. "I'm right here."

Charles looked at her, the palatable fear shone clearly in her eyes, her face a brave front. While she had slept, Lee had contacted him and said that though they hadn't found Seth or Kasha, but they had found Brother Barnett, placing surveillance on him, and one of Seth's personal body guards, who turned himself into authorities. Lee stated that he would be interrogating the guard himself and promised to call once he had more information.

Charles had just fallen asleep next to Deena when he felt her stir wildly then began screaming. Both Charles and Sweetie jumped, with Charles reaching for his weapon. He looked into her eyes and realized she had been having a nightmare.

"See, we're both here. We won't let a thing happen to you." He wiped away the tears with his fingertips. "You have my word, Deena. I love you too much to let anything happen to you."

Deena looked up into his dark eyes. "Do you really, Charles?"

"Do I really what, baby?" He tilted his head to one side.

"Do you love me?" She held her breath.

Charles pulled her onto his lap, one arm wrapped around her

waist, the other rubbing her back gently. "I think I fell in love with you the day you walked into my precinct and sassed me." He chuckled. "Woman of mine, you are so in here." He tapped the skin over his heart. "And yes, I do love you Deena. I'm in love with you and if you'd agree I'd like to try my hand at marriage again—with you."

Deena looked into his eyes. If she had ever felt love before, she surely didn't know what it was, for what she felt for the man holding her in his arms, willing to put a lot to the side for her, even willing to lay his life for her, was more than anything she'd ever experienced. Truly, she loved him unconditionally, with all of what made her woman. And she knew no matter what happened, she would never love another man like she loved Charles.

"Oh, Charles," she hugged him. "I love you so much." She touched the side of his face. "Thank you for taking care of me." She kissed him softly on the lips. "Thank you for loving me." she kissed him again as her hands rubbed across his curly hair. "And yes, I'd like to try marriage again myself—with you." She lay her head on his shoulders.

For an hour they lay next to each other, with Sweetie now lying at the foot of the bed. Charles had laughed when the dog jumped up and ignored his order to get down. "Looks as if you are marrying a dog as well."

They talked about all the things they really wanted in a marriage. Deena thought about what Dionne had said when she and Steve talked about the deal breakers. And it seemed as if she and Charles shared the same ones. When the conversation about children rose, Deena stated she wasn't sure if she wanted children of her own, especially with so many in both of their families. Charles had stated he wanted one more, but was willing to spoil all of his nieces and nephews. He also told her he was considering leaving the department to join the FBI in a less dangerous capacity. She agreed to support whatever he wanted to do, but admitted she'd sleep better at night if she knew he wasn't out chasing criminals. He also told her all he knew of the case. She had only smiled, glad that he knew as much as he did. She ended with telling him that she had decided to defend juvenile offenders once she got Kasha immunity that is if she even showed up.

"We're due in court on Monday."

Charles nodded his head as he slid down with Deena lying on top of him. "I know, but you have enough evidence now that points to her innocence. Besides, we're more interested in Barnett than anything."

They became quiet, eventually falling asleep in each other's arms.

Seth watched the streetlights shine eerily off of the hood of the car as they headed to their destination. Rolling by the high-rise, Seth could see Deena's sister Dionne as she carried a bag and the folder he had given the guards to deliver to her earlier. Dionne jumped into a Hummer and sped off.

"Follow that thing there," he pointed to the large military style vehicle. "And be careful. That one will kick your ass all by herself." He chuckled remembering that Dionne was a fierce bounty hunter and would present herself as a formidable opponent. He'd hate to meet her anywhere.

For nearly half of an hour, they followed the Hummer several cars behind. And when the large vehicle turned down a residential street, Seth had his guard to keep going, parking two blocks away.

"Stay here," he ordered as he climbed out of the Towne car and headed back to the block the Hummer had turned down. He walked quickly, the folder clutched under his arm. He thought of Brother Barnett and one of their last conversations where he had tried to get Brother Barnett to let Eric, his son, off the hook. Seth had even offered to pay the debt himself if he'd just allow him to live. Brother Barnett had laughed at Seth, accusing him of going soft.

Seth had left him that evening knowing he didn't have much time and headed to the hospital, his guard dressed as a Chicago Police Officer escorted him in handcuffs to the room. Their entry was easy, for the guard had left his post. Seth had slipped inside the room and looked down into the face of the young man who was his son, who had gambled and lost. Regret had never been a part of Seth's life, but for the second time in his life he felt the emotion. The first time had been his treatment of Deena.

Seth touched Eric's face, smoothed out the furrows from his son's forehead. He saw the likeness, the family resemblance. He spoke in his ear, telling him that he was going to try and right this wrong, how sorry he was that he didn't know who he was sooner and how he was going to take care of Kasha. Kasha had been part of the whole deal for Eric was going to make sure that Barnett didn't get anywhere near her by blackmailing him with the fact that he was engaged in child prostitution and slavery.

He'd gasped when Eric opened his eyes and looked at him, a tear slid down his face. Eric hadn't spoken, but his eyes told all as they looked at him with what seemed like fear. Seth kissed him on the cheek then slipped out of the room. He found the guard still away and ordered his own guard to stay until the other returned.

The next thing he knew both were dead and he knew Brother Barnett had killed them and was now looking for Kasha.

He slowed his footsteps when he spotted the Hummer parked in front of a house, the lights on in the front. He wondered if Deena was there and stepped into the shadows to think out his next move.

Turning quickly, he heard the footsteps behind him and came face to face with the man he had set out to destroy—Brother Barnett.

The sound of the doorbell woke Deena and Charles. Grabbing his weapon, Charles slid off the bed and headed toward the door. Sweetie shifted on the bed and took up the spot Charles had just vacated. Deena hugged the dog's head.

"I guess I am marrying you, too," Deena rubbed Sweetie's head and then listened as she heard her sister's voice. Sweetie looked up as Dionne stepped into the bedroom.

"How are you feeling?" Dionne said as she sat on the bed.

"Better. Where's Steve?"

"He got a lead on one of our fugitives, so I had him go chase him down."

Deena nodded and smiled thinking how Dionne and Steve were so perfect for each other.

"Did you get me some clothes?"

"Actually, I did one better, I went to your place and got you a few things."

Her eyebrows knitted together in concern. "Dionne, I hope no one followed you?"

"I don't think so, besides, you know I'd know something like that. Anyway, I also went to the police pound and got the folder." She handed it over.

"Let's go to the basement," Deena said as she climbed out of the bed and headed downstairs, Sweetie right behind her. "Charles," she called out to him. "Dionne and I are in the basement." He appeared and nodded his head.

"What's with the dog?" Dionne pointed to Sweetie as she walked behind them.

"I can't explain it. She hasn't left my side since I arrived. Charles seems to think she senses something and is staying close by." Deena rubbed the dog's head as she sat down on the couch.

Sweetie jumped up on the couch beside her and nestled her head in her lap. "Besides, Charles asked me to marry him today." She looked at her sister and smiled. Dionne jumped up, clapping her hands together.

"Did you set a date yet?"

"No, we didn't. We were talking about the deal breakers," Deena replied and then smiled, remembering their conversations, the ease and honesty in which they spoke of their needs and expectations. And they both had the same expectations—no verbal or physical abuse and no infidelity.

"We could have a double wedding, you know."

Deena shook her head 'no'. She planned on them being engaged for at least a year, seeing as how they had only been dating for two months.

Dionne shrugged her shoulders and sat back down. She looked at Sweetie and held her hand out to her. Sweetie sniffed then licked her hand.

"Well, I guess she likes you," Deena said as she opened the large folder and began to read what looked like financial ledgers with names and amounts of people paid and the reasons. The dates went back nearly twenty years and outlined what she assumed was every deal Brother Winston Barnett had ever made. Then there were the pictures of people and places, with names and date written clearly on the back of them. A few faces she recognized as high-ranking members of law enforcement, politicians and attorneys. And when she came across a sealed envelope with her name on it, she froze. She recognized the neat handwriting as belonging to Seth.

"My God, Deena, you have the entire illegal operation of Winston Barnett."

"This was what those goons were chasing me for? Did they have to scare me half to death to do it? Couldn't they have just walked up to me and said 'here'?" She shook her head and then handed the letter over to Dionne. "You read it."

Dionne opened the letter and then dropped the pages as shots rang out. Both hit the floor as Sweetie covered Deena with her large body. She heard Charles yell down to her in the basement to stay put, ordering the dog to do the same, as she heard his hurried footsteps overhead.

Deena watched as her sister began to crawl toward the lights and doused them right before she headed toward the stairs.

"Where are you going?" Deena yelled out to Dionne.

"Charles may need some help."

Deena saw her sister's form in the dark as she rushed to the stairs. "Crazy woman, get your ass back here." Deena then pushed at Sweetie. "Up girl, up." She felt the weight of Sweetie shift and they both headed quickly up the stairs behind Dionne. The house was dark as rounds of shots were heard in rapid-fire secession. Deena's eyes adjusted to the darkness and she saws the front door open and no signs of Charles.

Her heart beat hard in her chest, the sounds of sirens and lights could now be seen outside of the picture window at the front of his house. More shots, followed by screams came from near the left side of the house.

Deena grabbed Dionne's foot, pulling her backward, as she tried to scramble toward the front door. The sounds of angry words, more shots and screams were heard. Deena lost grip of Dionne's foot and watched in horror as her sister rushed to the front door. She heard the door open and then close as she lost sight of Dionne.

And then there was silence.

The silence was eerie and Deena reached beside her to feel for Sweetie. She inhaled deeply when her hand touched the side of the dog that was crouched down next to her. The sounds of shots and screams continued to ring inside of her head. Her mind raced wondering what had happened, where Charles and Dionne disappeared to. Rising to her feet, she propelled her body up and forward as she went in search of Charles and Dionne.

Slowly approaching the open front door, Deena peered outside the screened door to see Charles standing over a body laid out on the sidewalk in front of the house, his weapon resting at his side. She opened the door and ran outside.

Charles saw her running toward him and he stepped away from Seth Simon as she approached, intending on grabbing her before she saw his bullet riddled body. Several feet from him, lay an unmoving Brother Winston Barnett.

"Baby, don't." He said as he grabbed her and walked her back to the house. "It's Seth."

"Is he dead?"

"No."

Lee walked up to where they were standing near the steps of Charles's home. He motioned to Charles to come close. He shook his head and Lee came closer to them. "He's asking for Deena."

"Who?" Dionne said as she rounded the house.

They turned to see her as she came from the side of the house with a large folder in her arms similar to the one in Charles's basement.

"Seth," Lee responded just as the ambulance appeared.

Deena looked up at Charles. He nodded his head toward Seth's body. "Only if you want to. He's not armed."

Deena looked over at him lying on the sidewalk, his hand raised at the elbow. Her mind was unsure of what she should do. A part of her wanted to take Charles's weapon, but she knew that it wasn't worth the time of day or the jail sentence to go along with it.

For years she'd been so close to hating Seth for what he had done to her, for allowing herself to be robbed of the ability to love and trust. She looked at Charles again.

"If you want to speak to him, I'll be right there."

She put her hand out to Charles. He placed his weapon in the shoulder holster and then walked with Deena to where Seth lay. Lee and Dionne walked behind them.

She covered her mouth as she watched his struggle for air. He motioned to her and she knelt down beside him. His voice was low as he spoke to her about his daughter Kasha, asking her to take care of her. He tapped her hand when she looked away, the action causing her to meet his eyes.

"I'm…soo…sorry, Deena," he said as he breathed his last breath.

Deena stood and looked down at his face. She prayed for his soul then turned and walked back to the house without uttering a word.

Epilogue

"Deena," Kasha began. "I want to thank you for all of your help. I couldn't have done this without you." She hugged Deena tightly.

"No thanks necessary. I'm just glad you are okay."

It had been six months since the shootout between Seth and Winston Barnett that left both men dead. According to the accounts the FBI, Charles and Lee had pieced together, Seth had followed Dionne to Charles's house in hopes of handing her the envelope of information that would indict Brother Winston Barnett on a number of drug charges, racketeering, tax evasion, murder and child prostitution. In addition, the information pointed to his intent to take over Kasha's career and her brother, Eric wasn't having it and was blackmailing Barnett in addition to stealing from him. The night he'd been shot, Kasha arrived to talk to him about the crew she had seen him hanging out with. Juan-Carlos's murder was ordered by Barnett because of his desire of a larger share of the take from the prostitution ring.

"What are you going to do now?"

"My grandmother is living in Jamaica thanks to Seth, so I'm going to head down there for a while until the case dies down to a blip."

"That's smart. There are a lot of folks being brought up on various charges. No need to stay around." Deena knew the public knowledge of Kasha as Seth Scott's daughter; the media would hound her day and night. And with the first trial of a local alderman to begin in a few weeks, the last thing she knew Kasha needed was to be reminded of the types of activities her father and brother had been engaged in.

Deena was impressed with Kasha's ability to remain hidden. Kasha had informed her that she meshed back into the world she had come from—homelessness. Kasha had sought refuge and safety in a world many paid little attention to. The day before her bench trial she surfaced and when they appeared in court the next day, Deena moved to have all charged dropped in light of the new evidence.

"You know I knew you was dating Detective Harris."

Deena laughed. "How did you know?"

"Tommy," she responded and told Deena that Tommy was a fellow homeless friend. "He told me he saw the two of you together after when I asked him how he got a twenty spot."

Deena shook her head, remembering Tommy and his hustle. She looked up to see Charles walk into her office. Kasha rose and hugged him.

"And you are okay with me, Detective Harry." She smiled, the old joke caused them to laugh.

Deena hugged Kasha again as she wrapped up the paperwork that showed Kasha she was an exonerated woman.

"I'll keep in touch, Deena."

"Do that."

"Oh, and my grandmother sent you a message. She said she was wrong." Kasha hugged her and then walked out of the office.

Deena watched her leave, her head held high, and she wished the woman well as she walked out to begin a new life. Lee had agreed to see Kasha to the airport and on her flight without incident.

Deena thought about Seth. For years she held on to the anger. His words seemed to free her and as she and Dionne, joined by Karen, read the letter he had written to her once she returned to her home. She found the ability to forgive herself for all that had occurred between them and made a fire in her fireplace and burned the letter, finally free of him and there history.

She knew that her future was with Charles and Corbin. And they had decided to live in the penthouse, with Corbin making the decision that he'd prefer the top floor digs because he'd get a room that looked out over the lake. Charles had also decided to accept the position with the FBI and was working in their informant division.

"Ready," Charles asked her, his voice bringing her back to the present.

Deena rose and walked out of her office. She bid farewell to Kimmie and headed out of the office. She and Charles headed to her place.

She thought of Dionne's wedding, which took place a month after the shooting. The entire family, Karen and her husband, Gary, and Charles had flown to the Bahamas. While there, he asked her father for her hand in marriage. She laughed when Charles told her that Jedidiah Walls had told him he'd think about it.

Later, during the wedding reception, her father, while toasting Dionne and Steve, had also announced the engagement of Deena to Charles. And once they returned home, they met up at Charles's parent's house where they announced their engagement, Corbin and the rest of his family welcomed her. Deena knew right then, that this was her one in a million—she hadn't believed a love like this would come her way.

"When are we getting married, woman of mine?" Charles asked as they rode the elevator to the penthouse.

Deena smiled as he pulled to him and kissed her deeply, his lips doing that magic on her that it always did. She broke the kiss and looked up at him.

"How about next month?"

"Sounds, good, baby. Sounds real good to me."

And that's just what they did, surrounded by their family and close friends.

Author Bio

Barbara Keaton, a native Chicago, enjoys writing. Her first diary is dated December 1975. Since then, Barbara has written articles for *Today's Black Woman* magazine, *Chicago Reader*, *Chicago Crusader* and most recently, *True Confessions*. In addition, Barbara is an accomplished romance author, having seven titles to her name. Barbara credits her late grandfather, Thomas Hill, and the Oblate Sisters of Providence for instilling in her a love and passion for the written word. Visit her on the Web at www.bkeaton.com.

Parker Publishing, LLC

Celebrating Black
Love Life Literature

Mail or fax orders to:
12523 Limonite Avenue Suite #440-438
Mira Loma, CA 91752
phone: (866) 205-7902 fax: (951) 685-8036 fax
or order from our Web site: www.parker-publishing.com
orders@parker-publishing.com

Ship to:
Name: ____________________
Address: ____________________
____
City: ____________________
State: ____________________ Zip: ____________________
Phone: ____________________

Qty	Title	Price	Total

Shipping and handling is $3.50, Priority Mail shipping is $6.00 FREE standard shipping for orders over $30
Add S&H Alaska, Hawaii, and international orders – call for rates
CA residents add 7.75% sales tax
Payment methods: We accept Visa, MasterCard, Discovery, or money orders.
NO PERSONAL CHECKS.
Payment Method: (circle one): VISA MC DISC Money Order

Name on Card: ____________________
Card Number: ____________________ ____
ExpDate: ____________________
Address: ____________________
____
City: ____________________
State: ____________________ Zip: ____________________